"You want me to be your . . . mistress?"

"For the rest of the Season," he said. "Think of it, my Cat. What is one night? One interlude? A cruel tease when you consider it, no matter how satisfactory the encounter. Neither one of us expected to be in this position, but I, for one, am not about to relinquish you so easily."

Merriam shook her head. "You're insane."

Drake relaxed his hold, sensing the first signs of victory. She hadn't slapped him yet. "Stay."

She lowered her eyes and bit her lip, a habit he was coming to find dangerously appealing. Drake reminded himself that he was acquiring her as a tool and nothing more.

"It's too sudden," she whispered, looking anxiously back up into his eyes.

"It's not too sudden, Merriam." He pulled her against his chest. "You've waited a long time, I suspect, for a taste of passion, for an offer to experience true intimacy. Come on this adventure with me, my Cat."

A Lady's Pleasure

RENEE BERNARD

POCKET BOOKS

New York   London   Toronto   Sydney

An *Original* Publication of POCKET BOOKS

 POCKET BOOKS, a division of Simon & Schuster, Inc.
1230 Avenue of the Americas, New York, NY 10020

This book is a work of fiction. Names, characters, places and
incidents are products of the author's imagination or are used
fictitiously. Any resemblance to actual events or locales or persons,
living or dead, is entirely coincidental.

ISBN-13: 978-1-4165-2420-5
ISBN-10: 1-4165-2420-7

This Pocket Books paperback edition November 2006

10 9 8 7 6 5 4 3 2

POCKET and colophon are registered trademarks of
Simon & Schuster, Inc.

Cover illustration by Alan Ayers
Hand-lettering by Iskra Johnson

Manufactured in the United States of America

For information regarding special discounts for bulk purchases,
please contact Simon & Schuster Special Sales at 1-800-456-6798
or business@simonandschuster.com.

To my father, who though he has vowed never to read my books, couldn't be more proud of his daughter the writer. Only the best dad would cheer you on, even when you make him blush. I love you.

Your loving doesn't know its majesty
until it knows its helplessness.
—RUMI

One

I have no use for whey-faced widows or limp-boned virgins.

She recalled the biting words with acidic clarity. Moments after she'd met a man who had made her heart come alive with desire, and made her wonder if all the years of longing had ended, that very same man, Julian Clay, the Earl of Westleigh, had quietly spoken those words to a nearby companion. Unaware of the devastating blast he'd delivered to the trembling soul on the other side of the column, he had chuckled at his friend's mumbled reply and set the wheels of Fate in motion.

That the words referenced her own slight impact on the notorious rake was not in doubt. Or at least that was what Merriam told herself with the cruel precision of long years of practice.

Merriam the Mouse. It was a nickname her father had given her that had lingered throughout her youth, and even into the lonely nightmare of her marriage to an older and indifferent man. Her husband had teased her with the pet name, using it when he wanted to dismiss his quiet wife and return to more important and pressing matters: matters that included his business interests, endless correspondences, and sleeping with her maidservants.

But the mouse had survived him. And tonight Merriam was determined to taste the forbidden pleasures whey-faced widows and limp-boned virgins only dreamt of—lust and vengeance. Julian Clay would be hers, and she would show him just what a mouse was made of, then leave him wanting and aching—the satisfaction hers alone to savor. She would bring London's most notorious rake to his knees, and then . . . she would walk away.

Lord Milbank's Grand Costume and Masked Ball was notorious for its decadent and outrageous delights. No self-respecting member of London's high society would ever admit to attending it, which of course meant no one who received an invitation would dream of missing it. It was the most coveted invitation of the Season.

Merriam handed over her own gilt envelope tied with red ribbons, amazed at the steadiness of her fingers. For her, weeks of preparation would culminate in this one night. After days of careful study and nights of restless need, the mouse was transformed. Tonight, she would be the cat.

"Has Merlin arrived?" she asked.

"Yes, m'lady," the butler responded.

"Could you have one of the servers find him and tell him that his familiar is here?" She ignored the twist of the heated knot in her stomach at her brazen request.

He nodded. "As you wish, m'lady."

Merriam smiled. *Oh, yes, the lady wishes to teach the sorcerer a new kind of magic.*

In black silk and draped velvet, she entered the crowded room. Amidst costumes of blinding color and opulent flashes of jewelry, Merriam knew she would stand out. Her costume made a mockery of modesty, a widow's darkest weeds turned into a sensual invitation. Her black velvet mask and cat's ears were simple, but the black ties that held them on and laced through her hair were deliberately too long, draping over her collarbone, accenting her bare shoulders and the curved flesh above her bodice. Her figure of bold curves was displayed in simple lines, finished with a shocking glimpse of red satin beneath the black velvet, drawing the eye down to the flash of color that hinted at the shape of her legs and slim ankles through the strategically placed slits in her skirt.

She had even gone so far as to dye her brown hair to jet-black with one crimson streak to match her costume.

Madame DeBourcier's last bit of advice echoed in

her mind: *You must feel sexual, invincible. It will emanate from you like heat, the scent of a woman who is ready, accessible, and willing. You must feel this power, then draw him to you.*

She circled the room, avoiding small talk and ignoring the subtle bids for her attention from some of the bolder male guests. With every silky step, she felt a well of electricity start to pool between her legs and along the column of her spine. But several anxious minutes passed, and her confidence began to falter. She'd confirmed the layout of the house and even where the tryst would take place but. . . . *What if her information about his costume had been incorrect? What if he wasn't even there? What if—*

"You should be more careful." His voice came from behind her, the deep, masculine growl sending a delicious chill across her skin. "I thought familiars were supposed to stay close to their masters."

She turned to face him. "Ah, but then I am close, am I not?" He was taller than she remembered, but fear could color one's perception, and even as a cat, she knew this game could take many turns. He was masked, with his hair pulled back and powdered silver to match the gray silks of his beaded overcoat, embroidered with symbols of ancient magic and power. He was a strikingly handsome Merlin, and she made no effort to hide her appraisal, measuring him from head to toe as if Julian Clay were already hers.

At last, her eyes met the glittering heat of his through

the barriers of mask and costume, and she felt the first hint of victory. *Mine.*

He watched her, fascinated by the open challenge in her eyes. Who was this woman who presented herself, a sensual offering from gods he couldn't remember praying to? "You could not be close enough for complaint, my dear familiar," he countered softly, trying to recall that, no matter who she was, the rules of "polite engagement" would still apply.

She took a slow step closer, her face tilting up to look at him, and he felt his breath catch in his throat. She was like a magnificent panther, and his hands itched to stroke every sleek line of her body.

"No? Let us see then, Sorcerer, how close a woman can get before you . . . complain." With a subtle shift, she moved past him, then glanced back over her shoulder, daring him to follow, as she sauntered toward a private corridor, away from the lights of the party.

He followed without hesitation, dismissing any rational thought to caution or care. The truth of the rumors of courtesans and whores mingling amidst the Ton at Milbank's infamous affair appeared all too possible. He watched the hypnotic sway of her hips as this "cat" led him into the shadows of his host's hallway. He anticipated being led into one of the house's bedrooms, but she held out her hand and drew him into an alcove hidden by heavy velvet drapes. Moonlight through the window cast them both in shades from purest white through the gray of shadows to deep darkness, and he noted their small, secret space appeared to have a conveniently cushioned window seat wide enough to accommodate a tryst.

He drew the drapes and turned, reassessing this creature in velvet and silk, her skin like cream inviting him to drink and her chin angled with pure bravado. But instinct whispered that here was no courtesan, no jaded prostitute. In the light of the moon, he reveled in the details of his "seductress" as she bit her lower lip and seemed to struggle over what to do with trembling hands that conveyed inexperience. Her eyes caught the direction of his gaze, and she began to try to hide her hands in her skirts. But he caught them effortlessly, intent on uncovering the mystery that pulsed with raw need behind her mask.

Her hands were soft—her fingers long and tapered, her nails buffed smooth. They were the hands of a lady fluttering for escape, betraying her nervousness. No, this was no practiced whore, or even, he suspected, a wanton creature who had lost track of the lovers' beds she had visited. She was something else entirely. But exactly what, he could not yet say.

"How shall I please you, then, Master?" she purred, drawing his attention from her hands, forcing herself to face him in the cool and confined world of velvet and stone they would share for as long as the game lasted.

"Shall I tell you how?"

"Yes."

"And show you how?"

She swallowed, her heart skipping at the unbidden images the question evoked. After hours in Madame DeBourcier's parlor discussing the finer points of seducing a rogue, the time for talk was gone. Merriam wondered how she could ever have come to this place, could ever have conceived of anything so foolish, so laughable. But then he pulled her into his arms, and his mouth was on hers, tasting, teasing, consuming. She clung to the rugged heat of his chest and arms, feasting on the sensual fire of his kisses, devouring the raw pleasure, and gasping in shock to find, in just this first taste, that she may have underestimated her own need. Her own hunger.

He stroked the velvet of her dress with one hand. Finding the top of her bodice, his fingers dipped beneath the material to catch the peak of one nipple and free her breast from its confines. Merriam threw her head back, surprised at the streak of electricity that flowed from the touch of his hand on her breast, arching down to a sharp ache between her legs. God, she wanted his mouth there . . . everywhere.

"Who are you, Cat?"

She shook her head, fighting her need and the impulse to tell him anything . . . everything and anything he asked if only he would put his mouth against the sensitive coral tip of her breast. "Please . . ." The ragged whisper tore past her lips.

His mouth traced down the line of her jaw, guided by her desire. He gently took advantage of her exposed throat and followed her pulse to her collarbone, and to her breast to capture with his lips the impertinent peak that jutted into his fingers. He rolled his tongue around the flushed, taut flesh, mirroring the movement with his hand on her other breast, and grazed her with his teeth, nipping at the sensitive tip. She arched her back, her breath coming faster as he tried to teach his familiar about pleasure. Her own and his.

He tasted her breast, suckling her, drawing from her as if she were life and pleasure embodied. Her soft sighs and whimpers spun the heat and tension within him beyond his control—beyond recall or reckoning. He reached down to draw a hand along the outer line of her thigh, lifting one of her legs up around his waist and shifting back to press through the layers of her skirts. He worked his arousal against the damp core between her thighs. She bucked against him, and his lips released her breast as the eager, unpracticed message of her movements nearly undid him.

He took one of her hands, which were clutching the lapels of his coat, and slowly loosened her grip. His tongue flicked along each fingertip just as it had lingered on her breast, teasing each sensitive pad and suckling each indent between fingers until he felt a small measure of control return.

"I . . . I want to touch you." Her whisper ended his strategy in one swift intake of breath. The cat's eyes glittered in the moonlight, and he accepted a new definition for the word *surrender*.

"Then touch me."

He offered no assistance, beyond freeing the hand he had just worshiped with his mouth. A hand that now memorized the landscape of muscle and bone beneath the smooth folds of his shirt as she relentlessly sought her prize.

She prayed he wouldn't notice her trembling fingertips but forgot that concern when her touch encountered the unmistakable length of him, the straining power of his need against the buttons of his trousers. Merriam dropped her eyes from his, captivated by the sight of her hands shamelessly caressing and stroking him through the cloth.

Whose hands are so bold? Is this me doing this? Aching to touch more of him? To have all of him? Who is this woman?

The power of the questions made her giddy, and without the need for any more urging, she freed him from his pants. The buttons gave way easily. The stark light and shadows revealed his erection in all its beauty. Merriam smiled at the sight. She was surprised at the length and girth, for he was much larger than her late husband.

She ran her fingers along the silken skin, teasing then gripping, stroking his flesh, making his breathing change. The heat of him burned her as she reveled in the hardness and the way his flesh jerked against her palms, swelling and beckoning for more of her touch, more of her attention. Suddenly, she wanted more too. Madame DeBourcier had said there was one way to enslave a man, to drive him wild, but Merriam had privately dismissed that portion of the lecture as completely beyond the pale. Now, though—now, all she wanted was to taste him, to drink in the power of his flesh and to know what it would be to have the swollen, ripe head of him against her tongue and in her mouth. Merriam knelt down, her skirts fanning out around her.

"It's so beautiful," she murmured, and then she kissed him, slowly drawing one ivory pearl of moisture from the swollen tip and drinking in the sweet musk and salt before her mouth opened to enclose him.

He bit back a groan at the sensation, the sight of her on her knees, the unexpected brush of her breath against his erection, her whispered exclamation at his beauty. God, he wasn't sure how much longer he could keep from exploding. Her lips, her mouth, her tongue, so inexperienced, but God, she wrapped her fingers around him, the pressure exquisite, and the enthusiasm of her kisses made his thighs quiver. She closed her mouth over him again and pulled him slowly into its heat, the tip of her tongue flicking back and forth across the sensitive juncture at the tip of his shaft. His fingers tangled in her hair, his jaw clenched, determined to make it last.

Turnabout is fair play, kitten, he thought as he lifted her to her feet. Kissing her deeply, he used his tongue and teeth to seize control—her breath mingling with his until she sagged against him with a sigh. He held her upright while he reached down to cup the soft curve of her bottom, stepping forward until the backs of her knees met the window seat. Gently he set her down on the cushions, holding her so that she was balanced on the edge of the bench, and knelt facing her. His hands spread her thighs and reached to her ankles to push up the sensual barrier of her petticoats. The material trailed over her knees and brushed along black stockings secured by saucy red ribbons, revealing that his cat was a bold creature after all. For above her stockings, the receding line of black and crimson cloth showed that she wore nothing at all. Moist and glistening curls above her lush and ripe succulent lips beckoned to him.

"W-what are you d-doing?"

He grinned. Her naïve and breathless question made him wonder again at the mystery of a woman who would dress so provocatively, no undergarments but silk stockings and ribbons, yet tremble like an untried virgin at the prospect of his most intimate kisses. "I thought we were going to find out how close a sorcerer could get to a woman before he 'complained'?"

"Oh."

There was almost no sound behind her response as he deliberately held his mouth above her, the air from his words the first feather touch against the wet satin of her skin. "But if you're shy," he intoned softly, "let us see what we can do."

His hand caught at one of the layers of her red silk

petticoat and trailed the light material back over her, covering her with the thin illusion of a barrier against his touch. And then he lowered his mouth against the cloth and demonstrated how a sorcerer uses an illusion to achieve his desired ends.

His tongue traced the outline of her moist folds, the red silk wet within seconds from his mouth, from the liquid of her need, her body so slick, so ready to take him. But for now, there was only the tantalizing pressure of his tongue through her petticoat; heat and pressure, even the alternate cold and heat of his breath, all played against the silk. Merriam gripped the pillows, fighting and reveling in it all at once. To be touched there and not entirely touched. It was maddening.

"Are you shy?" he whispered against her, his tongue flicking over the tight bud of her clitoris. Merriam had to bite the palm of her hand to keep from crying out at the sensation.

The mouse was shy . . . the mouse would never spread her legs . . . would never pull them open so far that her muscles ached to give a man the access he wanted . . . she would never beg for him to penetrate her . . . to remove the damn silk . . . Ah, but tonight was different . . .

"I-I'm not shy," she managed to say through clenched teeth, her hips riding up to maintain the contact, cursing the existence of silk in the world.

The reward for the admission came quickly, as the wet cloth was dragged back across her skin, making her gasp when air struck the exposed and tender flesh. He blew a cool breath at the trailing edge of the silk as he removed it. And then his touch ignited her, the reality of his mouth, his tongue, his teeth against her—with nothing to keep him from tasting her fully, from exploring the contours and textures of her sex.

Merriam writhed against the cushions as she felt one of his fingers penetrate even as his tongue began to dance over her clitoris, a gentle and feathery flickering that contrasted with the increasing pressure and strength of his moving finger. A delicious tension, a red-hot coil, began to mount, and she gripped his head, her hands pulled at his hair, instinctively seeking more. More of the pressure. More of the teasing.

He added a second finger, stretching her. Pain and pleasure made her eyes fly open as the relentless dance of his tongue continued. Finally, the coil exploded. She bucked at the wave of ecstasy, shuddering as her muscles clenched against the fingers still pushing into her. Merriam cried out as the wave seemed to gather momentum. She arched her back with the ebb and flow, and he pulled his mouth away and drew himself up to kiss her—his fingers still penetrating and withdrawing—as she came. She could taste herself on his tongue, and the thought tugged at the coil of her release, the start of another cascade of explosions.

He pulled his hand away, and Merriam groaned at

the searing heat of his erection against her still shuddering flesh. She was still coming as he spread her legs wider and positioned himself to drive into her. Merriam felt a small lash of fear at the reality of his daunting size against her. She had a fleeting thought that her body couldn't possibly accommodate him. "W-wait . . ." She tried to catch her breath, to wriggle away but his hand held her hip, trapping her. He took his other hand and caressed her with his own swollen tip, and her body reacted, another tremor jerking her hips up and around him, and Merriam knew she wanted it. She suddenly wanted to claw him for more. Even if he rent her in two, she would have it all.

"Say yes," he commanded, pressing into her.

"Yes." His eyes held hers, her body tightening around the head of him, aching at the new presence, the first hint of the invasion that would come, writhing to escape even while a deeper drive made her hips quiver, tilting upward to try to take in all of him. He stopped, just barely inside her, and she could feel him trembling with the effort to hold still.

"Say yes," he commanded her again.

"Yes." And she was rewarded with just another inch, just one more thick, glorious inch of him, and he watched the realization come to her: that there was a great deal more of him and that the power was hers. Even as his body was held in a position to conquer, he yielded control to her to surrender completely and

take him, or even then, she had the power to refuse
him. So he asked, his voice rough and unsteady,
"Yes?"

"Yes! Oh, dear, yes, yes, yes!"

He plunged into her, driving himself in completely,
swallowing her small cry of shock and pleasure with
his mouth. Then slowly he began to move, his jaw
clenching at the molten heat and friction of her body,
so tight—the slick passage of a virgin, but no . . . She
wrapped her legs around his waist, her ankles urging
him to take her—deeper, faster, harder. His cat was no
virgin. She countered his every move, drawing against
him, pulling him in, crying for him to pound the in-
nermost core of her body, and he wanted it to last. He
wanted to make the magic last, the enchantment of her
scent and the feel of her beneath him, her hips rock-
ing him, her muscles contracting and milking him,
draining him.

"Oh! Oh, my!" Her fingernails dug into his shoulders, "I-It's happening . . . a-again!" Her innocent
shock at her ability to climax again stripped away his
last illusion of control. By God, he wanted her to
scream with it. He wanted to be the one to teach her
that she could come again and again—until the lines
between pleasure and pain were no more. He would
take her until there were no illusions between them,
nothing but the sustenance of need. And then he
couldn't hold it back any longer, a scalding orgasm
tearing from him, jetting into her as he ground against

her sensitive clit and felt the unmistakable grip and
spasms of her answering climax.

The game had definitely taken a turn, but even so,
Merriam's return to reality was slowed by the sweet ripples of her climax, the ache and burning between her
legs setting off another wave of desire when he shifted
slightly, withdrawing his still firm length a fraction of
an inch to take his full weight off her. A whimper of
protest escaped her throat, her legs tightening to hold
him captive. He kissed her throat and nuzzled her, apparently unwilling to beg for mercy. "Are you keeping
me, then?" he teased, and she tensed, all too aware that
he was not hers to keep, that it was time for the cat to
free her prey.

She pushed against him, shuddering at the sensation of loss, the ache between her legs, her flesh throbbing with hunger even now. She turned her face away,
seeking composure, repeating silently over and over
that victory is in the having, and that, at the very least,
she would have the memory of the cat to keep her
warm on the cold nights to come. Merriam the Mouse
straightened her dress and readjusted her bodice,
standing to shake the wrinkles out of her skirts, refusing to meet his curious gaze. The trembling in her
hands was the only sign of her turmoil.

"Tell me who you are," he said softly.

She stepped back with an odd smile and shook her
head. "I should thank you. I didn't know it could be
so . . . wonderful."

"This isn't amusing," he said more loudly. "I must know your name. I have to see you again."

Her chin came up defiantly; behind the velvet mask, her eyes shone with unshed tears. "You will, but you won't look twice. Let's just say that the next time you cut me in public, I'll have the pleasure of recalling this night and knowing that this is one whey-faced widow who is grateful to have had the honor of your attentions." Taking a deep, unsteady breath and squaring her shoulders, she transformed herself into a woman he could not touch, a woman who would never allow a man liberties such as moon-lit trysts and forbidden caresses. "Good evening, sir, and good-bye."

Before he could protest, she slipped through the curtains and was gone. *Whey-faced widow?* he asked himself. *What the hell was she talking about?* The next time he cut her? After eight years of self-imposed exile, he'd returned to England only two weeks ago. Drake Sotherton, the Duke of Sussex, found himself alone in the alcove, the scent of her clinging to his skin and clothes. He pulled a hand through his hair and tried to absorb the meaning of her parting words. He was a man who was used to getting what he wanted—and he'd be damned if he knew what had just happened, but she'd not escape him that easily.

Two

"You're a villain, Drake."

The duke smiled at his friend's wry accusation, aware that, in this instance, the words weren't intended seriously as they jested over a hand of cards. "Then imagine how grateful I am to have a saint like you who will admit in public to knowing me."

Lord Colwick's laughter rang out, drawing several disapproving glances from the other club members to the handsome pair as they sat by the fireplace. Whereas Drake's coloring was dark and forbidding, Alex's was much lighter. "A saint! Thank you, Drake! You shall be the first and last to mention my canonization, but I will take the inappropriate title happily. What would my peers say if they heard me brag of it?"

Drake shook his head, his smile not quite reaching

the darkening storm of his eyes, "They'd point out that saints are often martyrs, Alex."

Lord Colwick's merriment dissipated a degree, as he remembered the painful past that still haunted his companion. "You take too much to heart, Drake. It's been eight years, and clearly, you've atoned for whatever imaginary crimes you—"

"It wasn't an imaginary crime, Alex." Drake cut him off coldly, displeased at the turn in their banter. He gathered up the coins and notes from the table.

"It wasn't *your* crime, Drake," Alex amended. "Damn it! Let it go."

Drake stood and pocketed his winnings in one fluid movement, like a large jungle cat disturbed from his perch by the fire. "In time, Alex. All in good time, but for now, allow a villain to make his escape before I've done irreparable harm. I think you've been exposed to enough infamy for one night."

"Drake, hold on!" Alex stood, his stature and grace matching his friend's. "Leave if you must, but if I've overstepped by bringing up the past, then I apologize. We've been friends too long for this posturing and growling."

Drake nodded. "There was no trespass, Alex. I've been out of company too long and have no one to blame but myself."

Alex's stance relaxed, and he smiled. "Well, then. I'll free you to sulk, and when you wish another attempt at society, let me know." He bowed, releasing Sotherton to his mood and his own entertainments. From childhood,

Alex had respected Drake's desire for solitude, which no doubt accounted for the strong bond between the two men.

"Good night, Colwick." Sotherton offered him a half bow and turned to head out of the gentlemen's club and into the night.

The cool air was bracing, and Drake inhaled deeply in an effort to clear his head before climbing into his waiting carriage and ordering his driver home. So little had changed in the eight years since he had left England, but he acknowledged that, at the same time, a great deal had changed. *He* had changed.

He had prepared himself for the worst—and discovered that caution best accompanied wisdom. The Duke of Sussex was a novelty for the parties and salons of the Ton, but he was not considered respectable. Far from it. Drake's handsome features pulled into a humorless smile as he considered the odd notoriety of being the "Deadly Duke." The whispers that had driven him away eight years ago had been reborn with his return. Gentlemen kept their polite distances, except for the rare friend like Colwick who stood by him, but ladies without exception steered clear of his path. For what respectable woman could invite a murderer's attentions?

The memory of black velvet and the soft cries of a woman's release echoed in reply to his silent question, and Drake sighed in frustration. His mystery "cat" was an unwelcome distraction, but his body and mind

were unwilling to forgo the pleasure of remembering
the encounter. Now, when he was determined to stay
focused on his plans, he found that he was helpless to
ward off the intoxicating memory of her skin, the
taste of her climax against his mouth, the innocent
trembling of her fingertips as she reached for him.
*Who was she? Who was this creature who played such
games, seducing a stranger only to disappear without a
trace? Had he insulted her unknowingly and drawn her
to him?*

He shook his head at the absurd thought, convinced that he had never publicly cut any woman—
widowed or otherwise. So it seemed clear that she had
mistaken him last night for another man. She obviously didn't have much experience with these pursuits. Even so, the novelty of a woman who would risk
approaching a man in public like that was too delicious to ignore.

Drake took a deep breath and let it out slowly, wondering if a compromise would have to be achieved to
prevent this new mystery from distracting him from
current plans.

He smiled as the carriage pulled to a smooth halt in
front of his London home. Drake handed off his coat
and hat to a footman and headed for the quiet haven of
his study.

"Have you eaten this evening, Your Grace?" Jameson asked from the doorway, a loyal shadow that followed Drake into his sanctuary.

His master shook his head, "I wasn't hungry." He poured himself a brandy.

"I'll have dinner sent up—"

"No, Jameson," Drake cut him off. "I'm fine." He turned, deliberately softening his tone. "Thank you for the offer, but tell the kitchen staff they can have an early night of it. I won't ring the bell till morning."

"As you wish, Your Grace." Jameson bowed slightly, his expression hard to interpret, but Drake's jaw tightened at the telltale sympathy in his butler's eyes.

He turned his back, waiting until he heard the door closing before taking a long, slow drink from his brandy. The liquor trailed heat and languid potency down his throat, and Drake sighed in frustration as the amber spirit failed to take the edge off the restless tenor of his thoughts.

He sat at his desk and glanced at the ledgers and notebooks that lay in a neat pile awaiting his attention. The illusion of organization and control wasn't lost on Drake. He'd done well in the islands of the Caribbean, investing in various trade lines. His shipbuilding company in England had fed profitably into his interests in the Americas. His reputation for being ruthless in business had solidified with his personal woes. The rumors of his wife's murder had given him an advantage at the negotiation tables. Whenever he looked at a man coldly and informed him that he kept a close eye on his accounts and was unforgiving to those who tried to pick his pockets or take anything that was his, men believed him.

No charges had been filed. No one had ever been charged or convicted for the crime. Drake had been leagues away on business in Scotland, and the authorities had immediately dismissed him as a suspect. There was nothing for him to dispute or fight, but the rumors had been relentless, and his choice to leave, to grieve in peace, was in retrospect an almost fatal mistake. He had inadvertently played the part of a guilty man running from his crimes. And by the time he'd seen it, he'd been paralyzed by bitter memories and a stubborn desire to turn his back on all of it. He'd refused to dance for anyone's amusement.

And then, of course, there was Julian, the flesh-and-blood haunt that conjured up nightmares without effort. Julian Clay was untouchable, popular among his peers, and Drake had no proof against him, not a shred of evidence beyond instinct and experience. To accuse him openly would be a worthless exercise.

Lily.

It was Julian who had led the hue and cry against him, and Drake had come to realize that the source of his friend's venom was all too personal. Julian had loved her, or at least made a point of sleeping with her. And it had come to Drake over time that it must have been Julian who had taken her life. Perhaps in a jealous lovers' quarrel, or when Lily sensed that she was no more than a pawn in one of Julian's stupid schemes to hurt Drake. The reality was that Julian had been in town when she was murdered, had had access to the

house, and had been the first to cry foul and turn all
eyes to Drake.

They'd been friends and rivals, and before Lily,
Drake had laughed at Julian's urge to best him. He had
never imagined that the game would extend to murdering his wife.

All traces of her within the house were long gone.
He turned in his chair to study the room, with its dark
hues and strong lines. She had never really touched
this room with her feminine penchant for redecorat-
ing with colored silks, priceless porcelains, and endless
curios. He'd given her the run of every room but
two—his study and their bedroom. And after her
death, he'd ordered all his houses stripped to the walls
and redone. Every room but these two. Drake refilled
his glass as he faced the irony of that last decision.
After all, the bedroom was the room where she had
died. If he'd meant to banish her, he should have
started there. Perhaps, if he'd stayed in England, he
would have taken care of it. Instead, it was now a
shrine that he took odd comfort in keeping, even
though it scandalized his household to think of him
sleeping peacefully within the space.

But he hadn't returned to England to escape the
past. He'd come to embrace it.

A loyal business contact had sent word at the beginning of the year that Clay's fortress of wealth and
power had a fissure, a crack of vulnerability. It was the
first flag to draw Drake's eyes back to his beloved En-

gland. Julian, the untouchable, was weakening. It had been a matter of time, and he'd identified the one tonic to the obsession of long years of self-imposed exile and torment. Vengeance.

And now, when he'd intended to corral all his energies to this remedy, he was plagued by a masked woman with bewitching, trembling fingers that had traced his body with need and fear. God, he wanted her again, without the masks, without any barriers, to possess her again and find his release in the wet, silky flesh of her body.

Apparently dead men could still feel desire, something he didn't think was possible. He'd buried so much of himself and lost track of the times he'd raised his glass in a mock toast to the frozen stillness that infused him. The numbness was the proof that he'd lost more in these last years than his wife and his reputation.

He'd believed that it was the price to be paid—that, at last, Lily had exacted it for his neglect, for his failure as her husband and as a man.

A cruel and high cost, but then Lily had never offered him the chance for negotiation. If he'd known, would he have begged the Fates for mercy? Or, far more appropriately, would he have sold his soul simply to feel pain again, to experience anything beyond the wall that separated him from other human beings?

Even the desire for revenge, he realized, was a brush of ice in his veins. He would expose Julian and

destroy him—he would do this with the exacting patience of a surgeon. There was no expectation of pleasure in this accomplishment, no thrill in victory.

*Damn it! Who was this woman who had twisted him
into knots?*

She was a siren, and if he didn't get ahold of himself
soon . . .

The decision to take action was cemented in one
long, ragged sigh as his body tightened with need.

He'd pursue and discover his masked seductress and
put the question to rest. He told himself it was strictly a
matter of convenience and simple physical attraction.
He would unmask this "whey-faced widow" and then
move on to take his revenge and free himself from the
past. His spine stiffened with resolve as he took another
drink.

Merriam held still as her abigail finished arranging her
plain brown curls into their usual configuration and
fought the urge to cry at how easily her old self was
restored. Two days after Milbank's ball, her reflection
gave no hints of her feat. There was the mouse again,
looking back at her from her vanity's mirror. The
mouse had dull, brown hair and pale gray-blue eyes
that were a bit too large and owlish in Merriam's opinion. She looked at her lips, a bit too wide and not at
all formed in the desirable shape of a pouting little
bow. Merriam shut her eyes, unwilling to continue a
pointless inventory of her faults and shortcomings.

"Are you all right, madam?" her maid asked tenderly. "Is it another headache?"

"N-no!" Merriam opened her eyes, her cheeks coloring with embarrassment. "I'm just a bit tired."

Celia smiled, her expression relaxing with relief. "You were out unusually late the other night, m'lady. You're not used to such things!" The maid's fingers moved with efficient practice back to the task at hand as she talked. "Still, it was kind of you to offer to chaperone at Lady Palmer's. Did you enjoy yourself, m'lady?"

Merriam smiled and met Celia's eyes in the mirror, determined to carry it off. "Yes, it was lovely."

"I'm sure your new dress was much admired," the maid pressed innocently.

Merriam felt the heat in her cheeks but managed to keep a neutral expression. "The blue was a good choice, but I hardly think anyone notices a chaperone." She stood quickly, fearing she'd fumble the line of conversation if it wasn't diverted soon. Lying to the staff about her destination, changing in and out of her costume and disguise at Madame DeBourcier's bordello, the Crimson Belle, had been a necessary— and the riskiest—part of the plan. But now Merriam amended her opinion of which had been the riskiest moment. Arriving at the back door of a London brothel to transform into another woman seemed a simple matter compared with walking away from that alcove with her thighs trembling and her inner muscles aching from the surrender of her flesh to his.

She'd done it. Conquered one of London's greatest rakes, and walked away as he'd begged for her name. She hadn't exactly left him in a state of frustration as she'd planned, but wasn't it better to have taken her own pleasure? To have tasted the experience of letting go, reveling in her deepest desires?

"—dinner tonight, m'lady?"

"W-what?" Merriam's stomach clenched as she watched Celia's eyes flood with curiosity at her mistress's odd behavior.

"I wondered if you'd decided what you'd be wearing to the Markhams' for dinner tonight, m'lady."

"Th-the gray silk is fine," she answered quickly, hating the breathy fear that filtered into her voice. As if to counter it, she added more sharply, "That will be all, Celia. I'll take a light luncheon in my drawing room and let Geoffrey know that I'll want the carriage promptly at eight."

Celia gave a small curtsy and left in a hurry.

Merriam waited until the door had closed behind her before sinking back into her chair with a frustrated groan. It was all so boring. Dinner with the Markhams, old friends of her late husband's who out of pity included her in their gatherings. Then, in the next few days, she would make a round of required social calls, attend a lecture on musical themes, and participate in the Ladies' Charity Club's monthly meeting over afternoon tea. Then, in a fortnight, the Ladies' Botanical Society of Greater London was having their annual visit to the London Arboretum. Real life, the ordinary events of her schedule now seemed like a suffocating wave that threatened to drive her mad.

Instead of basking in the glow of her brief escape and lustful conquest, she wanted to scream at the colorless pattern of the days that stretched endlessly out in front of her. The memory of vivid black velvet and scarlet silk, of Julian's hands against her skin, it was like a dream that was already fading—teasing her just beyond her reach. Instead of having it to cherish, she wondered how long it would take before her body forgot.

No! It was over. She would make one last call to Madame DeBourcier to render her last payment for her lessons and to thank her for her help. She would shake her mentor's hand and then close the door on the entire episode. It was too dangerous to remember Julian. It was too dangerous to think that she could harbor such secrets. She would let the memory fade and forget that, for one fleeting moment, she'd come alive in a man's arms.

Three

"A what?"

"A widow," Drake countered easily, keeping his eyes locked on Lord Milbank's.

"I-it is an unusual request, Your Grace." Lord Milbank's voice was high, a soft, uneven pitch that betrayed his nerves. "My guest lists are a private matter, and those who attend . . . often trust me to protect their—"

Drake cut him off with a wave of his hand. "I have been away for many years, my lord, and have no desire to cause you any difficulties amidst your esteemed guests and friends. And I am not sure what to say to convince you without revealing too much of the nature of my search and its cause." He paused for dramatic effect, playing off of the infamous host's reputation for enjoying the intrigue and illicit romances that his parties generated. "But the lady . . ."

"Yes?" Milbank edged forward on his seat, an eager audience.

"Intrigued me," Drake supplied with an enigmatic smile, hoping that this strategy wouldn't later come to ruin, "and I simply must know who she is. I wonder if you could help me find her."

"It is a woman's prerogative to elude an admirer, Your Grace."

"As it is mine to pursue her. I can assure you, Lord Milbank, the lady gave a good indication that I am not an unwelcome suitor. But our conversation was interrupted by chance, and I lost her in the crowd."

Milbank's jaw fell open in amazement at such a delicious confession of romantic attachment—and from the Deadly Duke no less! Who would have thought it possible? Who could have guessed the—

"I take it you will help me then, sir?" Drake pressed, his eyebrows arched.

"Yes, of course!" Milbank moved with startling speed around his desk, despite his enormous girth. He pulled out the guest list with a flourish, his eyes glittering with anticipated pleasure. He scanned the sheets and named the women who might have caught the duke's attention.

"Hmmm." Milbank offered additional notes. "Too old . . . came as a mermaid, that one . . . was carrying a small dog, does that sound familiar?" With each additional bit of description, Drake was able to whittle the impressively sized list down until at last he had only two names.

Lady Millicent Forsythe.

Mrs. Merriam Everett.

"I don't recall either woman's costume, I'm afraid," Milbank remarked breathlessly, "but both women are still relatively young, if memory serves."

Drake kept his expression neutral. "And you're sure they were both at the ball?"

Milbank shrugged. "It is difficult to say, a room full of disguises and masks. They both sent acceptances and were expected. But honestly, if either woman were to be described as 'intriguing,' it would clearly be Millicent. She is a desirable and lively creature, very vivacious."

"Hair color?"

"Auburn." Milbank leaned forward in his chair. "Does that sound familiar?"

The recollection of a streak of red hair accenting lustrous black curls leapt to mind, and Drake felt a surge of relief that his search might be concluded so easily. "It's possible."

"I don't remember anything remarkable at all about Mrs. Everett. A rather plain and dull creature, I think."

"I'm surprised you would extend an invitation to a dull creature," Drake interjected dryly.

"Ah, well." Milbank shrugged again. "Grenville was an old friend from school, and it's not as if I expected her to actually attend! I met her at a gathering once and remember thinking that the drapery was more animated. But Millicent is a firecracker and would be my first and best guess!"

Milbank's glee at the possession of such valuable gossip was palpable, and Drake let him revel in the anticipation for just a few seconds before he closed this potentially dangerous loophole in his plans.

"I thank you for your assistance, Lord Milbank. Naturally, this matter will remain between us."

"Oh, naturally!" Milbank agreed quickly, his sincere tone fooling neither of them.

Drake's smile evaporated, his expression growing cold, a practiced look he knew had a potent intimidating effect. "If I hear of this matter beyond this room, I shall know that you are the source. And I will feel compelled to make it clear to anyone and everyone I meet that your private guest list for the Grand Masque is available to any who asks and that you have personally profited from sharing that list."

"Y-you wouldn't dare! It would be a lie!"

Drake threw a small leather purse of coins onto Milbank's desk. "Not at all."

He stood, and turned on his heels, and left a sputtering Lord Milbank bobbing behind his desk like a terrified pigeon.

Jocelyn smiled at her pupil's efforts to disguise her nerves as she put an envelope full of pound notes on the low table in front of her. Known as Madame De-Bourcier, she had developed an odd sort of friendship with this shy widowed lady who had sought her advice and guidance. With a trained eye, she noted the color in Merriam's cheeks and the averted gaze, which conveyed volumes of information to an apt teacher. "I take it the evening was a success?"

Merriam raised her chin, and Jocelyn saw a brief flash of triumph in her eyes. "It was—more than I'd hoped for."

Jocelyn watched the triumph fade and instinctively understood her pupil's new dilemma. She sank gracefully onto the divan next to Merriam, and gave her a few moments to collect herself by pouring them each a glass of sherry.

"Oh! It is too early for sherry and I shouldn't—"

"A woman can suffocate with the weight of *shouldn't* pressing down on her all the time. And we have already discovered that you are not a woman to shy away from a healthy rebellion or two." Jocelyn handed Merriam her glass, overriding the woman's protest with a soft clink of glass in a mock toast. "To conquest and the next battle."

"Th-there is no 'next battle,' Madame DeBourcier!" Merriam's spine stiffened in alarm.

"I see." Jocelyn leaned back, a study in languid sensuality, deliberately moving in contrast to her refined guest's nervously controlled gestures. "Perhaps I've missed something then. You said it was more than you'd hoped for."

"It was!" Merriam gripped the small sherry glass,

aware of the heat flooding her face. "But I thought I made it clear that this was to be just once."

"Twice a week for four weeks, we sat in this very room, and I am fairly sure that I was equally clear."

"Your instruction was . . ." Merriam struggled to think of an appropriate word to describe the impact their sessions had had on her. The simple act of sitting across from a known madam who ran a luxurious and infamous bordello had been daunting at first. But then to engage in frank and open discussions about acts that Merriam had only the vaguest knowledge of—it had been liberation itself. "Your instruction was invaluable."

Jocelyn tilted her head back and laughed. "You are priceless!"

Merriam's mouth dropped open in shock, then curved into a smile. The beautiful young madam's humor was dangerously contagious. "You'd prefer a different word of praise?"

Jocelyn recovered a bit, sipping on her sherry and then setting the glass down. "We sat here, that first afternoon, and I told you that each new experience, for better or for worse, changes a woman. I told you that you could have your rake, could have any man you desired, but not without letting go of your reserve—without tapping into your own desires."

Merriam blushed. "I did. It worked, and I have you to thank for—"

"No, wait." Jocelyn leaned forward to take the

sherry glass out of Merriam's hand and set it next to her own. "Mrs. Everett, I'm afraid there's no going back."

Merriam shifted away, the heat that flooded her cheeks withdrawing just as quickly. "You're wrong. This was . . . I've had my adventure, and now, unless I misjudged you and you're threatening my exposure, I have every intention of putting this behind me." She began to rise, but a hand caught and held hers.

"I threaten nothing." Jocelyn's voice was low but compelling as she held her pupil in place. "And you can run from this room believing anything you wish about my character. Passion transforms." She shrugged gracefully to accent her apparent disregard for the trappings of reputation and honor. "I am not wrong, Mrs. Everett."

Merriam shook her head. "It ends here. I—I've already risked too much. I'm grateful for your help and even more grateful that you never laughed at me, never mocked me for coming to you. But the transformation was fleeting, not permanent. I am still the same woman that I always was."

"I see." Jocelyn released her hand with a smile. "You'll return to your life then?"

Merriam stood and extended her hand. "I never left my life, Madame DeBourcier. I simply altered its course temporarily."

Jocelyn took Merriam's hand to shake it, accepting the formality of the gesture and the farewell it signaled.

"If ever you need me again, just send word. Good luck, Mrs. Everett."

Jocelyn watched her go and then walked over to pull the bell to order her evening bath.

Jocelyn was actually younger than her protégé. Still, a vast chasm of experience and status separated them. As she disrobed, she wondered if it were really possible to alter one's fated path. She thought of the odd twists her own life had taken, the layers of deception she'd mastered in order to survive. Then she pushed away the familiar regrets and doubt that began to nibble at the edges of her awareness. Jocelyn deliberately selected one of her most provocative gowns . . . like armor. She was a warrior choosing camouflage so that no one would guess her secrets.

She shook her head at the irony of Mrs. Everett's lessons. "So much yet to learn, m'lady," she spoke aloud in the empty room. "So much for both of us, I imagine."

Julian Clay leaned back in his chair, one eyebrow arching at the wretched spread of cards in his hand. He suppressed the urge to sigh. Apparently, his streak of bad luck continued and the gods of fortune insisted on dancing just beyond his reach. In the past, the taunt of the cards had been a thrilling siren's call, but recently, it was as if anything he touched guaranteed that gold would fly from his fingertips and into the pockets of his adversaries. Still, he was too experienced to let his anxiety show. He held on his face a fixed display of boredom to convey the impression of a man who had far more on his mind than a mere game of chance.

He managed a tired smile across the table at Lord Andrews, signaling the need for another card as he tossed out a coin to add to his bet. "Care to match it, old boy, or are you resting on your laurels?"

The gibe was delivered without venom, and Julian wondered if anyone else had noticed that he was losing so spectacularly in recent months. As used to the highs and lows of the gaming tables as he was, Julian felt a small shiver of anxiety at the thought of his financial straits being revealed to his peers. A wave of boredom and restless energy washed over him. He needed a distraction. "What news, Elton? You say little of the local gossip. It makes me wonder if your wife has kept you in too much lately."

"Sussex is back."

"What?" Julian's blood heated, and adrenaline surged through him. "That's impossible! It is a rumor not worth repeating, Andrews."

Jaded eyes hooded with a show of indifference met his without flinching. Lord Andrews was deep in his cups but still deadly with cards—and information. "Well, then I saw the rumor at a distance yesterday at White's. He was cutting quite a figure and a bit too substantial for me to dismiss as hearsay, Clay. I heard his fortunes have increased several times over from his ventures in the West Indies."

Julian's grip on his cards tightened, though his tone was mild and only softly dusted with disgust. "The exile returns. What a surprise."

"Seems he's returned to banish old ghosts. And with gold enough to make everyone forget why he ran off in the first place."

Julian's shoulders tensed. He knew from experience that there was little in a man's power that had the strength to combat and defeat the past—but if Drake had managed it . . . With the new knowledge that his old nemesis had reentered the game, Julian's sense of anxiety doubled.

He placed his cards facedown on the table and signed another chit to settle the evening's debts. "If you'll excuse me, Lord Andrews."

Without waiting for the older man's dismissal, Julian unfolded from his chair and made his way toward the parlor and through the velvet curtains that shielded the rest of the house from the gaming rooms.

"What is your pleasure, sir?"

He scanned the room, his eyes narrowing as he assessed the attributes of all the women, in various states of undress meant to arouse and entice men to select them for a visit upstairs to one of the brothel's many suites. Julian smiled as he spotted one prostitute, her strawberry blond hair and soft shoulders reminding him of a ghost that he and Drake had once vied for, fought over, and ultimately shared. "I'll take her."

Four

"Tell me again why we're here?" Alex asked archly, enjoying his friend's scowling response.

"You're the one who wanted me to get out more," Drake replied distractedly, his eyes already beginning to sweep the room. "Besides, you're also the respectable one with the invitation. How else am I supposed to assure the civilized beau monde that I'm a new man?"

"Ah, yes." Lord Colwick smiled. "Well, glaring like a lion searching for a wounded gazelle is certainly a technique I hadn't thought to recommend, but by all means, if the debutantes don't start bursting into tears or fainting, this should at least prove entertaining."

Drake sighed and amended his expression, chuckling at the realization that, once again, his friend was right. Beyond his quest, there were the very real consequences of his current reputation. It wouldn't help him to reinforce people's fears of the "Deadly Duke" by stalking around and frightening other party guests. Especially since he hadn't been personally invited and had come with Lord Colwick.

"Seriously, Drake." Alex leaned in and dropped his voice to avoid being overheard. "Why are we here? I'm having trouble imagining that you suddenly had an urge to waltz with simpering debutantes so you can send their mothers running for their smelling salts."

Drake shook his head, a wry smile lighting his face. "What? I love to dance."

"You loathe it as much as I do, and once told me that you would rather consume gravel and horse manure."

"True, and sadly, it's probably a statement I would still stand by. But since we are here, I may as well reacquaint myself with a few people and take one turn about the rooms. Then we'll make a quick escape before the debutantes realize there is an eligible saint in their midst."

"Very funny, though I'm glad you at least acknowledge the dangers I face on your behalf." Lord Colwick was indeed an eligible and vied for catch, and had it not been for Drake's insistence, this was a gathering he would have avoided. "Keep your secrets, Sotherton. One turn and I'll meet you at the library doors." Alex sobered as he spotted their host moving toward them through the crowd, and he signaled Drake. "Best go now while I divert Lord Chaffordshire, unless you want to spend the rest of the evening talking about the coffee trade."

Drake gave his friend a grateful look as he moved away, and began his search.

Lady Millicent Forsythe.

According to his discreet inquiries, she was supposed to be in attendance. Chaffordshire's respectable gathering was a remarkable contrast to Milbank's ball, and Drake wondered if his cat missed the freedom of her masked persona amidst the inflexible social rules that now surrounded them.

He drifted through the throng of guests, careful to keep his expression open and casual as he noted names and listened carefully for any indication of Millicent's whereabouts. Scanning the dancers, he was convinced that he would recognize her instantly, that he needed only a glimpse of her hands or the curve of her neck to be sure.

"What a lovely fan, Lady Forsythe!"

The syrupy compliment caught his complete attention, and Drake held still, his heart skipping a beat in anticipation as he turned in the direction of the male voice.

The sound of a fan popping closed and bouncing playfully off the shoulder of the speaker completed the scene and ended Drake's speculations.

"You weren't supposed to notice the fan, sir! I believe that was your cue to say something about my eyes," the lady chided.

Lady Forsythe was no more his mystery woman than he was the man in the moon. One glance assessed her fashionably petite stature, generously curved figure, ripe hips, and overflowing bosom, but the acid edge of her tones turned his stomach and sealed his unfavorable impression. When he heard the shrill laughter after her would-be paramour whispered some clever rejoinder into her ear, he removed her name from his search with the sweetest sense of relief.

Drake moved away quickly. So, it was the "plain and dull" Mrs. Everett after all—unless his costumed seductress had lied about being a widow and he was on a wild-goose chase. It was still possible that she was really an actress playing him for a tumble and a diversion. But that would mean his instincts had failed him completely, and Drake wasn't willing to entertain doubts on that account.

No, he reassured himself. There would be time enough to determine the nature of her deception and the causes behind it, once he'd found her.

The instincts he relied on echoed with a faint sense of warning.

He'd solved one half of the mystery, and with so little effort.

With too little effort.

His brow furrowed at the twofold revelation that followed the simple thought. First, that given the ease

with which he'd uncovered her identity, the elusive
Mrs. Everett possessed very little craft or experience at
elaborate deception. Her vulnerability made his throat
close with unnamed emotions, but Drake swallowed
hard and dismissed these feelings. After all, it was just
as likely that she wanted to be caught and had deliberately left an easy trail to continue her seductive game
with her intended victim.

He contemplated the second revelation. If Mrs.
Everett was one half of the mystery, then the identity
of the man she sought to seduce was the other. Without that piece of the puzzle, Drake knew the rules of
engagement could drastically change.

He replayed the simple chain of events at Milbank's
ball until his memory traced and recovered the thread
he sought.

A servant had approached and advised him, "Merlin, sir? The lady says to inform you that your familiar has arrived."

"My familiar?"

"Yes, m'lord. She is there, by the far tables. The
black cat, sir."

He'd spotted her, a still, dark form amidst movement and opulent color, and his blood had argued that
a man would have to be dead or his wits addled to ignore a woman's bold summons. And so he'd gone to
her side.

Merlin. The costumier had sworn that his choice
was unique, but clearly another man had made a sim-

ilar selection and abandoned it, or decided at the last minute not to attend.

He'd have her. But Drake decided that, before he cornered his quarry, he would be wise to discover the identity of her Merlin. He smiled darkly as he headed for the library doors to await Alex. If Lord Colwick had thought this evening's plans a bit out of the ordinary, Drake just hoped his friend didn't discover his plans to spend the next few days visiting costumiers and designers in London. He certainly wasn't about to admit to Alex that his remark about the hunt wasn't that far off.

Five

"Six hundred pounds!" Lady Sedgewold exclaimed, accenting each syllable to ensure that no one missed her point. "Why, when I heard that he'd given such a sum out of the kindness of his dear old heart, I could scarcely contain my admiration and astonishment!"

Merriam managed to make the appropriate response and sigh at her companion's husband's unheard of "generosity," all the while distracted by the pinch of her shoes and the dull throbbing behind her eyes. The squeak and chatter of the other guests at Lord Dixon's garden party made her jaw clench in frustrated determination. It had been a week since the masque, and this was the life she had vowed to Madame DeBourcier that she was all too happy to return to.

Merriam forced a smile to her lips. No one would be

able to look at her and see anything other than a woman perfectly content with the quiet, steady structure of her life; no one would detect the flashes of heat and fire that haunted her every time she thought of—

"The Earl of Westleigh! Look, my dear Mrs. Everett! It is the dashing earl I had the pleasure of introducing you to several weeks ago. Do you not remember? Oh, my! Isn't he handsome?"

Merriam felt as if all her limbs had simultaneously frozen and then caught fire. She glanced across the shaded lawn in the direction of Lady Sedgewold's gestures and saw him instantly. Julian Clay. The man she had vowed to seduce and humble. The man she had blatantly pursued and given herself to anonymously in a curtained alcove. She watched as he moved easily through the crowd, his figure lean and handsome, his hair the amber gold of a lion—his air sophisticated and all male. She traced the lines of his legs and felt her heart race at the recollection of how his muscled thighs had felt between her own, at how strong he'd been and how masterfully he'd—

". . . is it not?"

Merriam gasped at the realization that she had lost the train of Lady Sedgewold's comments, and worse, had failed to respond. Her cheeks stained pink in embarrassment. "I'm sorry, Lady Sedgewold. What did you say?"

Her companion laughed. "I shall take your distraction and inability to keep your eyes from following him about as signs that you are not entirely immune to the gentleman's charms."

Merriam stiffened in protest and forced her gaze back to her companion to prove her point. "You misinterpret my actions, Lady Sedgewold. I was merely trying to place Mr. Clay in my memory and recall the introduction."

"Ah!" Lady Sedgewold offered, clearly not fooled. "Well then, let us see what we can do to reacquaint you."

Before Merriam could compose a protest, Lady Sedgewold had lifted her hand in an imperious wave and summoned Julian over. Merriam gripped her parasol handle as if it were the hilt of a sword and vowed to give her entire fortune to a charity of the Fates' choosing if only the ground would swallow her whole before he reached them.

Her thoughts raced in panic. *Will he remember me? Will he realize that I am the woman who led him into that alcove? Will he make some indication? Will I be able to tell?*

"You honor me, Lady Sedgewold." Julian bowed smartly as he drew near and gave them both an easy smile.

"You remember my friend Mrs. Everett, do you not, Mr. Clay?"

"But of course," he answered and took her gloved hand politely to complete the required ritual, his expression neutral and unaffected. As he straightened and released her numb fingers, Merriam realized it was worse to be invisible once again in his presence after what they had shared.

She bit the inside of her lip and silenced the contrary sting of her pride. Hadn't she nearly had a heart attack at the thought of him seeing through her disguise? This was a sign that she'd been right to put her dangerous escapade behind her. The mouse knew when to be still in order to survive.

Lady Sedgewold sighed, long used to Merriam's shyness. "You shared a waltz at my annual gala."

"Yes, charming. How could I forget?" His handsome eyes diverted briefly to Mrs. Everett as if to prove his polite powers of recollection, and Merriam lifted her chin, determined to prove her own strength as well. She managed a smile before she realized that Fate was even crueler than she'd anticipated.

Although Julian Clay was more handsome than she'd remembered . . . this wasn't the same man!

A rush of details assaulted her senses. A wig would have explained the difference in hair, and the mask had concealed a great deal from her study, but there was no disguising the unmistakable fact of his height. Unless Julian had lost several inches in height, she had seduced the wrong man.

No! It wasn't possible! Merriam had met him only once before the masque. She'd thought he was the most handsome man she'd ever seen and he'd insulted her. But at Milbank's, she was sure he'd been taller.

She'd thought it was fear that had made him seem taller and his shoulders broader than she'd remembered. After all, it had been one brief encounter. If this was hysterics and he'd been in some kind of heeled boot the night of the masque, there might still be hope. Her brain grasped for logical threads to lead her away from the nightmare conclusion that she'd made a terrible mistake.

"I am glad to see you out in company, Lord Westleigh. My husband said that you were a man who seemed to count the days till 'tedious Society' freed you to hunt and play," Lady Sedgewold continued, oblivious of her young friend's struggles.

"Not at all. I find myself unable to leave the pleasant society of London. Time enough for hunting and manly pursuits when the weather turns in the fall."

Oh, God. Even the voice is different. How could I have been so stupid? Merriam chided herself silently, her knees starting to shake as she became more certain of her error.

His hands, though lean, weren't the hands she remembered. These weren't the long fingers that had stroked her skin and tugged her nipples free from her bodice or spread open her thighs and the soft flesh between her legs . . .

The world receded to a dull gray.

"My dear! Are you unwell?" Lady Sedgewold's voice pierced through the fog, and Merriam realized that she was now sitting on a stone bench with Julian Clay in polite attendance.

"I'm—I'm fine!" Merriam kept her eyes away from Julian for fear of setting off another dangerous wave of panic.

"A glass of punch?" he offered. His expression was pure courtesy, but Merriam noted with despair that his eyes reflected boredom and disinterest.

"No, b-but thank you, sir." She pushed away Lady Sedgewold's supportive hands to demonstrate her independence. "I am completely recovered and wouldn't wish to impose."

Oh, God. It hadn't been Julian . . .

"I am glad to see that you have. Well, if you will excuse me." He nodded, seizing the opportunity to move away. "I will leave you ladies to enjoy the rest of the party." He bowed again to Lady Sedgewold and turned to make his way toward a colorful group engaged in livelier pursuits.

Merriam watched him go, trying to swallow the fiery ball of resentment that threatened to choke her. The blasted man could at least have argued! He could have insisted on attending her! Apparently whey-faced widows fainted in his presence on a regular basis, giving him another reason to avoid the tedium of her company.

The flash of anger faded quickly as she returned to the stark horror of her actions at Milbank's. If not Julian—then *who?*

"You should have sighed and accepted his offer of punch, my dear," Lady Sedgewold advised at her elbow, her voice lowered conspiratorially. "You chased him away."

"I'm sure I didn't chase him away." Merriam stood, determined to put as much distance as possible between herself, the dowager, and any other "friend" who was in the mood to offer advice. "And I most certainly didn't summon him!"

Lady Sedgewold's mouth fell open in a shocked gasp, and Merriam's hands clenched into tight balls of frustration.

"I apologize, Lady Sedgewold. I— A headache has contributed to my ill humor, and I'll take my leave." She curtsied and picked up her parasol to make a dignified march from Dixon's lawn and away from her peers. It was either march or run, and Merriam doubted either method would put any distance between herself and the day's revelations.

She'd seduced the wrong man! A wave of nausea assaulted her as a dark, cold part of her brain pointed out that if it wasn't Julian, it could have been almost anyone. A stranger whom she didn't know—or worse, someone she did know. The husband, brother, or father of an acquaintance. What if he recognized her in public?

Cold sweat broke out across her forehead, and Merriam leaned against the verandah railing to catch her breath. Seeing him again was inevitable but she'd been so confident of her disguise, so sure that he wouldn't be able to single her out later. Only her parting words might have betrayed her if he'd recalled the insult and connected the events. But now . . .

Madame DeBourcier's words came back with prophetic weight. *There was no going back.*

Patience. Drake was doing his best to keep a tight hold on a virtue he had never entirely mastered. His informant, Peers, had an ambling style that rankled him, but the man was one of the best at what he did. The duke had made his own efforts, even tapping his friend Alex to make inquiries to anyone who might not be amenable to sharing information with a man of Drake's reputation. The idea of tracking down the sorcerer's costume had produced a mountainous list of shops and potential leads, and he was grateful to his friend for pitching in—even if Lord Colwick had no real idea of his intentions.

Peers finished his "report" on Mrs. Everett's general background, aware that most of the information wasn't the useful tidbits a man in the duke's position was hoping for. He took a deep breath before continuing. "Her servants are loyal and a bit protective, but I did manage to learn the lady has quite a full schedule. Mrs. Everett volunteers for charities and events and recently took on a new project, some kind of lecture series. Early Tuesday and Thursday mornings at the Chesham Science Hall."

"No offense, Peers, but if this is supposed to make my heart race with excitement and me beg you to take a bonus payment, then I think you've omitted something, or been drinking."

"Except there ain't no morning lecture series at the Chesham on those days. And nothing the four weeks she was 'out.' One of the kitchen maids thought the mistress had herself a beau and said they had their fingers crossed she was off meeting some lover."

Drake's eyebrows rose in interest. "An affair?"

Peers nodded, his confidence bolstered by the duke's expression. "Over, apparently. But a respectable suitor would've called at the house, seems to me. If she were meetin' a man for a bit of clandestine fun, it'd be outside the reach of the eyes and ears of her staff."

A lover? Had she thought to meet her secret paramour at the masque? Wouldn't she have been able to distinguish a stranger from her regular lover?

"Any chance of discovering where she was going during those weeks?" Drake couldn't stop himself from pressing for more information.

"Already on it. It's not going to be easy because she seems to have been extra cautious, hiring hacks and not using her regular driver on those mornings. It's why they made such a point to recall it, I'd say."

Drake had an odd flash of a possessive emotion. *His* cat had met someone secretly, had eluded her own staff, and was playing at some game. He instinctively knew it had everything to do with her Merlin. He tried to ignore the irrational hatred for his rival, but the man's identity was still a necessary piece of the puzzle. He was already on unstable ground in London, and he wanted to be sure of any potential pitfalls in his path. He couldn't afford a misstep that would interfere with his true goal.

But he also wasn't about to relinquish his temptress.

"I know you'll do your best, Peers." Drake stood abruptly, impatient to conclude the game and claim his prize.

"Aye, Yer Grace. I'll get back to you as soon as I get something."

Drake handed over an additional payment, the amount generous enough to guarantee that his runner would make this search his only priority. "Hurry, Peers," he advised as the man took his leave.

Drake turned toward the windows, his thoughts circling round and round like the widening gyre of a falcon searching for its prey.

A knock sounded at the door, and he guessed Jameson had once again decided to ensure that he was eating.

"No dinner, thank you," he asserted without turning around.

"Damn! And I'm famished too!" Alex's easy manners exiled the last remnants of Drake's dark thoughts. "God, man! You owe me a decent meal after all the traipsing over London I've done for you."

"I owe you more than a meal, Colwick."

"Agreed, but we saints must take the crumbs offered to us." Alex threw himself elegantly into a chair next to

Drake's desk, unfolding his long legs in an exaggerated show of exhaustion.

"I'm sure the staff will be happy to scrape up a crust of bread and some cold broth to accommodate you." Drake moved toward the bell pull to order a decidedly more sumptuous meal than he'd described for his guest.

"Wait."

The command was quiet but unexpected, and Drake's hand dropped before he'd touched the embroidered rope.

Alex straightened in his chair, his demeanor becoming serious. "You may not want to linger at the dinner table after . . ."

"After what?" Drake made it clear he was in no mood for guessing games.

But Alex was not a man to be intimidated by Drake's moods. "What are you doing back in London, old friend? What are you up to?"

Drake froze for a moment, then moved to take the seat across from Lord Colwick. "Nothing that need bother a saint like yourself."

"You'd hinted about putting your past to rest, Drake. I can't help but think that it would be wise to do so. But if it's vengeance—"

"What the hell are you talking about? What is inspiring this?" Drake's voice was inflamed with guilt. He made no attempt to conceal it out of respect for his friend, but the errand he'd asked Alex to complete had nothing to do with vengeance. It startled him that Colwick would bring it up, but he'd be damned if he was ready to admit his plans. Even more important, he didn't want his friend implicated if things went badly later.

"The costume you were seeking," Alex began calmly. "I was at LeBlanc's. He said he'd had an order placed for Milbank's and that it was never picked up."

"By whom?"

Lord Colwick just looked at him and waited for the storm.

It hit Drake almost instantly.

"You can't be serious."

Alex's mahogany gaze never wavered.

"Damn it! If you're trying to tell me that Westleigh—"

"What's going on?" Alex pressed again. "It's not as if the earl is in hiding. Why go to such elaborate lengths to find some stupid Merlin costume he may or may not have worn to a party? Of all the people to seek out, why in God's name would you be looking for him?"

"Leave it, Alex!" Drake's fury shocked them both.

Colwick held his breath for a moment, letting the silence bring a new calm into the conversation. "No, *you* must leave it, Drake. Whatever plans you've made, you cannot think that this can come to any good."

"I can think what I wish." Drake steadied himself. "I'm asking you as a friend to respect my wishes and drop this matter. You are the last true ally I have on this earth. But I will not explain my actions."

The men stared at each other, a tentative truce building between them.

"I see," Alex supplied and stood in one fluid movement.

"I apologize." Drake's voice was barely audible. "If I'd known it was him, I would never have asked so casually for your assistance."

Alex pulled air through his teeth at the sting of his friend's admission. "You don't deny that you have plans . . . only express regret that I have an inkling of your intentions. You wound me, old friend. I'd have thought I had your trust by now."

"Then I regret it even more." Drake wasn't about to back down.

He let Alex leave without another word exchanged and could only hope that Lord Colwick didn't cut him publicly the next time they met. But concern over their friendship was overtaken by this new twist of the game.

The second half of the mystery was resolved, to Drake's fury but also to his bitter triumph. So, his cat was a woman who sought to give herself to Julian Clay. The coincidence was too bittersweet. After years of denial and punishment, he had unwittingly taken something from Julian. In the past, Drake had always been the one to lose—though he had never realized just how serious the game could become. Not until he'd found his wife dead.

Was this widow already Julian's? Were they in league

somehow? Had Julian anticipated his return and used this woman to reach him? Distract him?

His return to England wasn't exactly a secret. Drake had deliberately tried to give the impression that there was no stealth or subterfuge to his actions—no hidden motives behind his return to society and his efforts to reestablish himself. No one knew of the private theories he harbored about his wife's death or his desire to drive Julian to ground.

But keep your friends close and your enemies closer—and in either case, it would get that sleek, little, trembling body closer to him. His temptress was no longer a distraction to be dealt with before he could seek revenge. She had just become the centerpiece of his plan.

It was a brief dilemma, how to approach her. She was as much a mystery to him now as she had been that night, perhaps even more so. She was tied to his greatest enemy, but he wasn't sure of the true nature of their relationship. He couldn't believe she'd ever slept with Julian—perhaps it was to have been a first clandestine meeting, the initiation of a seduction, or even the culmination of an ongoing flirtation. But then the manner in which she'd left him seemed off.

Then again, perhaps that show of temper had been a rehearsed display. A wry grin emerged as he realized what an effective method of ensnaring a man's attentions that haughty little escape had been. Hell, *he* was certainly determined. But she'd have more than she bargained for . . . and he would have the means to reach Julian's back.

How exactly did a man call on a woman he'd never been introduced to? Even if it was a woman he'd undone and tasted, a woman whose soft cries still haunted him when he thought of how his release had taken him—exploding inside her as her spasms of pleasure gripped them both?

He glanced at the elegant brownstone with its respectable little wrought-iron gate and plain windows. Mrs. Everett was a woman of moderate means, and he'd learned from Peers that she lived well within them. Her husband had eccentrically seen his property entailed to her sole control upon his death, motivated, it was said, more by a fierce hatred of his distant male relatives than by a love for his bride. Her fortune was solid enough to attract men of greed. But the widow had kept to her somber garb for two years now and shown no interest in another marriage. She was careful of her reputation and guarded in relationships. The dull list of her meetings and associations made him shake his head in amazement. As the dusty facts of her existence accumulated, Drake had had more and more difficulty reconciling the two views of her. Only the horrific memory of Lady Forsythe's shrill cackling urged him to stay his course rather than admit that he might be in error. He needed only to see her to be sure.

Seeing her, however, was proving to be a minor challenge. He'd left his card, certain that his title alone would earn him an audience. But the housekeeper had made it clear that Mrs. Everett was not currently receiving callers of any rank or title without references.

His temptress was evading him.

The very thought made his blood race with heat; he was a hunter drawn to the chase.

His plan had been to confront her casually and test her mettle within the confines of a drawing room, to see if she would offer him tea and serve him cakes. He wanted to see if her hands would tremble or her face grow pale at the mention of the Earl of Westleigh. How many seconds or minutes would it take her to recognize him? Would she play the reserved lady of quality and deny all, or confess to her wanton behavior and seduce him again?

Now he sat in his carriage, his fantasy of a drawing room confrontation fading quickly. His eyes narrowed to study the upper windows. "Hide, Mrs. Everett. But you'll come out eventually, and I'll be waiting for you."

After days of waiting, Merriam's frustration gnawed at her nerves. She needed to act. She interrupted her pacing to stand at a window overlooking the unkempt flower garden alongside her neighbor's wall. The scandalous consequences of her unsuccessful adventure loomed, but when would the blade fall? She wondered if men condemned to die felt this horrifying sense of limbo between their sentencing and the brutal end.

She hadn't left the house since Lord Dixon's garden party. Since her last humiliating meeting with the dashing Earl of Westleigh and the revelation of just how much of the forbidden path she'd explored, Merriam wasn't sure what to do. She'd found herself a prisoner of fear, waiting for the worst.

Her last interview with Madame DeBourcier replayed endlessly in her head. "Passion transforms," her mentor had said as easily as if she'd been announcing tea. But Merriam hadn't wished to transform. She'd wished only to sample a life she'd envied—and prove to a rake like Julian Clay that she wasn't a woman to be underestimated. She closed her eyes at the memory of a masked man leaning down to lick her, the sight of his head between her thighs laving her until she begged for—

"Beg pardon, m'lady." Her maid's interruption turned her on her heels, and Merriam did her best to compose her face into a modicum of serene calm.

"What is it, Celia?"

"Mrs. Hamlett bid me bring you these cards from this morning, madam. Shall we continue to convey your regrets then?" Her maid held the small platter bearing the cards and notes from her employer's small circle of acquaintances.

Merriam waved it away, unwilling even to look at

the meager stack. "No callers. T-tell them that I am in-disposed."

"Yes, madam, as you wish." She curtsied, her eyes flashing with pity.

At the sight of it, Merriam's spine stiffened. "Celia?" She stopped the girl on impulse. She knew she was committing a breech in protocol in the carefully orchestrated relationship between mistress and maid, but days of isolation and mental tempests pushed her to continue. "W-what do they say . . . downstairs?"

"Pardon, madam?" Celia's confusion was evident.

"About me . . . what do they say?"

Celia colored prettily, but she bravely answered. "We worry 'bout you, ma'am. For a while, it seemed you were . . . happier, and there was some that guessed you'd a suitor as you were out a bit more, and seemed a bit . . . livelier. But now . . ." Her voice trailed off, unwilling to hurt her mistress.

"But now?" Merriam urged her on gently.

"It's not my place to pry, and I'd not wish to add to the gossip—but you've grown as quiet and lost as I've ever known you to be these last few days. Whatever hurt's been offered, I'd hate to see you give up. Th-they wish you happy downstairs, m'lady. You're too young to be so alone . . . i-if you ask me." Celia curtsied again, a miserable bid for her freedom.

Merriam numbly nodded her dismissal, and the maid left as quickly as she could manage. *They wished her happy.* Merriam held her breath for a moment, absorbing the insight. She had wished herself happy, hadn't she? She'd longed for it and then . . . Was it happiness she'd felt in that anonymous stranger's arms? Lust, sweet release, freedom, hunger and unmistakable satisfaction—she'd felt all those things and then abandoned them to return to her "life."

"I'm a fool," she told the wild garden beneath the window. Merriam felt some of the burden lift, the tension ease from her shoulders. She'd punished herself enough for one lifetime, hadn't she? She'd yielded and sacrificed and conformed, and she hadn't considered the cost of compliance. Her father's drinking, bad investments, and mounting debt had led to her arranged marriage at age seventeen to his business partner, Grenville Everett. In gratitude for being given so biddable a young bride, he'd forgiven her father several loans and freed him to drink himself into his grave. Sold like stock, Merriam wasn't sure what had been worse. To be so indifferently handed over in marriage, or to discover even more indifference in one's husband. She'd been the dutiful daughter and wife, and once— just once—she'd been a wanton lover without shame.

She took a slow, cleansing breath and smiled. Fear loosened its grip on her. The temporary madness that had initially fueled her fantasy was forgotten. Seeing Julian Clay in that garden, so handsome and so aloof, she'd accepted that no deceptive game would change the course of his life to bring him to her side. He would never learn of the woman who had turned hunter and dreamt of his capture. No, the Earl of Westleigh would go on with his shocking love affairs, and she would gasp in pretended horror when the sordid details were whispered in drawing rooms and dinner parties.

Are you shy? Her masked lover had asked, and oh, how she had reveled in the denial of it—in proving that she could be so much more than the shy, forgettable woman who was afraid of her own shadow.

Whoever he'd been, she would never see him again, and he certainly wouldn't be looking for her. Even if he experienced some fleeting curiosity, she was confident that her disguise had been effective. He would look for the cat in the theaters, or the burlesques, not on the conservative, tree-lined streets off Bellingham Square. He would seek a woman without shame who wore velvet and no underclothes and could marvel openly at the beauty of a man's cock in her hands. The cat didn't wear gray gabardine and spend an hour each day penning useless chatter to dusty, distant relatives or mediate arguments between her housekeeper and butler over the cost of coal and candles. If, seeking her, he scanned the faces of women he saw in the crowds at Covent Garden, he would be diverted and forget her quickly enough. There would be no scandal, no repercussions.

It was over.

Six

"**I**s that not the most impressive Apostasioideae?"
The question was laced with dry authority that
didn't invite a response. The Dowager Lady Florence
Corbett-Walsham led the group of women in their
muted widows' tweeds through the London Arboretum, a plain gaggle of geese in the wake of her broad,
burgundy skirts and stiff petticoats.

The Ladies' Botanical Society of Greater London's
outing was an orchestration of a year's planning and,
Lady Corbett-Walsham was quick to remind them, a
banner day for women of good breeding with a fashionable interest in an acceptably genteel science.

The glass and wrought-iron greenhouse was one of
the largest in the world, displaying plants and trees, and
even birds from all corners of Her Majesty's vast empire. Although it was usually crowded with visitors, the

ladies of the club had secured a private stroll during one of the afternoons on which the arbor was closed to the public.

"Come, ladies!" The dowager sniffed. "Their orchids are touted as the most complete and beautiful in England. But then, my own collection wasn't taken into account, I'm sure."

"Oh, no! If the curator had seen your *Cypripedium,* I'm sure he would have pleaded for your secrets!" one of the older women cooed on cue, aware that the only interjections their hostess and president invited were ones that praised her tastes or her hobbies.

"I should never tell, but you are dear to have recalled the supreme prize of my hothouse." Lady Corbett-Walsham swept her gaze over the small sea of bobbing heads, enjoying the consensus and attention that were her due until she noted that one member had yet again allowed her attention to wander. "Mrs. Everett!"

Merriam jumped at the sound of the woman's bark, flushing as eighteen pairs of eyes bore down on her with varying degrees of disapproval and amazement. "Pardon me, Lady Corbett-Walsham . . . I . . ." She bit her lower lip, unsure whether she'd missed a question or should just chime in with her usual, "Yes, how lovely!"

The dowager's bosom heaved with the force of her impatience. "You drift again, Mrs. Everett. If the exhibition of nature's flora in all its wonder cannot hold your attention, I wonder what would succeed in that quest."

Merriam wouldn't have offered a suggestion for all the treasures in the world. "Please excuse me, Your Ladyship," she murmured. The heat in her cheeks retreated, and she felt her spine prickle in a flash of temper. She stifled the emotion, her face impassive from long years of practice. "I was feeling unwell. It's overwhelmingly beautiful, but the damp, warm air leaves me short of breath. I just need a moment to rest, but I shouldn't wish to hold up the group. Please, go on without me and I will catch up with you presently."

The dowager appeared to be appeased. "Don't dawdle too long, Mrs. Everett! You'll miss the exhibit of South American ferns."

Merriam waited until the group had moved away before stiffly settling on a stone bench to "recover." The lie about being unwell bit at her conscience, but an hour of Lady Corbett-Walsham's monotonous diatribe seemed a justifiable recipe for a splitting headache and the vapors for any woman of sense.

Merriam indulged in a mischievous smile at the echo of Her Ladyship's voice coming through the thick trees as the tour wound its way up the brick path. "Of course, as something of an expert, I can appreciate the unique shades of green that distinguish the *Vanilla planifolia* from a common hedge. But alas, not everyone is blessed with my keen eyes."

"Or lungs with the ability to heat a greenhouse," Merriam muttered to herself.

"Such irreverence from a lady," a man's voice interjected, and Merriam jumped up with a startled cry, turning toward the intruder.

He stepped out from the curved path. No gardener or exhibit curator—he was a gentleman, his impeccable dress, the cut of his breeches and coat proclaiming his wealth and tastes. His broad shoulders and height were secondary to the rugged, masculine beauty of his chiseled features and the paralyzing intensity of his gaze. His hair was coal black, and hazel eyes gleamed under perfectly arched dark brows. His open study of her sent the already accelerated rhythm of her heart into a sustained race. She tried to read his expression. Was it disapproval of her remark? Did he, unaware of her club's authorized presence, think her a common intruder? Never before had she been the object of such a man's scrutiny.

He continued, his eyes warming with a flash of humor. "You have a wit, Mrs. Everett."

Her intake of breath betrayed her surprise that such a man would know her name. "I have"—she lifted her chin an inch, treating him to her most prim and forbidding look—"though I'm not sure who you are to make comment, sir, on any trait I may possess." She waited for him to look chastised, or even offended at a dowdy scrap who dared to stand up to him.

"We are not unacquainted, Mrs. Everett." He took a step toward her.

She took a step away to try to regain the insulation of space, only to find the paved path's edge at her heel. To retreat into the greenery seemed overly dramatic, but she was alone and out of sight of the others. What was his—

Her eyes widened as the first glimmer of an unthinkable possibility flitted across her mind. He couldn't be!

Merriam stared. She looked at him again, as if for the first time. His smile weakened her bones and set fire to her flesh. The square jaw, the shoulders of a certain width, his height—the memory of a man's overwhelming and delicious height and heft as his body pressed her into silken cushions—and finally, her eyes dropped to his hands. His strong fingers, lightly bronzed, the shape and contour of them unmistakably familiar, unchanged from the erotic memories that haunted her dreams.

Merlin.

Her first instinct was denial. "I-I've never met you before. Y-you're mistaken . . ."

His expression was pure sin, and Merriam's whispered lie died in her throat.

He wouldn't! He—in the afternoon light and in such a place? He wouldn't dare!

"Step back this instant or I shall . . ."

The space between them evaporated as he pulled her into his arms.

His mouth covered hers, and the rush of desire he evoked wrenched a moan from her. She responded, blind to everything but this man who filled her vision and conquered her senses. The dance of his tongue pressing into her open mouth, the delving exploration so sweet, the taste of him all the sweeter as her body clamored for the release that he promised. Everything he had awakened in her at the masque, everything she had since smothered, returned to glorious life in his arms.

His hand moved down her back to press her against him, his thigh shifting to nestle her closer—through layers of petticoats and her thick, serviceable gabardine, she could feel the raw power of his arousal. The slick, liquid hunger that begged to be filled, to be satisfied with the force of him and the depth of his strokes, the strength of her need forced her back to reality.

She pushed against him, and he released her instantly, stepping away with a calm grace that belied the outline of his massive erection and the erratic pulse visible at his throat. Although she'd been the one to resist, his withdrawal left her feeling bereft and even more confused. Her cheeks flushed with embarrassment as she tried to recover her balance. It was harder than she wanted to admit, especially now, when she was faced with the sight of him looking at her calmly—as if he were unaffected by what had just transpired between them.

Fury pounded on the heels of her astonishment, and Merriam gave it full rein. "What are you doing?" she hissed. "Just who do you think you are to accost me—"

He was next to her instantly, his fingertips against her lips interrupting her tirade only because it shocked her how casually he reached for her and how instantaneously her body responded to his. He lifted his other hand to his own mouth, in a mirroring gesture. "Shhh, the ladies will hear you."

Icy panic overtook indignation. She'd completely forgotten the women at the far end of the greenhouse. "You—" Merriam caught her breath and started again more softly, terrified at the idea that Lady Corbett-Walsham herself might be turning back at any moment to witness this humiliation. "I want you to leave."

He didn't move. He continued to look down at her, as if this were the most natural thing in the world—to steal the air out of a woman's lungs by looming over her, to stare into her eyes with such open heat that she was having trouble recalling why this was all impossibly wrong.

Merriam forced herself to hold his gaze, determined to prove that, if it were a duel of wills he was after, then this was one mouse who could hold her own. "I said I want you to leave."

"Is that all you want, Mrs. Everett?"

The unexpected question froze her in place. "I . . . I want . . . to be left alone."

One eyebrow arched at the obvious falsehood. Other than that, her handsome tormentor made no effort to withdraw.

Merriam's ire returned. "Don't ignore me!"

At the flash of pain in her eyes, his stillness ceased. His hands framed her face, the warmth of his fingertips making her gasp. His hold was gentle and compelling. "Never. I promise that, of all the things I am going to do to you, I will never ignore you, Merriam."

His mouth slowly lowered, and her eyes started to flutter closed as she anticipated a kiss, then flew wide open in shock as his mouth instead grazed her lips and the tip of his tongue traced the outline of her sensitive flesh before moving to her throat.

She fought the urge to moan, but when one of his hands brushed over the crest of her breasts, its heat searing her even through embroidered gabardine and corset, she gasped and pushed against him. "Y-you go too far, sir!"

He withdrew with a chuckle. "We have been much, much further, Mrs. Everett."

The slap was inevitable. Though he seemed far more prepared for it than she was. Shock at the gesture made her mouth drop open, instant regret warring with the fury that had spurred her action. She'd never struck anyone before, had never dared. Merriam took one long breath to steady herself, determined not to apologize for the angry red mark her fingers had left on his cheek. "I believe I made myself clear, sir. I wish you to go."

"The only thing that is clear, Mrs. Everett, is that you"—his eyes narrowed dangerously as he maneuvered her off the brick path and into a sheltering cluster of palm trees, until her back met the immovable bark of an Arecaceae—"are wearing the wrong costume." He drew his hands across her prim dress, from the high collar down over her breasts. "This role doesn't suit you at all." One hand pressed against her belly, his splayed fingers sending fireworks throughout her body. "I prefer the one you were wearing"—the other hand started to lift her skirt, skimming above her stockings to the soft, bare flesh between her thighs—"the night of the ball."

Her eyes fluttered closed at the magic of his fingers on the slick silk of her folds. "N-no," she whispered, even as her hips bucked against his restraining hand, her treacherous flesh wanting friction against the hard bud that now pulsed with anticipation.

His fingers found the opening in her underclothes easily, his thumb moving over the ridge of need and across the swollen tip of her clit in soft, quick strokes that made her sigh with pleasure. "Say no again, Merriam, and I will stop instantly," he warned as his fingers increased the tempo of their dance. "Or lift your leg and put it around my waist and let me show you how merciful I can be."

"Oh, my!" Her body obeyed before thought could catch up to the breathless coil of tension increasing beneath his hands. Her legs parted, and he moved to put her stocking-clad leg along his hip, steadying her against the tree and rewarding her instantly for her boldness by slipping one finger inside her. He shifted so that his thumb continued the relentless movement over her sensitive crest.

It was magic—mindless, powerful magic, the sorcery of his hands, the pressure and movement of his touch. He pulled his finger out, then pressed back into her, a slow withdrawal and equally slow invasion that made her bite her lip to stifle a moan. Then he repeated the movement, a little harder, a little faster, a little deeper, each time increasing the pressure until he added another finger and she bucked again, arching into his hand, silently begging him for more.

"Still want to be alone, Merriam?"

"Who are you?"

The fan of his breath against her throat was another caress. The need for release was so sharp, so sweet that Merriam thought she would weep. And then he stopped, withdrawing his fingers and hands. Without a word, he gently lowered her leg and slowly straightened her skirts. "We should finish this discussion later, don't you agree? After all, I wouldn't want you to accuse me of ignoring your needs or being capable of satisfying you only when we are in public. My card and address, Mrs. Everett. I'll hope for you at midnight."

And he was gone.

That bastard! How dare he? Her fury was boundless. Merriam slammed and locked her bedroom door behind her. With a strangled cry of frustration, she ripped her bonnet off and threw it against the wall.

I'll hope for you at midnight. Let him hope he didn't die waiting for her to come to him! He could rot an eternity at his cursed house! She wanted nothing of his arrogant smirking mouth—his mouth with its firm lips and treacherous tongue, to say nothing of his hands . . .

The sharp ache between her thighs and the still wet flesh that pulsed and burned mocked her outrage. Merriam shuddered with the frustration of desire denied and the unmistakable truth of her body's needs. Who was he? It was clear that his insistence on a meeting at such a scandalous hour and at his private residence had nothing to do with an honorable relationship. He'd recognized her hunger, and he knew her secrets, inviting her to walk further down a path that could only lead to ruin.

But, oh! What a sweet walk it would be . . .

She had already risked everything, given herself to the wrong man and exposed herself to the worst possible censure—and for what? To be publicly reminded, yet again, that Julian would never see her for more than a drab widow not worthy of his time or attention?

But this man wanted her.

No! Merriam sank down, sitting on the padded seat at the foot of her bed, shaking her head slowly. No, let the arrogant sorcerer wait in vain. Who was he to insult her with his vile suppositions and insinuate himself into her orderly and respectable life? He could wait an eternity, she vowed, ignoring the pulse between her thighs and the restless tautness in her breasts. Hell! That impossible man would turn to dust before she'd darken his door!

Seven

Drake poured the brandy, watching the amber liquid swirl in miniature currents in the crystal glass. He tried to ignore the chime of the clock in the downstairs hall as it rang the hour. Midnight and she had not come.

He reminded himself with a slow, deliberate taste of the potent spirit that the odds of Mrs. Everett coming to him had never been substantial. A woman's sensibilities could override even the best-laid plans of seductive—

"A lady to see you, Your Grace." Jameson trailed off, unwilling to elaborate on his opinion of women who presented themselves long after most sensible and respectable ladies had retired for the evening.

"Show her up, and see that we are undisturbed," Drake instructed.

The butler made a brief bow, and within moments,

she was there. Trembling and unsure, in her widow's weeds, with a pale face and luminous eyes that defied him to find traces of the woman he had met at Milbank's. He watched her as she took fewer than six steps into the room and stopped, holding herself ramrod stiff, unapproachable. But she'd miscalculated. Everything about her beckoned to him.

"I . . . I came to . . ." She held out his card, her fingers unsteady, and Drake felt his body tighten and harden as she bit the ripe, plump flesh of her lower lip, betraying her nerves. He forced himself to focus on the stiff slip of paper in her gloved hand. Her eyes dropped, following his, but then lifted to make her plea. "Whatever games you think to play, I came to tell you that I am not interested, sir."

He held still, studying her and wondering how it was possible that such a woman could affect him so profoundly. She was ultimately not an unparalleled beauty. Her coloring was soft, and in the shimmer and flash of the Ton, he could see how she would be overlooked. But then, most men would miss the subtle beauty of a pearl amidst cut glass and worthless paste. Drake's fleeting pleasure at recognizing that he was *not* "most men" faded quickly as he recalled that he was not entirely alone in his appreciation. Julian Clay must also have noted her. The thought strengthened his resolve—and made him want her more. If she'd allied herself with Clay, she deserved no mercy. She was no innocent.

As at the arboretum, he admired the delicate balance of her features, her arched brows and wide eyes. Her lips were a full, lush line that was currently pressed tight in nervous disapproval of him. Her skin was cream, and he remembered the feel of it against his fingertips. She'd chosen her dress for modesty, he was sure. But no amount of cloth could conceal from him the sweet curves of her body. He'd seen far too much of her to be fooled.

She ignored his inspection, moving farther into the room and closer to him. "I came to give you your card back."

He shook his head, taking the card out of her hands and dropping it onto the carpeted floor. "That's not why you're here, Mrs. Everett."

"Of course, it is!" Merriam held her ground, her chin lifting another inch, daring him to call her a liar. "Who are you?"

"Did you wish a complete list of my titles and holdings? Glowing references will be hard to come by, but if you insist, I can have them fabricated."

"Stop it! If you mean to humiliate me, I'd say you've already accomplished your goal. You've had your amusement at my expense, sir. Now I beg you to end this game."

"No games, Mrs. Everett. Since the ball, when you refused to give me your name, I've been . . . intrigued."

"It was a—mistake," she countered quickly, hating the ripples of desire that worked their way through her body at the mention of that fateful night. "A mistake I don't intend to repeat."

"Really?" Drake watched her cheeks pulse with tell-tale color at the lie, then he deliberately moved past her to the chairs by the fire as if he had no concerns regarding the matter.

The ploy worked brilliantly. Her confusion was so easy to read he had to bite the inside of his mouth to prevent a triumphant smile from spoiling the delicious illusion he'd created as she moved closer still.

"Really," she echoed. She squared her shoulders, deciding that this duke couldn't possibly be taking her seriously. "It was a singular moment of weakness that I would never—"

"And the arboretum?" he interjected casually.

"Y-you ... caught me off guard." Merriam's eyes dropped guiltily to the patterned carpet at her feet. Even while she knew he was no gentleman, his readiness to bring up her illicit reactions to him made her feel defenseless. Damn it, she reminded herself, this wasn't about his seductive skills! "You have a wrong impression of me, Your Grace."

"Do I?" Drake leaned against the mantel and gave her his complete rapt attention. "And what impression is that?"

"Y-you seem to think that I ..." Merriam faltered, wondering how on earth she had come to this place, to this conversation, to this moment in time. "I don't ... it is not my custom to ... approach strange men at social gatherings—or to allow them to . . . in public . . ." She stamped her foot in frustration. "You know very well, you cad, what impression! You are deliberately trying to make this harder for me!"

He shook his head. "Not at all. Should I tell you what impression I have, Mrs. Everett?"

She shook her head, but her feet didn't move.

He simply smiled. "If you insist." He moved closer until he was standing directly in front of her. His eyes caressed her face and then moved over her body as if she weren't wearing several dowdy layers of rogue-repelling gabardine and sensible wool.

Merriam held her breath at the sensation of being both vulnerable and, at the same time, powerful.

"I saw," he began simply, "a woman who wanted to explore her needs and who wasn't afraid to be desired. I saw a woman who was being very brave."

She gasped at the unexpected impact of his words. "I'm not brave, sir. I'm not—"

"And yet you came willingly tonight, knowing that it would be a risk, even dangerous. But that didn't stop you, Mrs. Everett. Not exactly the actions of a woman who is completely bound by the rules of society."

"Dangerous?" she asked with a soft laugh. "I'm sure the situation doesn't call for more drama than is warranted. You're trying to make more of this than—"

"I'm the Duke of Sussex, Merriam. Are you saying you haven't heard the rumors?" His eyes darkened, and she felt a chill whisper down her spine.

Rumors? What could he be talking about? She'd never been keen on gossip, but... the name and title sounded vaguely familiar. Still, at the moment she couldn't link him to anything of note. She studied him, her head tilting as she contemplated the puzzle. "I must have missed the tales of you lurking behind Brazilian palm trees in English greenhouses and stalking widows."

He shrugged, his stance relaxing slightly as he circled closer. "Ah, fleeting fame."

"What do you want?" she whispered. "I mean... surely your 'curiosity' has been sated. You discovered who I am, you've forced me to admit my... indiscretion... proven you can—" she cut herself off, unwilling to voice what he'd demonstrated at the arboretum that he could have her at will.

"I want you," he replied, the heat in his eyes increasing.

"Wh-what?" She shook her head in disbelief, then giggled nervously.

His brow furrowed. "You find that amusing?"

"I... I was expecting something along the lines of blackmail, sir." She swallowed hard, the grip on her reticule betraying its contents to him instantly. The cat had foolishly brought cash to buy his silence.

"Blackmail?" Drake didn't bother glancing at the sumptuous riches of his room or alluding to the grandeur of his house. "Appearances can be deceiving."

"Perhaps not out of financial need but for sport then . . ."

"Is desire so unbelievable a motive?"

"You're not serious!" Merriam sat down on one of the matching chairs, her knees finally giving out under his piercing gaze. "You have a wicked sense of humor, sir."

Drake smiled at the turn of phrase. "Wicked," he repeated it, slowly. "I'm sure I'll take that as a compliment."

"Take it as you wish." She drew another steadying breath, giving him her primmest and most daunting look. "I . . . I came here to settle this matter with you. T-to put it behind us. I'm sure you are as wary of scandal as any man and—"

"No."

"W-what?"

"Scandal is the least of my worries. Would you like something to drink? Brandy? Sherry? Or some port perhaps?"

"No, thank you!" She forced her hands to be still in her lap. "I don't understand what you meant . . ."

He dropped the topic of scandal deliberately. "What were you doing at Milbank's, Merriam? What were your intentions that night?"

"Oh!" It was as if he'd commanded the world to stop. "I . . . I hardly think it relevant . . . to—"

"It is relevant to me," he interrupted softly, and she suddenly recalled his warning that it was dangerous for her to have come to him. His gaze was compelling, as if he wanted her but also as if he might want just as readily to snap her neck.

"I . . ." The urge to lie was too powerful. She would rather die than admit the whole truth to him—a man who already knew too much about her. "It was a childish rebellion . . . I thought . . . I would see what it would be like . . . not to be me for a night."

His gaze never wavered. "So your choice was random that night?"

"Yes!" She seized the assistance in constructing her tale. "I-I saw you and thought you . . . very handsome. I never . . . thought you'd . . . try to find me afterwards . . ."

Drake drank in the lie, tasting the bittersweet confirmation that she was not what she seemed.

He'd intended to draw things out, to outline his "plans" and then win her compliance by whatever means necessary. But suddenly there was no thought of strategy. Frustration and lust twisted into a primal need to claim her, to punish her for the lie, to try to drive every trace of Julian Clay from her mind and body. She looked at him, trembling and defiant, so beautiful and lush that his flesh ached, and he hated her for it. She'd touched him when no other woman would—and now he wanted her to scream with her desire to have him touch her again.

He stood up and moved behind her, placing his hands on her shoulders with the lightest pressure.

"You shouldn't—"

He leaned down to whisper in her ear, ending her protest. "There is no such word, Cat. No *should* or *must* here. Not in this place. Here we will finish what we started this afternoon . . . here"—his tongue traced the outline of her ear and then pressed against the pulse behind it—"is where my Cat has no need for masks."

"Oh, my!" *My Cat,* her heart skipped a beat at the words.

She was playing with fire, her hands twisted together in her lap, and it struck her that there was nothing to keep her from standing—from putting a halt to this. But his hands moved from her shoulders, his fingertips brushing lightly up her throat, then back down, skimming across her collar and teasing every inch of bare skin he could reach. Her eyes closed as she leaned against the chair back, begging for a bolder exploration.

His fingers never stopped moving, each light circle across her flesh pushing her gently toward surrender.

His voice came again, soft and deep against the shell of her ear, sending shivers down her spine. "Undo the buttons."

"Oh!" The exclamation was barely audible, the shock of his words offset by the rush of heat through her body. Her nipples hardened against the rough material of her corset. She wanted his hands everywhere. She wanted his fingers to touch her breasts and tease each sensitive crest. But to undress for him . . . to be so brazen in the glow of a fireplace? There would be no shadows to shield her from him. She felt vulnerable, but as his hands continued to tease, power surged through her as well.

"I'll touch no part of you that you yourself don't bare for me, Merriam."

He would touch only what she bared for him. As on the night of the masque, he had put her in control.

She moved slowly, pulling off her gloves and dropping them on the floor next to the chair with her reticule. A part of her marveled at how easily her bare fingers could work the small buttons and loosen the bodice of her dress, baring her skin to him.

His fingertips followed the path of her labors, drawing sighs as he caressed her shoulders and gently drew his palms down to the ripe curves of her breasts above her corset. She shifted in the chair, anticipating his touch on her, preparing for the sweet jolt of his hands dipping down and freeing her nipples, only to gasp as she realized that his fingers were retreating to her bared shoulders. "But—"

"Only what you bare for me, Merriam."

The corset's hooks and tapes were harder to manage, frustration and desire making her hands shake. Self-doubt and insecurity began to creep in. As if sensing her inner battle, Drake leaned suddenly over the chair's back, his lips finding her ear again, his tongue working fire and wet heat through her until there was no thought but freeing herself for him. No arguments against his hands as they cupped her breasts, his fingers finding the taut, jutting crests that pebbled at his touch.

Merriam moaned, arching her back, pushing her breasts harder into his hands. He rewarded her, caressing her flesh, pinching the nipples gently, and making her shudder with pleasure. His hands left her nipples, teasing the warm undersides of her breasts and then explored her rib cage in feather-light touches that made her wriggle in the chair. Boldly she lifted her own hands to cup her breasts, offering them up for his worship. "More . . . please . . ."

His tongue laved the shell of her ear in rhythm with the flicker of his thumbs across her nipples, and Merriam cried out, imagining his mouth latching on to each of her breasts, suckling her as he had that night.

His touch was wonderful, but it wasn't enough.

She'd bared herself to the waist, and his fingers were applying the most delicious pressure she could imagine against her breasts and nipples, but it wasn't enough.

God help me, it isn't enough. Each pinch of pleasure-pain sent bolts of white-hot need into the aching well between her thighs and her throbbing clit. "More," she begged breathlessly, willing him to understand and take control. "Touch me . . . I need you to touch me."

"You know the rules, my Cat," he countered, moving to her other ear and letting his fingers dance along the top edge of her skirt and the waistband of her petticoats. "Pull up your skirts, Merriam. Slide them up slowly, and then spread your legs for me."

Disobedience was a distant and unthinkable choice. There was nothing but the surge of wanting and the new experience of submission——not to his commands so much as to her own needs. This moment was unlike any other in her life. His hands touched her ceaselessly, his lips moved along her ears; the only part of him she could reach was his hands, but she had no intention of interfering with their successful efforts to drive her wild.

There was no retreating now. Her fingers tugged on the gathers in her skirt, and she pulled the layers up to her waist. She winced as she exposed her staid and practical stockings gartered above the knees and her pantalets. Perhaps he couldn't see much of the plain linen from where he stood . . . perhaps he would just pull her from the chair and carry her to the bed.

"Only what you bare," he whispered, his breath hot in her ear. "Hurry."

She untied her drawers and lifted herself a few inches to slide them to the floor, then pulled her ankles out of the confining material. The sensation of her bared posterior against the smooth silk upholstery was decadent. She began to untie the ribbons of her garters when he stopped her. "Leave them."

He teased her nipples again with ghostlike touches, and her hips bucked in reaction, her legs parting, inviting him to sample what she had stripped bare for his attentions. "Drake, please."

"Spread them wide for me," he countered. "I want to touch you, Merriam."

She pulled her legs farther apart, daring to hook her knees over the chair's low, padded arms. Merriam felt completely vulnerable, so exposed and open to him. The heat from the fireplace danced across her skin, and she could smell the soft musk from her body. There was nothing to disguise her heightened arousal from him. But the daring, the naughtiness of it all, infused her with a new flood of courage. "Yes," she whispered. "Touch me."

She heard him kneel, the whisper of his clothing against the chair's back and the carpet. Merriam closed her eyes impatiently, awaiting the invasion of his fingers, the caresses and friction that would finally give her the release she craved.

His hands moved over her bunched up skirt and petticoats, teasing her hips and the outer curves of her bare thighs, working inward until one hand splayed against the swell of her stomach to hold her in place while the other delved into the velvet of her slit. With one finger, he traced up and down, pooling honey at her opening until it coated her entirely and she could even feel it weeping into the virginal pucker of her backside, as if there would be no part of her that didn't beg for him. Up and down, but never touching her hardened bud, he worked her until each time he moved toward the top she began to lift her hips, guiding him to her. She cried out in frustration.

At last, his fingertips stroked the swollen length of her clit, moving against it gently, keeping his pace measured and slow, giving her just enough sensation to make her writhe.

And then she felt it—the instant the coil within her began to tighten, the tension so exquisite and taut that tears sprang into her eyes. Merriam realized that this pleasure was hers alone and that, when the release came, it would be hers to seize and revel in.

He'd said he would touch nothing she didn't bare for him.

She released her grip on the chair's seat and with trembling hands reached up to follow the path his hands had taken. She cupped her breasts and marveled at the sensation of their weight in her palms, slowly daring to test each peak, moaning as she tugged at the tips, pinching them in rhythm with the teasing touch that continued between her legs.

She trailed her fingers lightly down to find his. To add the soft weight of her hands onto his, to guide him gently against her hungry flesh.

Faster and faster his hands worked against her skin, softer and softer against her hardened bud and harder and harder into the hungry opening that she bucked and shimmied against his touch. The angle was awkward and new, and her body seemed to revel in the magic of this game of hidden lovers and self-discovery.

To be with a man and not be with him . . . Drake was inaccessible to her touch. The only thing she could reach was her own body, and it was pure indulgence.

A game that a mouse would never play.

Oh, but a cat would, she countered with a slow smile as the first tremors of her release began to cascade along molten paths from his hands to hers, from her wet flesh to the heated peaks of her breasts.

She came in a rush of sensation, crying out at the force of her release, the flash of ecstasy ripping through her frame and making her tremble and writhe against Drake's hands.

Her eyes fluttered open as she realized he was moving to face her, felt the brush of his coat against her thighs. Even as the aftermath of her climax made it difficult to focus, the shift of his presence, and its implication, startled her. She started to close her legs and push her skirt down, aware only that he would see her wet, swollen flesh, that nothing was hidden from his hungry gaze. Even at her boldest on the night of Lord Milbank's ball, she had relied on the shadows for courage. "You mustn't—"

His hands held her knees firmly. "No, Merriam. You're wrong. I must." With gentle pressure he began to push her legs apart, and then his hands slid her skirt upward, revealing everything that she had tried to hide from him. "I must see you, and touch you, and taste you, until you're so ready and eager for me that you'll beg me to take you."

She gasped as his hands brushed her inner thighs again, his elegant fingers so strong and dark against her soft, white skin. The sight of him kneeling between her legs, like a predator ready to devour her, made her body ache to cradle him inside. The inequality of his state of dress only made her hungrier for him. "Take me," she managed, her voice ragged with need. "I . . . I'm ready, Drake, don't—"

His smile was like a bolt of wicked lightning, and she knew he wasn't going to relent so easily. Before she could compose another plea, or think of a way to entice him to hurry, his head lowered, and he traced her sex with the tip of his tongue, starting from the bottom and ending with a firm flick against her distended nub.

Merriam pushed against the chair's arms with her legs, lifting her hips, unwilling to lose the contact with his tongue and lips. The sweet play of his mouth increased its pace, and she knew that, whatever control he had given her, he had now easily wrested back. She would do anything to relieve the growing tension inside her, to achieve the release that only he could provide. Her fingers wound into the silken curls of his hair as she gripped his head and held on, her breath coming in jagged gasps at each movement against her tender skin. Merriam threw her head back and sensed the luscious wave overtaking her.

Drake fought himself for control as she gave in to him, arching against him, her taste so intoxicating and rich against his tongue it made him want to lap at her until he had drunk every heady drop of her arousal. The game of pleasuring her with the chair between them had nearly driven him over the edge. But this was an opiate whose power he had underestimated. She was mindless with need, mewling softly as her excitement grew, and Drake wasn't going to be able to wait much longer.

He lifted his head, using his fingers to ensure that no momentum was lost. He took in the sight of her, spread and ripe, the beautiful, glistening petals of her sex open to him, her breasts high and firm, and the gray-blue eyes that met his, half-lidded with fire and wantonness. She'd transformed again, from a fluttering, shy priss into the glorious creature he had first tasted through red silk, and he wanted to shout at the triumph of it. Game or no, she was his—for now.

"Drake, please," she begged softly. "I'm . . . I'm going to . . . come . . ."

"Damn it," he cursed, unable to hold himself back any longer, his thoughts so primal, so raw that he knew there would be no gentleness in this joining. He wanted to bury himself to the hilt inside of her and plow her until she screamed with it. Civilization and schemes were lost in the face of his desire to plunder the searing confines of her body.

He shifted up onto his knees and, with his free hand,

released his hardened cock. It jutted from his hips, so taut and swollen he wondered if he would spill himself at the first touch of her. Her eyes widened as she seemed to drink in the sight of him, leaning forward and licking her lips in anticipation of what was to come. Her eagerness was the last whip against his frenzied need. He didn't bother with his clothing but reached up to slide her onto the chair's edge, taking her legs off the arms. Then, without a word, he lifted her onto his lap, impaling her in one deliciously hard stroke. Her legs fell around his waist as she cried out, and Drake moaned at the impossibly tight grip of her muscles and the searing heat of her body around his cock.

The world had narrowed to this woman in his arms. Merriam began to ride him, moving up and then letting herself slide back down, and he knew it would be a close race to a climax. Drake held her hips, matching her movements and increasing the friction, driving himself up into her. He lost himself in the taste of her breasts in his mouth, the first spasms of her release as he penetrated her so deeply that the sensitive head of his cock was touching the entrance of her womb. She bit his shoulder, and he came in a shattering torrent, his hot crème jetting into her as she cried out, his hips continuing to move against hers, unwilling or unable to stop, Drake couldn't say.

After a few moments, he slowed, letting them both recover their senses a bit.

"Oh, oh my!" she sighed softly, and he ducked his

head into her breasts to shield his smile at the faint echo of innocent shock in her voice. It was impossibly alluring, this gift she had for feigned naïveté.

His cat had her charms.

He leveraged himself up without releasing her, his semiaroused flesh still embedded inside her. He cupped her bottom and chuckled at her gasps.

"P-put me down, Drake!" Her arms tightened around his neck as she clung to him to keep her balance. Despite her protest, his pulse jumped as she shimmied her hips against him.

He stood carefully and began carrying her toward the four-poster bed. "In a moment, my dear."

She glanced over her shoulder, then looked back at him, her eyes widening, "D-Drake . . . I don't think I can . . ."

He silenced her with a slow, tender kiss as he laid her down on his bed. The feeling of her underneath him made him thicken inside her. "Too many clothes. This time," he whispered as he nuzzled her ear, smiling when she tilted her head to give him more access to her throat and breasts, "new rules. You shed those clothes, then undress me, and we'll determine together what you can do if you set your mind to it." He trailed kisses down to one rose-hued, taut nipple and let his mouth hover over it, his breath teasing her as each rise of her rib cage brought her closer to his tongue but never quite achieved its goal. "Yes?"

"Yes," she purred, arching her back and finding his mouth to suckle her.

Drake reveled in the word and began the next round of the game . . . *yes, yes, yes.*

He awoke before dawn, his every sense on edge. In the soft, gray light of the room, he marveled at how innocent and vulnerable his familiar looked. Merriam had curled up in her sleep against his side, her ankles crossed in a way that made him smile. She was a study of gentle curves and sweet, inviting crevices, the scent of her perfume and the faint musk of her sex already permeating the bed. Her long hair was an indescribable color, a light brown streaked with muted mahogany and copper. He had the odd thought that it suited her better than the dramatic black and red dyes she had used at the ball. He studied her imperfections and found himself drawn to her even more. He admired the tiny lines of her face, a small, acorn-shaped birthmark beneath her right breast, and the asymmetrical arch of her brows . . . even the thin, willowy shape of her hands awed him. She was the most unlikely seductress he could have envisioned. But then, he reminded himself, appearances were always deceiving.

He moved carefully, so as not to disturb her, and extricated himself from the bed, ignoring the heavy weight of his stiffening cock and the desire to awaken her by easing himself back inside of her. No, he forced himself not to look at her again. He wanted to gather his strength and brace himself for the morning ahead and the next small battle, when she realized just how much ground she had given up to him. She would awaken and, no doubt, try to escape.

He had other plans.

He found his robe and put it on, then walked in bare feet toward the door, only to stop as something foreign pressed against his instep. He looked down and saw the pale outline of his card against the carpet. He bent to retrieve it, smiling at the memory of her holding it out to him. He shook his head, and spotting her reticule under the chair, he knelt to slide it inside the embroidered pouch. He would let her return it another day . . . but not today.

Today, she would agree to be his.

And then he would use her to lure Julian out into the open.

Eight

Layers of dream drew back slowly, and Merriam became increasingly aware that the sensual memories of her sleep were more than the usual illusions of her typical mornings. She sat bolt upright, sunshine blazing along the edges of the draperies and slanting into the room and across the bed. Her heart raced as the flood of reality washed over her. She was alone, stark naked under silk sheets in *his* bed, in *his* bedroom, in *his* house! She had come to him last night and presented herself like a brazen whore. She had denied him nothing, begging him to take her again and again, proving his power over her. She became aware of the tenderness between her thighs and the faintest bruises on her skin from the fury of their coupling. Merriam's face burned. She frantically scanned the room for her things.

I came to end it, she lamented silently, but another

part of her instantly squealed at the lie. *You came so that he could finish what he'd started in that greenhouse. You came so that you could play the wanton and have his hands on you again and feel that incredible cock of his between your legs.*

She moaned, pushing away the internal debate regarding her incredibly unladylike actions, and gingerly slid out of the bed, pulling the sheet with her for modesty, and began to search for her clothes. She would dress and leave this place, and if Drake Sotherton so much as glanced in her direction in public, she would freeze his blood with one look. She would—

Be forced to leave the house wrapped in a sheet if her clothes didn't appear soon! Merriam bit her lower lip, losing some of the momentum of her self-righteous internal tirade. Her clothes were gone. The idea of facing him in a state of undress was unacceptable.

She forced herself to sit, determined to apply cool reason and recover at least a small amount of her pride. She silently reviewed her options. She could ring the bell and demand that whatever servant responded promptly produce her clothes. She winced at the humiliation of admitting to a servant that she had obviously lost her clothes in the master's bedchamber. Her mind turned to her second choice. She could try to sneak about and find her clothes, hoping to avoid Drake and his household staff altogether. A shaky smile escaped her lips at the image of her tiptoeing down hallways in a bedsheet.

How in the world did I come to this?
Willingly.

Madame DeBourcier's gentle warning came back to her instantly: *Each experience changes a woman. There was no escaping it.*

Merriam worried her bottom lip with her teeth as she considered the dilemma that she alone had created. But had she changed the night of Milbank's masque, or had she somehow always been this woman who was starving for a man's heated attentions? A woman who would do anything to ease the gnawing emptiness between her thighs?

"Beg pardon, miss," a young female voice interjected softly, making Merriam yelp in surprise and leap to her feet, pulling the sheet tighter around her as her cheeks flamed in embarrassment.

The maid eyed her warily for a moment from the doorway. "Didn't mean to startle you, m'lady. I'm Peg."

"N-no! I'm . . . I was just . . ." Merriam swallowed hard, horrified and relieved that, one way or another, the stalemate of what to do next had been resolved. "I was just looking for my things."

The maid, petite in stature, strawberry-blond curls framing blue eyes, stayed in the doorway. "They're being pressed, though His Grace said you'd have no quick need of them. I'm to fetch you a dressing gown and escort you downstairs for breakfast."

Merriam had to bite off the acerbic rejoinder to His Grace's audacity in decreeing that she wouldn't need her clothes. But she could feel the increased color in her face as she struggled with her temper. "I-I'm not hungry, Peg. Please fetch my clothes and see to it that—"

"Oh, no!" The maid shook her head vigorously, fear lighting her eyes, as she scurried into the room. "He was very clear, and I'm afraid that's that, as they say."

Before Merriam could think of the proper argument to negate the odd logic of "that's that," Peg went on. "Please wait here and I'll be back with a wrapper for you." The girl was gone through a paneled door near the fireplace, and Merriam was left alone in solitude, her fury increasing. The man's arrogance knew no bounds! He'd taken her clothes deliberately and now seemed to think she was just going to waltz downstairs wearing nothing but a wrap and join him for breakfast. Well, she'd borrow a coat from his butler and walk out the front door before she'd set one toe inside his—

Peg's return interrupted her fantasy of a mad dash out into the streets of London wearing little more than a butler's coat. "Here you are, m'lady." The girl held out a bundle of beautiful lavender silk with layers of French lace and organza flounces. "This will suit you, I think. And there's matching stockings and slippers."

"Whose are those?" Merriam's stomach churned at the sight of the garment, proof that another woman existed within these walls. "Is . . . His Grace married?" she whispered in horror.

"No, madam." Peg continued to hold out the gown for her. "These were purchased years ago but never worn. Please. He'll be waiting."

It seemed self-defeating to refuse the items when her only other choice was a bedsheet. Merriam started to take them from her, but Peg drew her over to the screen in the corner. "Here, let me help you, m'lady." The maid set the pile of items over the screen and moved swiftly to unwrap Merriam from her protective cocoon.

Modesty lost the quick battle with Peg's efficiency, and Merriam was amazed at the girl's skill at dressing her in a fluid dance that wasted no time or energy.

"It's lucky for me that His Grace employs such a wonderful lady's maid." Merriam spoke, wondering if that meant she was one of many female visitors to his chambers.

Peg's eyes dropped to the carpet. "Not at all. His Grace is generous to keep me on since it's been a long time since we've had a woman in the house. Or anyone for that matter."

"I-I . . ." Merriam steadied herself, feeling a bit foolish and relieved. "How interesting."

"There you are, my lady." Peg's cheeks colored a bit. "All ready, I'd say."

Merriam looked down and admired the dressing gown. Lavender silk caressed her body, and the wrap accented her figure with its wide, matching sash and flounces. Stepping forward, Peg completed the ensemble by tying a lavender ribbon choker around Merriam's throat. Merriam reached up to touch the soft strip of material, realizing that, despite her protests, she felt impossibly pretty.

"Is there anything else, my lady?"

"No," Merriam managed to reply, still fighting the unreal sensation that her life was no longer her own. Well, breakfast with Drake would resolve that. She would offer him a polite farewell and then get as far away from him as humanly possible. And so long as he swore not to attend any more meetings of the Ladies' Botanical Society, she doubted their paths would cross again. She ignored the nervous lump in her throat and squared her shoulders. "I'll finish myself, and then, please, escort me to His Grace. I—I have a full schedule this morning and will need a carriage to get home."

Peg nodded.

"Can you help me with my hair? I usually just have it in a simple—"

"Ah, trust me, my lady." Peg cut her off gently. "I've an eye for these things." She pulled a comb from the pocket of her apron, and Merriam submitted to her ministrations. The young maid was managing without a single cruel yank or tug and working very swiftly.

"All done then," Peg announced a few moments later, putting away her comb and hairpins. "Slippers then, and he'll be waiting."

Peg put the slippers at her feet and helped her into

them. Standing to go, Merriam caught a glimpse of her reflection in a full-length mirror across the room and froze, taking in the image of an attractive woman in romantic lace and elegant flounces. Instead of her usual style, with her hair parted down the middle and pulled back into a roll, Peg had woven a simple braid over her crown and created a loose chignon with the long plaits.

The woman in the mirror bore no resemblance to her. Her lips were still swollen and stained from a night of sensual indulgence, her eyes wide and unashamed.

Where was the mouse now?

Still there, a part of her whispered softly. *Just hiding.*

"If you'll follow me, my lady."

Merriam lifted her chin and followed Peg along the grand halls and down the sweeping staircase, winding through the Duke of Sussex's ostentatious and beautifully appointed home. She gritted her teeth, recalling her premature suspicions that he was a blackmailer after ready cash. She averted her eyes as she passed a few of the staff busy with their assignments, all too aware of how she would appear to them. Her temper began to reassert itself as she started constructing the lecture she would give her audacious host on his high-handed hospitality, forcing respectable women to parade through his home indecently attired.

"Right inside, madam." Peg's instructions wrenched her from her thoughts, and Merriam felt the first flash of nerves at the prospect of facing him again. Still, there seemed to be no other option. It was just that in that instant she realized she truly had no idea what to expect from him. Would he thank her for the evening's pleasures and make polite small talk before dismissing her? Would he express regret for his actions? Or worse, say nothing of what had happened between them and expect her to do the same? Before last night, she would have welcomed the last option, but now she wasn't sure.

She pushed through the doors and stopped at the sight of the table and chairs set out in the center of the solarium. Unlike any other room she had ever seen, it was appointed like an Arabian oasis, inviting and soothing, with long, colorful silk panels shielding the sunlit interior and invoking a Bedouin's tent. A woven rattan rug and small Oriental and Eastern touches delighted the eyes, and she wondered at the eclectic tastes of her strange host.

She walked toward the table, set with crystal and silver service for two, wondering what Drake would think of a woman who used her most common dishes whenever she was alone, economy and restraint ruling even her choice of tableware.

Well, she amended with a sad smile, economy, restraint, *and* a fear of her husband's ghost returning to haunt her if she broke one of his hideous china plates. In truth, nothing had ever looked palatable on Everett china.

"I was beginning to think I was going to have to

carry you downstairs, Mrs. Everett." His voice came from behind her, and Merriam slowly turned to face him, the impact of his presence striking her senses. He was impeccably dressed in a proper morning coat, as if he expected guests at any moment, his handsome face set in an expression that was difficult to read.

"I had nothing to wear until your maid provided this and said you were insisting that I join you for breakfast. Well?" she demanded in her iciest and most commanding tone.

His eyes appraised her, openly warming at the sight of her in the dressing gown he'd provided. "You are a vision, Merriam."

She wanted to scream as his words brushed over her skin and brought a flush of heat into her face that he couldn't help but notice. Damn the man! Couldn't he look a little less virile and stop distracting a woman from putting him in his proper place? "I want my clothes back, please."

"Whatever for?" he asked in mock innocence. "This color is far more flattering and, by the looks of it, much more comfortable than that whalebone-lined woolen prison you'd encased yourself in."

"We are not discussing my fashion choices!" She crossed her arms in a fury. "You have no right to keep me here! I need my clothes."

"As you wish. You can wear anything you like. It makes no difference to me, since I believe I am far more interested in seeing you out of your clothes than in them. Come, Merriam, you know at least that much by now."

"I know nothing except that my servants are likely to think I've been kidnapped!"

"Not at all," he answered, unruffled and unhurried. "I took the liberty of sending a note that you had been called away and had decided to stay with a friend. My man should be returning within the hour with your things. So please, sit and have something to eat, Merriam. We have a great deal to talk about, you and I."

Her mouth had fallen open in shock at his calm announcement. He'd taken a liberty, he'd said. Her legs felt numb, and she sat gracelessly in the chair he offered her. It took a few moments to collect herself before she could respond. "I-I am not staying here. I cannot possibly stay here!"

He took the seat opposite her and began pouring them each a cup of coffee. "Cream? Sugar?"

Her eyes widened as she noted the sensual curve of his lips, his calm oblivion to the disaster that she was facing. "My reputation, Drake! If it's discovered that I came here, alone, and stayed . . . People will think . . . They'll realize that we . . ."

One black eyebrow arched at her inability to name their "crime." "You worry about the wrong things, Merriam. And while I know that the sting of people's opinion can be a brutal lash, it is an empty threat as far as I am concerned."

"An empty threat? The scandal! Drake, please!"

"Ah, the scandal," he echoed, his eyes lit with playful disregard. "I'm afraid I meant what I said last night. It is the least of my worries." He leaned back casually, noting that, as he did so, her eyes were drawn to his legs and the outline of his hardening shaft. The sight of her in that gown was making his pants uncomfortably tight, but he was determined to see the conversation to its finish. "I see no need to spend my life avoiding scandals when they are apparently inevitable."

She forced her eyes back to his face, her cheeks patched with bright color. "Scandal is not inevitable. You are deliberately . . ." She stood from the table, determined to ignore the hungry look in his eyes, which was creating waves of heat inside her. It was broad daylight, and the setting was so genteel, so elegant and extraordinary; and all she could think of was how she wanted to feel his mouth on her again, to have his hands up her skirt and— "I'm going home."

Drake was next to her instantly, the façade of lazy disregard gone. He held one of her arms, his expression somber. "Stay."

"I . . . I can't . . . I'll be ruined. People will talk . . ."

"Let them," he urged softly, his voice seductive but firm. "What exactly is it about the quiet, drab existence of a lonely young widow that you are trying to protect, Merriam? Will you miss the committee meetings? Tea with musty dowagers and forlorn spinsters?

The piteous looks from acquaintances who then put you in a corner at gatherings and forget you're even there? Or perhaps you'll miss the insidious hints that another passionless match is all you could ever hope for?"

Tears welled in her eyes at the painful queries, each one cutting her to the bone as she heard the all too dreary highlights of her life laid bare by his caustic words. At that moment, she hated him for it. "Let go of me, Drake."

"You aren't that woman anymore, Merriam. Perhaps you never were."

Her breath caught in her throat. "D-don't." She choked on the protest, unwilling to lie. "What do you want from me?"

"I want you, Merriam. I want you in my bed. I want you in my house." His grip on her arm tightened possessively. "Stay."

"And play at being your paramour?"

He smiled at the word on her lips but decided that his cat needed to accept the rules of engagement. He would feign no false emotions or ply her with empty romance. But he had no intention of letting her leave. "You won't be playing."

She gasped but didn't pull away from him. Drake felt the moment stretch out as her mind struggled to begin to grasp the implications of what he had proposed.

"Y-you want me to be your . . . mistress?"

"For the rest of the Season," he pressed on, following his instincts to seize the advantage that came with the element of surprise. "Think of it, my Cat. What is one night? One interlude? A cruel tease when you consider it, no matter how satisfactory the encounter. Neither one of us expected to be in this position, but I, for one, am not about to relinquish you so easily."

She shook her head. "You're insane."

Drake relaxed his hold, sensing the first signs of victory. She hadn't slapped him yet. "Stay."

She lowered her eyes and bit her lip, a habit he was coming to find dangerously appealing. Drake reminded himself that he was acquiring her as a tool and nothing more.

"I know almost nothing about you," she argued weakly.

"I'm sure by the end of the Season we can rectify that." His hands moved down her shoulders to caress her arms. "Of course, for each question you ask, I shall expect you to answer one as well."

Merriam's brow furrowed a bit at his last words; she felt no desire to share the dreary facts of a mouse's life with this vibrant man. Perhaps questions could wait for now. "It's too sudden," she whispered, looking anxiously back up into his eyes.

"It's not too sudden, Merriam." He pulled her against his chest. "You've waited a long time, I suspect, for a taste of passion, for an offer to experience true intimacy. Come on this adventure with me, my Cat. I know it's a brave step to take"—Drake kissed her softly on the forehead before continuing—"but I've seen you take other ones, and this time, you aren't entirely alone."

She tilted her head. "The risk . . ."

"Is nothing," he lied smoothly, kissing her temples then looking directly into her face, willing her to see the possibilities. "Afterwards, your calendar will be less cluttered with dreary luncheons and soirees where you'd be asked to chaperone ferret-faced debutantes, but your life will be there waiting for you just as you left it. In the meantime, we shall set the Ton on its ear with your beauty, and everyone will wonder how they could have missed the Incomparable on my arm."

The power of his words, the delicious sanctuary of his arms, and the gentle, almost innocent kisses he pressed against her skin eroded her desire to argue. What was she defending? He was right. She'd miss none of the dreary rewards of her quiet, respectable existence. All her life, she'd followed the rules and become so adept at blending in and avoiding trouble that no one even bothered to look at her anymore. Ruled by fear, Merriam had retreated from any threat to her precious routines and sedate schedules. The mouse had accepted her fate.

Until Julian Clay. Until she'd ignored the rules and stumbled into Drake's arms.

"I-I don't want to upset the Ton, Drake."

He lowered his head until his lips hovered above hers, his breath mingling with hers until there was no room for fear. "Then think only of me, Merriam. Be with me."

"This is insane, Drake." Her voice was soft but steady. "I'm twenty-nine. There are younger women who could . . . please you. And I am no beauty to——"

He kissed her, a consuming, searing taste that swept away her protests. Merriam gave in to the onslaught of his mouth, her tongue meeting his and moving against it, suckling it, as if drawing sustenance from his touch.

As her knees buckled, he released her lips, his smile a bone-melting promise of what was to come if she agreed to his wicked proposal. "Let me give you passion, Cat," he whispered, his voice rougher, his hand pulling hers down to the ridge of his shaft so that she could feel his arousal through his trousers. "One decadent London Season and I'll let you go. But for the few remaining weeks of the Season, you agree to be mine—completely."

"Yours *completely*?" Her voice was soft and steady, trying to imagine giving him more than she already had. What more could there be?

"Completely," he growled with finality.

She would be his . . . for the Season.

Her clothes from home arrived later that day, and Merriam's courage faltered a bit at the sight of her trunks and baggage. They were lifeless sentinels from the world she had agreed to abandon temporarily, but their appearance made things all too real, yet unreal at the same time.

Peg supervised two undermaids as they shook out the garments, hung them in the wardrobe in the dressing room, and organized her possessions.

Clothes. Merriam sighed, miserably wishing that she had pushed a bit harder on the topic when Drake criticized her wardrobe the night before. Now, as she surveyed the dreary tide of gray and black garments, she admitted that her practical and sturdy dresses were not exactly suited to the adventure she'd just agreed to. Each gown highlighted just how unsuited she was to this impulsive path.

Too late. Even if I ordered them to repack everything and send it all home, the servants will talk and everyone will know what I've done.

Merriam shook her head at the flurry of activity around her as Peg opened the last of the trunks and made a silent inventory of her less than fashionable wardrobe. Unlike most of her fashion-obsessed peers, Merriam had always dreaded selecting anything new, shying away from the ruthless assessment that seemed to accompany each measurement and adjustment. Every dress involved a dozen decisions, and she equated the process with sheer drudgery. If she had mastered any art in fashion, it was the art of camouflage.

Drake came up behind her. "I'll send for a modiste. You should have a few new things."

Merriam's hands gripped the bedpost so hard her

knuckles shown white. The man was impossible! Not that she'd planned on running, she reminded herself. Damn him.

Drake watched the flash of spirit in her eyes and briefly contemplated how much he enjoyed the lively play of her struggles to hide her temper. But he knew better than to waste her fire on these initial battles. It was time to soothe and placate his familiar. It was the inaugural day of their arrangement, after all.

He approached and leaned down to kiss her chastely on the cheek, lingering to tell her softly, "Relax, my Cat."

He felt some of the tension leave her frame at his words, her eyes meeting his, full of unspoken questions but willing to wait. "I hate getting fitted for new clothes, Drake."

"Then let us see if we can't make this an enjoyable experience for you. Perhaps once the maids leave, I shall help you with your selections." His look triggered pure, fiery mayhem down her spine. The man was just too attractive, and the experience of having him take charge was overwhelming . . . and liberating.

Merriam gasped. "Ladies do not allow . . ." She lost momentum at his amused look. "I meant, I don't think it would be appropriate for you to—"

"I promised you a decadent Season."

"Yes, but I don't see what that has to do with clothes, Drake."

"And you promised to be mine completely." He

lifted one of her hands to kiss her bare fingertips, then without looking away from her, he spoke to the maid. "Peg, that will be all. You and the others can finish later."

Within moments, they were alone once again.

He stepped back and began to survey the collection of items on the bed, lifting one of her simple linen pantalets and examining it with mock curiosity. "Perhaps we can forgo replacing these when we order your new clothes."

Merriam took a step toward him, a hint of rebellion in her eyes. "Drake, undergarments are hardly optional."

"I want you as I found you, Merriam. Ready for me at all times."

"You are incorrigible."

"I'm not convinced you would prefer me if I were better behaved, Merriam."

The color on her cheeks gave him the answer he sought. "Behave better, and you might be surprised."

She contemplated him, still trying to convince herself that the turns of her life in the last twenty-four hours were entirely real. At this hour yesterday, he'd mastered her in the greenhouse and sent her world into a wild spiral of desire and fulfillment. It didn't seem possible that, even now, she was free from her life as a mouse and was Drake Sotherton's mistress.

"What are you thinking, Cat?" He watched her warily, his uncanny ability to read her making her pulse jump. Her Merlin had his wicked ways.

"I'm wondering if you are a sorcerer after all. I cannot believe any of this . . . No one will believe . . ." Her words trailed off miserably as she found herself unable to voice her fears. She fingered one of the black paramatta and crepe gowns on the bed. "People have discreet affairs, Drake. I . . . I think I am more suited to . . ."

"Secrets?" His expression became harder to read. "Desire is not fed by shame, Merriam. Guilt is a temporary enhancement at best. And I see no need to embrace the shadows because of circumstances I cannot control. Are you so quick to turn your back on your promises, Cat?"

"No! It's not that." She watched him, wishing his eyes didn't have the power to dim all the logical arguments in her head. She was ruined. She should be tasting ashes and crying, not blushing and counting the seconds until he touched her again.

He moved to sit in front of her on the bed, pulling her hands into his. His large, masculine fingers gently engulfed hers as he spoke. "The world will wait, Merriam. Time enough to worry about dresses and details. Shall I distract you from your thoughts?"

"You do so already, without any effort," she chided him, a blush betraying the honesty of her admission. "Perhaps, as your mistress, I shall learn to return the favor."

He laughed. "I'll look forward to such deliberate torment, my dear."

A mischievous smile lit her face as a bold idea occurred to her. "I was thinking of how, just yesterday, you deliberately left me wanting in that greenhouse." She lowered her chin and gave him a coy look through her lashes, doing her best imitation of a practiced coquette. "I was thinking of how I'd sworn one day to pay you back in kind."

His breath caught in his throat, and Merriam marveled at the delicious thrill of knowing that she could affect him. She moved toward him, more deliberately, to stand between his knees. She knelt on the rug at his feet, her eyes never leaving his.

"You intend to leave me wanting?" he asked warily, wondering if she could fathom how hard it had been to abandon her in the greenhouse.

"I intend to punish you. Perhaps it is your turn to beg, Your Grace." Merriam put her hands on his knees, marveling at the sight of him, her eyes locked on her reward. His trousers were tented with the unmistakable outline of his swollen flesh. She smiled, licking her lips in anticipation of the touch and taste of him. Before Milbank's she had never been so daring, never even considered that a man's erection could hold such appeal.

She bit her lower lip, then made her decision. Every game must have its rules, after all. "You must keep your hands at your sides," she commanded him with a purr. "If you move to touch me or interfere, I shall cease immediately."

"Wicked creature," he countered but instantly moved to comply with her instructions, his grip falling to the bedding and the dresses beneath him, bracing himself to withstand her tender assault.

She slid her fingers up his thighs, shy determination in her eyes.

Yes, it was his turn to beg, though she doubted that either one of them would be left wanting this time.

She dragged her fingernails lightly over the contours of his balls, relishing his body's reactions to her ministrations. His breathing was already ragged, and she could feel the heat of him through the material under her fingertips. His shaft so hard and eager to be freed, the ripe head of it was barely contained by the buttons of his breeches.

"Enough torture, Merriam," he moaned, his hips bucking up against the whisper-light pressure of her hands spread on either side of his length. "Touch me."

She grinned, a merciless, beautiful grin that made his blood surge and boil, her fingers slowly moving up toward his buttons. Her tongue darted out to trace the outline of her upper lip as she tugged just enough to liberate the first button. She paused to ensure that he understood just how cruel she could be.

"Merriam, I am officially begging."

She laughed, low in her throat. "You cannot pretend to beg just to have your way, Drake. But I suppose since you've been so good . . . so far . . ."

She began to work at the buttons, the second, then the

third, then the fourth, faster than before but still maintaining a deliberate pace that pushed him to the edge.

Damn it, she'd learned too quickly how to drive him mad.

Merriam found her own breath coming a bit faster; she was unable to disguise her excitement. His cock was so impossibly gorgeous, the heated tension between her hip bones throbbed and pulsed at the raw power and strength of it. Her fingers followed the graceful paths of veins and sinew, luxuriating over the velvet sheath of skin so soft and sweet it made her weep to think of him driving it inside of her. She tightened her grip and moved it up and down over his thick, hardened core—it was the ultimate battering ram of pleasure and pain, and the sight of it in her hands made the silky flesh between her legs wet.

The color of it was so deep, his tip almost purple against her palms, jerking and pulling at her touch, as if it possessed a will of its own that she hungered to consume and overpower.

The game was forgotten as she leaned forward to use her mouth.

Her lips moved against him in a kiss, so soft, dragging the sensitive contours of her lower lip against his swollen tip, until the pink of her lips was coated with the silky salt of his desire. Then she deepened the kiss, pulling him into the warm and waiting pocket of her mouth, worshiping the strength and beauty of his body.

Tasting him, savoring the burning touch of his head

against her tongue, Merriam used her hands to encircle his length, stroking down the rest of him, then swirling lightly with her fingers over and under his sac, feather-light caresses that contrasted with the firm massage of his shaft. His hips moved against her hands and mouth, straining for control. His response guided her actions and spurred her hunger for him beyond any thought but their mutual pleasure as she worshiped his flesh without any restraint.

Merriam took more and more of him into her mouth, her tongue flicking across the sensitive juncture of his shaft and swollen tip, then down the underside, increasing the pressure as his moans and breathing kept pace with her own desire.

"Merriam, wait—"

But there was no waiting. She knew what was coming and she wanted all of him. She wanted his surrender, his release. She wanted to drink the sweet, hot essence of him and drain him completely. She moved faster and faster against his erection, oblivious to anything outside the small circle of sensation that she had created.

He let go of the bed, heedless of the consequences. His hands wound into her hair, pressing her against him, losing the fight to delay or deny the unstoppable force of his climax. He came in explosive bursts that made him cry out as Merriam relentlessly drew out each spasm and drank his orgasm until he swore his heart would shatter from the sheer rapture of it.

At last, his mind rejoined his sweat-covered body and Drake opened his eyes to take in the alluring and unforgettable sight of a very smug and satisfied Cat wiping some of his crème off her lips, only to lick the last drop from her fingertips.

"Merriam?" he whispered, his throat dry.

"Yes, Merlin?" she asked, eyelashes fluttering playfully.

"Now may I beg?"

As she laughed, shamelessly basking in her victory, he pulled her into his arms.

Nine

"**S**till nervous?"

Merriam tried a cavalier laugh but managed only an unsteady hiccup. Denying the existence of dozens of icy-scaled dragonflies battering along her rib cage, she forced herself to brazen it out. "Not at all!" She gave Drake a wry look. "Which makes me wonder what you put in my tea this morning at breakfast."

"I'll never tell. A magician must have his secrets, my pet."

They were in Hyde Park, their first public appearance since she had disappeared into his house over a week ago. Merriam knew that if someone had told her a month ago that she would be riding shamelessly at a man's side as his mistress in front of the elite of London society, she would have seen them off to bedlam in the blink of an eye. She wasn't oblivious to the stares and whispers around her, but Drake was the ultimate portrayal of nonchalance. She could only pray his ease would bleed over to soothe her own raw nerves. After all, what was there to fear when he was so openly unconcerned?

Everything!

But she was determined not to fail now.

Drake cut a fine figure on his black steed, and everyone's eyes followed the pair, trying to guess who she might be and where they may have seen her to wrangle an introduction. The plain widow at his side was probably a novelty, she speculated. She only hoped she didn't look too out of place.

It was ridiculous—and erotic. He had relented on his requirement that she wear almost nothing under her clothing and allowed her riding habit to be an exception. She wore breeches underneath her skirt, but the exception was more maddening than she'd anticipated. She'd grown accustomed in the last few days to nothing against her delicate folds and the soft curve of her backside. The doeskin leather of her pants was making her squirm, the pressure against her keeping her in a constant flush of constricted desire. Worse, if he noticed her wriggling, he gave her a look that promised to see her out of her clothes at the earliest possible moment.

Her lover was proving wonderfully distracting. Drake had sworn she would know passion, and Merriam wondered how she had ever lived without it. Her husband had informed her that a true gentleman didn't "bother" his wife more than once or twice a year. And since Grenville's visits to her bedchamber during the ten years of their marriage had essentially been little more than a bother, she'd never thought to argue even though he saw fit to "bother" her maids far more frequently. After he'd died two years ago, Merriam had been sure that her own longings were aberrant. The quest that had brought her to Milbank's should have confirmed it. Instead, she'd learned that there were rewards for a woman's rebellion.

After over a week, Drake's appetite for her was unabated, and the mouse had discovered that her own capacity for pleasure was apparently unlimited. She was insatiable and eager for him, though she wondered if there was a balance to be found between insanity and discretion. She looked over at her lover, her body tightening with longing, and she couldn't stop the smile that leapt to her lips.

Drake inconspicuously kept an eye on Merriam as she perched, straight-backed and proud, on her mount. No matter what she'd said, he knew that this was a huge step for her. A woman who had apparently lived a life ruled by the defining niceties of society was being openly naughty. Her secret parlor games with Clay couldn't have prepared her for the maelstrom to come. But he forced the thought away. He didn't want to think about Julian this morning. Time enough for his opponent to make the next move. Drake simply wanted to focus on his current goal of exposing his lovely sorcerer's apprentice and ensuring that word spread that the Duke of Sussex not only was back in England, but also had resumed his life in full force.

He smiled back at her, his Cat in her sedate velvet riding habit. She had made an effort to break from her mourning hues by adding a turquoise silk scarf. The color set off her eyes and skin perfectly, and made her look almost ethereal. She was radiant but not vibrant. No, Merriam shimmered, her beauty soft and difficult to define. He'd insisted that she would stand out, but as a priceless pearl and not a cheap bauble. Peacocks and popinjays rode past them, dyed feathers in bonnets and jewels shining, ostentatious accessories and impractical designs. But the mourning dove on her white mare at his side made them seem tasteless and vulgar.

The ploy was working.

Drake noted the ripples of speculation about the elegant creature next to him.

It was perfect.

Now, he needed only wait until . . .

"Your Grace!" The hail came as if on cue, and Drake slowed to allow Lord Andrews to catch up to them. "I knew I'd seen you at White's earlier in the month. Few acquaintances believed me, but now there will be no arguing the point."

"And why would anyone doubt my return?" Drake countered.

Andrew's face lost a measure of its joviality. His expression became more guarded, wary of offending the "Deadly Duke." He shrugged, "Who can say? I for one am glad to see you back amidst good society."

Drake chuckled. "You may be the only one, Elton." Lord Andrews's appraisal of Merriam was impossible to miss. Drake took advantage of the unspoken opening to attend to his social duties. "Forgive me. Lord Andrews, may I introduce Mrs. Merriam Everett? Mrs. Everett, this is Lord Andrews, a man I should warn you will do his best to induce you to share all your darkest secrets so that he can distract people with them while he plays cards. A devilish trick, mind you. Does it still work, Elton?"

"Like a charm, Drake." Andrews beamed, then tipped his hat to Merriam. "His Grace exaggerates, Mrs. Everett."

"Does he?" She looked at Drake, her eyes openly speculating. "I'm never sure."

"I have never in my life induced anyone to share their secrets," Lord Andrews continued. "I simply have a trustworthy countenance that inspires confidences."

Merriam had to bite the inside of her mouth to keep from laughing at the jest, since Lord Andrews would never have been mistaken for a priest or confessor. He had the look of a man who had indulged for too many years to account for.

Drake shook his head. "As I said, a dangerous man to know."

Lord Andrews smiled. "Not at all." He leaned forward to make eye contact with Merriam. "As his friend, you must convince him to brave my den. Or if he won't, then perhaps you can set an example for the duke, defy him and come without him. At a dinner party next week? Say, Thursday evening at eight?"

"Are you questing for confidences, Lord Andrews?" Merriam asked.

"Never, but if you have any, be sure to bring them along. I'll send the invitation and hope to see you there." He spurred his horse forward and left the pair alone to their morning's outing.

A few moments of silence passed before she asked Drake quietly, "Why would Lord Andrews be the only one glad to see you amidst good society?"

"I wasn't being literal." Drake fought to hide his admiration of her agile mind and tried to deflect her curiosity. He reached over to squeeze her gloved hand, seeing her eyes warming as they met his. "You had him feeding out of your hand, Mrs. Everett."

She blushed. "He was just fishing for gossip."

Drake let go of her hand, straightening to get better control of his mount. "You are the loveliest fish in the pond, my dear. How does it feel to be the center of attention?"

She stiffened, scanning the faces in their vicinity warily. "I don't think I qualify as the center of attention, Drake."

"You underestimate yourself, Merriam."

"Andrews was right," she retorted. "You do exaggerate."

He just smiled for a moment, enjoying the exchange.

"Mrs. Everett!" A woman's astonished exclamation from a parked, open carriage instantly attracted Merriam's attention, and several heads swiveled in their direction as the greeting carried in the morning air. "Is that really *you*?"

Merriam's brief burst of confidence evaporated at the sight of the familiar face in the stylish carriage. Manners dictated that they stop to exchange words, overriding her own instinct to spur her horse to a gallop to escape the inevitable. It was Lady Sedgewold. Merriam hadn't seen her since Lord Dixon's garden party and her disastrous second meeting with the Earl of Westleigh, when she'd uncovered the truth of her encounter at the masque.

More important, unlike the strangers she had passed in the park, Lady Sedgewold embodied the forces that would set ablaze every path she knew back to her quiet, respectable life.

"Lady Sedgewold"—she managed to keep her voice level—"what a pleasant surprise."

"That scarf," Lady Sedgewold didn't hesitate to comment, "is a remarkable color for you. Such high fashion flatters you, but what a change! I would hardly have recognized you." Her voice trailed off as her eyes scanned Drake, eager like a baby bird for an explanation of his presence with her unchaperoned friend. "Introduce your companion, Mrs. Everett."

"Lady Sedgewold, may I present His Grace, the Duke of Sussex."

Her gasp was one of pure shock and malicious discovery. "He isn't!"

Drake tipped his hat and gave Lady Sedgewold a slight bow, interjecting calmly, "He is."

Lady Sedgewold wasn't won over by the gesture. "What an unexpected thing! And to be introduced by my dear young friend." Her eyes narrowed, the path of her thoughts all too clear. "Mrs. Everett, you never told me that you were acquainted with the Duke of Sussex. I cannot believe you would fail to note such an *illustrious* connection."

"I . . . I . . ." Merriam was not entirely sure why the identity of her companion was a cause for such reaction.

"We are newly acquainted," Drake intervened smoothly. The only betrayal of his displeasure at Lady Sedgewold's tone was the darkening of his hazel eyes. "Since my return to London, I find that Mrs. Everett has been kind enough to add her circle of acquaintances to my meager ones. It is an honor to meet you."

It was apparent that it was an honor Lady Sedgewold would have happily forgone—her eyes darted from his face to Merriam's, incredulous at the link between the two. "I understood you have been away from England for some time, sir."

"Eight years," he supplied. "But I grew too homesick to remain away."

Lady Sedgewold looked unconvinced but also seemed at a loss for a reply. Finally, she found her voice and spoke directly to Merriam. "I will call on you tomorrow, Mrs. Everett." It was more of a warning than a promise.

"Oh!" Merriam was paralyzed at the lightning speed of her downfall.

Drake, by contrast, was angry enough to increase the pace. "Then by all means, you should direct your coachman to my residence, Lady Sedgewold. I'm afraid your lecture won't reach its intended audience otherwise."

Merriam's intake of breath overshadowed Lady Sedgewold's. Any last trace of playful bravado was gone from her frame as she watched the lady take in the impact of Drake's words. The world seemed to slow as the seconds unfurled. She was officially "ruined."

"Come along, my dear." Drake's gentle command reached through the fog of her emotions, and they moved their horses away from the stunned woman.

Merriam kept her spine ramrod stiff, fighting for composure.

Drake wisely gave her a few minutes.

At long last, she sighed and gave him a tentative smile. "You certainly have a way with words, Drake."

He shrugged, pleased to see her spirits rebounding.

"It's a gift." He lowered his voice conspiratorially. "In the interest of spoiling the old bat's fun in being the first to tell this tale, I could start introducing you as my mistress for the rest of the ride."

She managed a weak laugh but playfully swatted him with her riding crop. "Thank you, but no, that won't be necessary."

"Had enough for one morning?"

Merriam shook her head, unwilling to admit defeat. "Let's finish the circuit. Unless someone starts throwing rotten fruit, I can't imagine that things could worsen. Besides, I think I'm surviving the ordeal, don't you?"

"With unqualified composure," he readily agreed. "Remind me to reward you later."

She unconsciously squirmed against the saddle. "You're incorrigible."

"You keep saying that as if it is a terrible thing, Merriam."

She smiled, her mood lightening a few more degrees. "Wicked man."

"You have no idea."

They continued on without talking, letting their horses set a leisurely pace, winding through the traffic of the Ton as around them introductions were made, invitations extended, and connections established and broken. Merriam observed it all and felt some comfort in the larger picture. Her own drama was just one inconsequential moment in it all. Lamenting her choices was pointless. This was a storm that would pass, and Merriam reminded herself that, after all, she had been the one who had once prayed for rain.

At least, she told herself, *I'm through the worst of it now.*

And then she saw him.

It was Julian Clay. Astride a bay stallion, he was riding on the other side of the wide path, heading toward them from the opposite direction. The Earl of Westleigh was difficult to overlook, with the rakish angle of his hat, the gleam of his golden hair, and the attractive lines of his coat across his broad shoulders. If Drake was a meticulous study on brooding, dark, rugged sensuality, then Julian was surely a casual sketch of elegant male beauty.

Merriam ducked her head, ignoring the logical voice inside her pointing out that he would never remember or recognize her, much less bother to acknowledge her. And she didn't want him to! She'd hoped never to see him again after the humiliation at Dixon's. Now to meet him as Drake's mistress—it was impossible!

A few more steps and he would be past them. Merriam held her breath.

"Sussex!"

Julian reined in his steed and crossed the path toward them. The trio came to a conspicuous halt in the grass, the parade of riders continuing without them and Merriam's grip on the reins of her horse making her fingers numb.

"Westleigh," Drake returned the greeting, his voice level but soft. "I'd have never considered you a man interested in making the morning rounds of Hyde Park. Desperate for social engagements?"

Merriam gasped at the open insult, as surprised by Drake's animosity as she was to discover that the men knew each other.

Julian's eyes darted to her at the sound, then shifted back to his antagonist. "Interesting that I could have said exactly those words and been far more accurate in the guess."

Drake's eyes narrowed dangerously, then he let out a long exhale, his brow clearing. "I've returned for a fresh start. Forgive old habits, Julian. They die hard."

Clay's look was wary as he measured the potential sincerity of Drake's speech. It was an unexpected olive branch. "They do indeed."

His eyes were drawn back to Merriam, and she knew the exact moment he recognized her. Heat flashed across her skin, and she was reminded of all the reasons she had set her mind on his conquest. Julian's mild shock and open approval of her new fashion set her heart racing. He'd looked at her before, but this was the first time she'd ever really captured his attention. Weeks ago it would have seemed like a triumph— but with Drake at her side, it felt more like a bizarre nightmare.

"Mrs. Everett, wasn't it?" the earl prompted politely, his gaze intense, ignoring Drake for the moment.

"Yes." Merriam made a miserable attempt to sound neutral. "Though I'm surprised you'd remember me."

"Not at all," Julian refuted her with a gentle smile. "Perhaps it was the unusual heat that day in the garden. I trust you've fully recovered."

Her eyes widened at the reference. She was flattered, despite the circumstances, at his recollection. Her cheeks flamed at the flirtation in his eyes and the waves of jealousy she could sense coming from Drake. It was a revelation for her. To acknowledge the small thrill at this glimpse of Julian's charismatic powers; to feel Drake's eyes on her burning with possessive heat—it was a new experience and one she hadn't foreseen.

Have I become this wanton? Can a woman desire two men at the same time?

Drake's gruff interruption ended her speculation. "I'm afraid we're running late, Julian. Good day." He yanked on his horse's reins, forcing the Earl of Westleigh to retreat to avoid a slight collision. There was no mistaking Drake's disapproval of Julian's attentions toward her or the warning look he gave his rival. "Come, Merriam."

He set off at a brisk canter, and she was forced to follow. "Good day, sir."

Julian Clay watched in bemusement at their hurried retreat.

So, the Deadly Duke wanted a fresh start, did he?

Ah, but habits do die hard, my old friend. And Drake knew it. Julian had seen the flicker of fear in his face. Apparently, Drake didn't want to play another round. He must have thought to choose a plain creature who wouldn't stir up the past, one who wouldn't draw his attentions. Poor Mrs. Everett. Who would have guessed that under those wretched sacks of wool was a creature worthy of seduction?

Julian smiled and spurred his horse back onto the path.

He would see to it that Mrs. Everett fell into his bed, and ensure that no one, least of all the Duke of Sussex, forgot the past.

Eight years of exile was nothing, Drake. Murderers should pay with their lives or, at the very least, enjoy no mercy.

They left the park in silence, Drake's ominous expression an impenetrable force that kept Merriam quiet. When they reached his mansion, she fully expected him to dismount and storm into the house without her.

But then Drake had a talent for surprising her.

He was off his horse before it came to a halt and signaled to the footman that he would personally be seeing to Mrs. Everett. His expression was unreadable as he approached her, and Merriam felt a small shiver of fear and desire at the sight. Whatever misapprehension he had of her conversation with Julian, she was sure she could resolve it quickly once they were alone. But she knew better than to attempt it in front of his servants.

She released the reins and put her hand into his to allow him to help her down. Instantly, Drake took a firm step forward and, with a viselike grip on her wrist, pulled her over his shoulder in a tumble that reduced her to an undignified weight against his back. She squealed at so unexpectedly having her head hang down with her bottom in the air, her hands forced to push against the small of his back to maintain her balance. "Drake! Put me down this instant!"

Instead, he clapped a hand firmly against her bottom to hold her more securely and, without a word of response, marched into the house and began to climb the stairs.

Instinct to struggle wisely gave way to a desire not to send them both tumbling backward down the staircase. But the cat wasn't about to go quietly. "Drake! How dare you treat me like this . . ."

Her tirade faltered as the hand on her rear squeezed her through the layers of velvet and cloth while the other slid up her skirt and moved against one leather-clad thigh. "D-Drake . . ." Merriam pushed against his firm backside to try to lean upward, determined not to encourage him. "Stop that! You cannot just drag me upstairs as you wish."

He reached the first landing, demonstrating that he wasn't out of breath from his exertions by replying tonelessly, "Yes, I can."

Merriam floundered for the next logical thing to say to a man who held the upper hand and seemed in no mood to relinquish his control.

He pushed through the bedroom door and kicked it closed behind him, the sound and vibration renewing her fears. "What are you doing?"

His momentum continued forward and she recognized the path to the bed.

"I'm punishing a very naughty girl."

She thrilled at his words; a part of her was convinced that, at least from this point forward, she was on familiar ground. His jealousy had spurred him to desire. Within minutes, he would fill her with that beautiful cock and she would have the release she craved. "Yes," she purred, "but put me down first, Drake. I want to—"

He set her down for the briefest instant, and while the blood rushed from her head and she wobbled a bit at the sudden movement, he tilted her world yet again, pulling her facedown across his lap as he sat on the bed.

Merriam yelped as her feet once again left solid ground. "Drake!"

She teetered; the reality of finding herself bottom up across his thighs, her skirts draped over his legs, her breasts suspended above the floor as her fingers clutched at the bed and his boots, was dizzying. There was nothing to push against for the leverage to fight him to stand. She was helpless as he pressed one hand against her spine, the other splayed firmly against her rounded backside.

"Drake, let me up!"

His thighs parted slightly, giving her torso more support and steadying her against him. The hand against her bottom lifted, and Merriam felt the velvet of her long riding habit start to rise as he uncovered her legs. He made quick work of her riding boots, and she stopped struggling.

Her pulse leapt at the erotic sensations his actions evoked. Her next words died in her throat, overtaken by a moan when his hand slid over the warm leather breeches, back and forth across the curves of her bottom, tracing the seam of her pants against the damp crease between her legs. "Oh, my!"

Drake's hand was relentless, reaching around her hip to tug at the fastenings of her breeches. She lifted her bottom to assist his efforts, eager to be bare for his pleasuring fingers. He used both hands to peel the offending barrier from her, letting his hands drag across every inch of skin he revealed. He tossed her breeches across the room and she bit back a giggle at the sign that she wasn't alone in her desire to rush.

Still, she tried to twist around to see his face. "Drake, this isn't exactly the best position for—"

The sting of his palm against her bottom was a sensation like no other.

She arched up, the jolt of it robbing her of speech and thought.

It had never occurred to her that the punishment he had in mind would involve a spanking. In her naïveté, it was a scenario she had never in her wildest imaginings envisioned. Not once in her life had she been spanked, not even as a child. The shy mouse hadn't needed correction—until today.

The offending hand that rested against her lifted again and landed with sweet precision against the ripest part of her flesh with a resounding smack. Merriam's breath hissed through clenched teeth at the heat that radiated through her. She braced herself for the next blow, only to have his fingers begin softly to caress her sensitive curves. He circled her stinging cheeks, and then his other hand was parting her thighs a few inches, his fingertips grazing against her honey-coated slit, deliberately avoiding her sensitive nub. Confusion swirled through the haze of sensations, but desire asserted itself, the undercurrent for whatever was to come.

"Time for your punishment, Mrs. Everett." His voice was a menacing whisper that made her even wetter, her body surrendering to him.

His fingertips lightly teased her slippery folds while his other hand worshiped the pinkening halves of her bottom, circling each and then playfully striking them with his open hand to increase her arousal. Electric arcs moved from each point of contact into her sensitive nipples and her throbbing clit, her body losing the ability to distinguish the sources of sensation, all of it happening too quickly. Everything he was doing to her translated into the sweet tension that was building inside, and added to the force of the climax to come.

At last, his fingers moved up to the top of her slit, uncovering and covering her nub with light pressure and quick, tiny strokes that made her whimper and buck in his lap.

"More . . ." It was humiliating to beg, but pride was an easy sacrifice to make.

He spanked her again, slightly harder this time, and then his caresses soothed each blow. His breath kept pace with hers, her excitement fueling his. The intermittent, jarring addition of pain and the ripples of fire that his finger against her clit only seemed to feed drove her to the edge. She writhed against him and then shrieked at the glorious invasion as he slid a long, thick finger inside her wet passage. "Yes! Drake . . . please!"

She begged him for more, uncaring what her pleas might earn her. The rhythm of his hands changed as he manipulated her flesh and increased the friction that she desperately needed. He added another finger, giving her just a few strokes to adjust before he added a third—stretching her, pounding into her as she rode his hand, urging him on while his other hand slapped her firm bottom each time his fingers buried themselves to the hilt of his hard palm. Harder and harder, deeper and deeper his fingers worked her inner passage, and he began to spank her with equal fervor. Pain and pleasure became one, and she could feel the steely length of his cock against her stomach. The speed increased, faster and faster, until she screamed at the shattering release that ripped through her, her inner muscles clenching in spasms of molten ecstasy.

Drake's stomach tightened at the feel of her release against his fingers, the scent of her musk so salty sweet, he knew he'd passed the limits of his own endurance. The "punishment" could have only one conclusion.

He lifted her off his thighs only to push her roughly facedown on the bed's edge. She was still writhing and crying out in the midst of her orgasm, almost unaware of him. Drake surveyed her beautiful body as she gripped the bedding. Her skirt was pushed up, her bottom pink and swollen, the marks of his hand evident against the rich cream of her twin curves. Her slit gleamed with her release, strawberry ripe, open petals begged wordlessly for his cock.

He ripped open the buttons of his breeches, freeing his engorged flesh. He pushed her legs even farther apart, pressing his shaft against the liquid heat of her silky opening, aligning his body with hers.

Without hesitation or tenderness, he drove into her in one long stroke, groaning as he savored the tight grip of her sheath against him. She cried out, and he could feel her continuing to climax around him.

But then even her cries became distant and secondary as a wave of lust overtook him and wrested the last of his control from his hands. He drove into her, faster and faster, giving in to his darkest primal need for release. She moved against him, lifting her hips to allow him access to her deepest core, the only sounds in the room their ragged breathing, the slap of his flesh against hers, and the wet collision and withdrawal of his sex from hers.

He spilled himself inside her, his release seeming endless. Drake saw stars as the force of his climax overtook him until he collapsed onto her.

He lifted himself, gently disengaging from her body's hold on him. He smiled at the luscious vision she made, rolling over in her crushed velvet riding habit, her ginger movements a telltale sign of the roughness of their encounter.

"Are you . . . all right?" he asked tentatively, aware that, at some point along the way, he'd lost all perception of himself as a civilized human being. He only hoped he hadn't truly hurt or frightened her.

Her blush made him start to harden, but he shifted his hand to keep himself in check and shield it from her. "I'm not sure I'll want to go horseback riding in the next day or two," she answered shyly, then smiled. "You're incorrigible."

He ignored the odd flutter in his chest at the now familiar accusation. He had to be careful. She was too alluring, and any attachment to her could be fatal. He gently pushed her toward the edge of the bed. "Go.

Perform all of those mysterious female ablutions." He kissed her hand. "Then come back to bed and laze with me."

She rose, her look grateful that he'd anticipated her needs. Peg had set up the screen for her privacy, and Drake undressed and climbed back into bed to wait for her.

She returned quickly and slid the riding habit off her shoulders, baring herself but leaving on her half corset and silk stockings, aware that he enjoyed the sight of her in them and nothing else. She joined him underneath the coverlet, curling naturally against his side. Drake stroked her hair and bare shoulders.

Shafts of the early afternoon sunlight slanted into the room, ethereal pillars that glowed as he watched her fighting sleep in his arms.

"Drake?" Her voice drifted up to him, heavy with sated exhaustion.

"Yes, my Cat?"

"Why are you so angry with Westleigh?" she asked softly, on the brink of dreams.

The name stung him. He'd just conquered her body and exhausted them both physically, and somehow, it was still Clay she was thinking of as she slipped into sleep. He closed his eyes and resigned himself to the punishment of a half-truth. "An old debt, nothing more. Now sleep, my naughty familiar."

She smiled against his chest and obeyed with a sigh of pure contentment.

Ten

The next morning, Drake found himself pacing in his study, turning over and over the encounter with Julian in the park. He replayed the scene in his head, stumbling on each little gasp and change of color that had betrayed his Cat. He retraced the possible nuances of each threat and reviewed his own performance. Even though he'd known that Merriam and Julian were intimately connected, it had affected him to witness the undeniable reality of it firsthand. There was no mistaking her interest in Julian, nor his in her.

Drake's reaction to their heated glances and the "punishment" that had followed had caught him by surprise almost as much as they did Merriam. But Drake was determined to keep to his chosen course from this point forward. He'd vowed not to let his emotions get the upper hand again. He summoned the icy resolve to destroy his wife's murderer as the shield that would keep him from wavering.

The outing had achieved his goal far faster than he'd ever dreamed. After Lady Sedgewold had huffed and puffed her worst, he'd been about to take Merriam home, satisfied that the thread of gossip would take less than forty-eight hours to reach Clay. Instead, the devil himself had made an appearance.

Drake had thrown down the gauntlet and, once again, put a woman between them, challenging Julian to the hunt. If Julian had been surprised that Drake had usurped his prize, he'd barely disguised it. He'd admitted to knowing her, and Merriam's blushes had confirmed Drake's suspicions that they were more than acquaintances. Julian may have initially thought to school her, but it was Drake to whom she was apprenticed at present.

Drake had flawlessly played the jealous lover and put the pieces on the board in motion.

He would keep them apart but deliberately dangle Merriam just beyond Julian's reach. If the earl pursued her, the diversion would make Drake's other efforts to destroy him easier to accomplish. If Julian intended to use Merriam's hold on him as a weapon, Drake would let him learn the hard way that he had chosen the wrong lever to pull. He would continue to keep Merriam close and make sure she had nothing useful to report to Clay. He simply had to ensure that Merriam wasn't making plans of her own.

Drake tugged on the bell pull and waited mere seconds till Jameson appeared in the doorway. "Yes, Your Grace?"

"Has Mrs. Everett been sending any correspondence from the house?"

"No, sir," Jameson answered without hesitation. "Nor received any that I am aware of."

"If she sends letters or notes from this house, you are to pass them to me first, understood?"

"Understood, Your Grace," Jameson agreed, not a trace of judgment in his tone. They'd been together too many years for Drake to expect anything else. He waved the butler out of the study and sat down at his desk, leaning his forehead into his hands.

Unbidden, memories of Lily and a similar edict he'd made came back to haunt him.

"I want to see every letter my wife writes and receives, do you hear me, Jameson?"

"Yes, Your Grace."

So little had changed. Perhaps he was destined to come full circle after all.

No, Drake amended the thought. *To hell with circles and destiny!*

It was an old debt . . . nothing more.

And Julian was the one who would pay.

"Lady Sedgewold to see you, Mrs. Everett." Jameson's announcement was level and undramatic, but Merriam was sure she was in danger of a genuine faint.

Even though Lady Sedgewold had threatened to call when they had seen her in Hyde Park, Merriam had been sure that the lady wouldn't risk calling on her here. Drake's scandalous behavior had pushed the possibility from her mind, but apparently it took more than that to frighten off a woman of Lady Sedgewold's constitution.

"Is the duke upstairs?"

"Yes, madam, in his study. Shall I advise him of the visit?" Jameson offered.

"No! I mean I'm sure His Grace would prefer not to be disturbed." Merriam smoothed her skirts with nervous hands. "I'll entertain her in the solarium. See that tea is provided, won't you?"

"Of course, madam." Jameson bowed formally and withdrew to assure that all was prepared for this impromptu visit. If he'd noticed her trepidation, he gave no sign of it. Merriam could only hope that Lady Sedgewold would have come and gone before Drake was aware of her call. Another scene between the lady and Sotherton would only make things worse.

As would keeping the outspoken lady waiting any longer than necessary. Merriam made a quick check of her hair and gown and hurried to the solarium, slowing only at the last moment to catch her breath and compose herself. After a careful count of three, she pushed through the ornate doors with a silent prayer for strength.

"Lady Sedgewold, it is a pleasure—"

"Nonsense! You are as horrified to receive me as I am to be here." Lady Sedgewold launched her attack without preamble. She stood apart from the elegant table and chairs as if by refusing even to sit down she had avoided contaminating herself with Merriam's disgraceful state.

"Oh! I'm . . ." Merriam was at a bit of a loss. "I'm very sorry for your trouble, then."

"Had I not sworn to myself to look after you when your dear Grenville met his untimely end, I shouldn't have troubled myself for an instant." Lady Sedgewold took in one long breath to regain her momentum, and Merriam began to wish she'd allowed Jameson to fetch his master. Any hope of a gentle reproach was dashed in the next instant. "Tell me you have lost your senses, been drugged on opiates and kidnapped by this fiend; that you have forgotten your own name or, even better, that you are an impostor pretending to be my sweet, quiet, and unassuming young friend who has been seduced by an utter rogue!"

"I hardly know what to say. I know this must seem—"

"Incredible? Utterly insane for a woman in your position simply to walk away from her good name and respectability?" Lady Sedgewold suggested icily.

"Drake is hardly the fiend you suggest," Merriam choked out.

"What has happened to you? You didn't seem the type for personal ruin and romantic attachments. I warned Grenville that you spent far too much time with your nose buried in novels. Sussex is exactly the sort of villain those things glorify!"

"Drake is no villain, and I am sure that my choice of reading material had nothing to do with—" Merriam cut herself off, aware that all roads seemed to lead back to dangerous confessions. "I'm happier than I have ever been. Please . . . understand."

The woman was not swayed; her lips pressed together so tightly the line of her mouth seemed to disappear before she replied, "You are blind, Merriam. What can I say to make you see reason and accompany me right this instant from this house?"

"I . . . I realize that we might have been a bit m-more . . . decorous . . . in this relationship. I don't think it warrants your . . ."

Lady Sedgewold raised one patrician eyebrow, as if daring Merriam to continue defending the indefensible.

What could she say? That if Lady Sedgewold knew the whole truth, no vow on earth would have made her attempt Merriam's rescue? That Merriam had willingly stepped beyond the pale when she'd stepped off that garden path? That she'd placed her own desires above everything else and ignored the costs? That Drake was becoming more and more vital to her existence, and that even if he were the devil himself, she would seek his touch and fiery kisses? That she knew it would end in tears and didn't care?

The urge to grovel or apologize evaporated as an odd detachment washed over her. "You are a good friend to have come, Lady Sedgewold. You risked your own reputation to reach out to me, and I shall never forget your kindness." Merriam dropped her eyes and curtsied, by custom ending the exchange.

Silence reeled out, and Merriam could only wait. At last, the older woman cleared her throat and took a step toward her. "I . . . I care for you, Mrs. Everett. I beg you to abandon this. To leave him while you still can."

Despite her conviction that she'd chosen the best path, Merriam felt her eyes fill with tears. But she kept her head down, unwilling to let Lady Sedgewold glimpse the myriad complex feelings she was experiencing.

"As you wish then. I'll not be the one to further foul gossip and spread insidious tales, but I will make it clear that my good name is no longer connected by acquaintance to yours. It is ruin, simple enough, madam. But it is ruin that you have brought down on yourself."

Lady Sedgewold's footsteps withdrew, and Merriam heard the doors shutting firmly behind her. The peaceful quiet of the room enveloped her. Still, she remained stock-still, awash in her emotions. It was done. The committees and the clubs, the teas and the social calls around which the mouse had built her life. And all the empty ties that had made her feel connected to the world had been rended apart at last. She hadn't felt the weight of it until the moment she had seen Lady Sedgewold standing amidst Drake's Arabian silks and gilt solarium. And miraculously, she was still breathing, still standing, something the mouse would never have thought possible.

The doors opened behind her, and Merriam spoke without looking up. "We won't need the tea after all, Jameson."

"Are you sure?"

She turned at the unexpected caress of Drake's voice. He stood framed in the door, holding the tea tray out like a pagan offering. "I added your favorite cakes."

"You would make an excellent footman." She bit her lower lip at the charming picture he presented as he set down his burden, arranging it for her easy reach. She felt fragile and a little uncertain after the storm of Lady Sedgewold's disapproval and the strange pull of her offer of escape. Merriam knew her wet cheeks would convey the worst of it, perhaps mislead him about her regrets.

"Come, sit with me, my Cat, and let us have tea like civilized people." He invited her to take a place on the embroidered silk cushions. He began to pour, allowing her time to compose herself. She sat gingerly and took in the dance of his hands, strong and masculine, holding the delicate, pale china.

"I have a feeling it would take more than tea to make you civilized." She sighed.

"Ah, but it gives me pleasure to pretend on occasion." He handed her one of the fragile cups. "It keeps my enemies guessing."

Merriam started, as the thought struck her that now

she had enemies as well. "I'm not sure you would have fooled Lady Sedgewold, though tea may not be what she expected."

"I could have shocked her and offered whiskey," he countered drily, dropping a lump of sugar into her cup. "Or strolled downstairs wearing nothing but a grin."

Merriam squeaked in horror, then managed a giggle at the image of Drake in all his glory taking a turn in front of the dusty old prude. "I wouldn't put such a thing beyond that wicked mind of yours."

"Alas! I'm afraid you inspire me." He took a careful sip from his cup, his eyes warm and approving over the rim as they met hers. "If nothing else, you've regained some of the color that your friend's visit took away."

Merriam put a hand to her cheek. "Oh, well. There is that childish rhyme about words and the wind. I should keep it in mind the next time I cross paths with her."

"Wind can sting and do a bit of damage. You should have sent for me. There was no need to face her alone, Merriam."

She rewarded him with a shy smile. "I was protecting you."

"From Lady Sedgewold?" His expression betrayed his surprise.

Merriam's chin rose. "Never underestimate a dowager, or a widow."

Drake's eyes narrowed, and she felt an unexpected chill at the sight, but his expression changed again before she could absorb the shift. "I will never underestimate you, Cat. Never."

"Well, then." She did her best to recapture the fleeting playfulness between them. "I shall endeavor to fend off the rest of the Ladies' Botanical Society when they emerge with parasols and smelling salts at the ready."

Drake wondered if his familiar had any idea of the dangerous game they played. She must have. His mistress was proving a quiet puzzle in many ways, and at every conflicting clue, he had to believe that she was more than a pawn. It was only a matter of time before Clay would attempt to contact her. Perhaps another public appearance or two would prove too much of a temptation. In the meantime, he was determined to keep her close.

"Was she a dear friend?" he inquired gently.

Merriam's eyes dropped to her hands. "I suppose not. She was my late husband's godmother and always took some interest in our lives. She was a source of advice and would readily take charge." She set down her tea. "Most of our social circle was a bit older. Grenville thought it suitable."

"Suitable?"

"To our social standing, for his business, and . . . I was hardly a glittering hostess. Grenville said I was as vivacious as a mop." She shrugged, her hands waving off the past as if it were some unseen gnat she could dismiss. "He wasn't wrong, but secretly, after his death, I realized I wasn't ready to be consigned to the status of decaying matron."

"Of course he was wrong. I'm having trouble believing any man could possess you and not see the fire latent in your soul. You are a passionate and beautiful woman, Merriam. Drowning in black wool and surrounded by prudes, you just lost sight of it."

She touched her cheek, heat suffusing her face at his compliment. "Oh, please!" She laughed. "You didn't know me before . . ."

He tilted his head, openly studying her as if they were opponents across a field of battle and not lovers sharing a simple cup of tea. "No, I suppose not. It does make one curious."

"Curious?"

"To consider what it would have been like to watch."

"What on earth would you have been watching?" she asked in astonishment.

"You. It was such an amazing step you took that night at Milbank's. In light of your past conduct . . . such a leap, Merriam, from quiet frustration to stunning temptress, I wonder at the inspiration for it all."

"Oh." She appeared to have no ready response, her color deepening. "I . . . I'm not . . . sure. Perhaps all women . . . wish secretly to change and be at liberty."

"Ah, yes, liberty." He set down his cup, wishing he had the sorcery to make her confess her relationship to Clay. Hearing her admit to the conspiracy would release him from any guilt that tried to press in during unguarded moments. She had the power to make him forget, and Drake had vowed never to forget . . . or forgive. "You are a rare creature to be so independent. So many women seem doomed to wait for rescue, to be inspired or driven to change by someone else. They have not the courage to act entirely alone."

She averted her gaze for a telltale second, and Drake's stomach filled with a chilling weight. It was her passion for Clay that had drawn her out. And now she would lie to him.

"You make me feel very brave," she admitted, looking at him with shining eyes that threatened to undo his every plan.

It was too much. He managed a smile, then stood to escape. "I should return to my work upstairs." He kissed her forehead, withdrawing before the scent of her hair and the simple touch of his lips against her skin could arouse him. "I will rejoin you this evening."

"I will look forward to it," she answered softly and gave the flattering impression that she was disappointed to see him go. The sweet show of sentiment made him feel raw and strangely cornered.

Unable to explain his reaction, he was forced to turn and leave without another word.

Eleven

Peg stood behind Merriam as she sat before the ornate dressing table in the bathroom, twisting curls and ensuring that her hair looked its best. Drake had said they would attend the opera that night, and Peg was determined that her new mistress would hold her own among the opulent attendees. Grenville had taken Merriam to the opera house once when he was assured that it was considered entirely respectable. But she was certain that an evening on Drake's arm would bear no resemblance to the dull outing she'd endured with her husband.

Nothing about Drake reminded her of her husband.

"You're so skilled, Peg," Merriam complimented her, watching their reflection in the vanity mirror, mesmerized by the intricate pattern of the maid's hands as she worked the plaits of her hair. "Have you been with the duke's household a long time?"

"Ten years," Peg responded softly. "I was his wife's personal maid."

Merriam didn't need the mirror to tell her that her face had gone pale. She could feel the blood draining into a churning, cold storm in her stomach.

It was ridiculous. Why shouldn't he have had a wife? She'd had a husband, hadn't she? What difference did it make? How could a man like Drake not have been married? The man's appetites made any notion of a life of solitary self-denial laughable.

She couldn't say why it mattered so much. Jealousy didn't seem an inappropriate description for the strange unease and possessiveness that flashed through her. She knew so little of him. Almost nothing. His name on a card. That he'd been gone from England and only just returned. Drake had shared nothing of his past and she had never pressed, so relieved not to relive her own, so distracted by the changes in her circumstances.

But now she knew that Drake had once had a wife, Merriam was compelled to know more.

"The duke is a widower?"

Peg nodded, her look distant and sad. "Eight years ago. We don't speak of it, madam."

"You're so young." Merriam floundered, wanting very much for Peg to speak of it. "I hardly believe it."

Peg smiled. "I was fourteen when she came here. She chose me for my gentle hands, she said."

"You have a light touch," Merriam agreed softly. "Was she a good mistress?"

Peg shrugged, her expression shuttered. "She was very beautiful."

Merriam wondered if the twist of a cold knife would have been less painful. "Oh," she breathed. Her eyes dropped from the reflection, unwilling to face her own shortcomings against the imagined enchantress who crept into her mind's eye. The dressing gown that had never been worn—it must have been *hers*. Her curiosity about Drake's dead wife evaporated at the prospect that answers to even the most basic questions might prove even more difficult to hear. Did she really want to hear about the woman's accomplishments and graces? About her tastes or remarkable qualities?

No. The mouse stood firm. This was not a conversation for the weak of heart.

"I like the twists you added." Merriam reached up to touch the back of her hair. "They make me feel very regal."

Peg's eyes brightened. "I'm glad, madam. Come, let's get you dressed."

Merriam stood and moved toward the fireplace, holding out her hands to warm them while Peg fetched the gown that she'd selected for her appearance at the opera. The maid returned quickly and began her work, dressing Merriam in front of the bright blaze.

It was one of her very best evening gowns, though a

bit austere by most standards. Without ornamentation, it was gossamer silver-gray with a soft blue underskirt that shimmered when she moved. The colors matched the gray-blue of her eyes and made her feel other-worldly. In keeping with Drake's request, she had for-gone a full corset and undergarments and wore only a half corset, which accented her figure but left her feel-ing naked beneath the illusion of cool elegance. Under-neath, she was wickedly exposed. She was coming to love the combination.

"He'll change his mind and keep you in tonight when he sees how lovely you look," the maid warned with a smile.

"Thank you, Peg." Merriam blushed. "That will be all for tonight."

The maid curtsied. "Enjoy your evening, madam." She lingered for a moment, as if she wanted to say something else but then turned and was gone.

Drake had never spoken of his wife. There were no relics or mementos in his house to signal that she had ever existed. He had forbidden the servants to speak of her.

Merriam sighed.

Drake must have loved her very much, she con-cluded. A flash of pity seized her. She had never loved Grenville, had never known what it was like to be "in love." To lose a soul mate was a pain she couldn't fathom, and wasn't sure she wanted to. It was frighten-ing to think of that kind of vulnerability.

The jealousy that had flared in her initially was set aside by an act of pure will. Drake would tell her when he wanted to—*if* he wanted to, she amended quickly. The late duchess was not the concern of his current mistress. If he'd forbidden the servants to speak of it, he certainly wouldn't welcome an inquiry from her on the topic.

Besides, what would she say? *I understand your wife was beautiful?*

No, she didn't want to pry. She wanted to earn his confidence and his trust. He deserved at least that much for all he'd given her. He'd offered her an escape from the suffocating confines of her life. She stared into the fire and realized that she had spared little thought for how she would return to the life she'd abandoned. There'd been no time to catch her breath since she'd entered the house. A telling sign, she suspected.

Do I truly miss any of it?

She silently pondered the question as she returned to the bedroom and waited expectantly for a tug of regret. The ache came, but not for the security and quiet of her routines or the lost invitations. It came instead for her friendship with Madame DeBourcier and the singular lessons and conversations they had shared. She felt isolated. There was no one to really talk to about the transformations she was experiencing or the strange turns of her relationship with Sotherton. But Madame DeBourcier would understand. Perhaps she would slip out to—

Drake's appearance interrupted her reverie.

She made a mock curtsy as he openly admired her modiste's latest effort. "My familiar looks enchanting this evening." He kissed her gloved hand before she could protest.

"Thank you, Merlin."

From behind his back, he brought out a small black satin box. "For tonight."

He opened the box, and she reacted precisely as he'd predicted to the jeweler.

"Oh, my! It's too much, Drake!" She took a step back even while he noted that she couldn't take her eyes off the glorious strands of pearls accented with garnets and silver filigreed elements that would drape over her collarbone. The necklace was perfect for her evening's ensemble, the luster of the pearls and garnets enhancing the color of her skin.

"Merriam." He kept his offering in front of her. "You're mine for the Season, remember?"

The question captured her attention. "Y-yes, but I fail to see what that has to do with you wasting a small fortune on—"

He stepped forward and pulled her into his arms, claiming her lips with his, his tongue working against hers and tasting her until she sighed against him. He lifted his head slowly. "My mistress, Merriam, to desire and worship, to dress and spoil and *decorate* and *display* as I wish."

"But—"

"You promised, Merriam. And I swore to provide you a decadent Season. Now, how can I do that if you refuse even a small gift such as this?" He held up the box again before she could argue with his definition of the word *small,* his eyes full of triumph and mischief. "If you don't accept things from me, Merriam, I am likely to feel slighted."

Her head was still swimming from his kiss, and his logic was impossible to follow but wonderfully sinful. She finally laughed and surrendered to his generosity. "You're incorrigible." She let him help her with the jewelry, his kiss at the nape of her neck as he sealed the clasp drawing a sigh from her lips and igniting a trail of fire that traveled down her spine to pool between her legs.

She moved to the mirror to admire the gift, her eyes catching his watching her in the reflection. The man was truly gorgeous in his evening coat, and when he looked at her, his hazel eyes a storm of molten desire, he banished her insecurities and fears.

She was his. The necklace was a symbol of her new status. She was a woman who had stepped away from all that was respectable. She didn't need the pronouncements of someone like Lady Sedgewold to grasp the implications. But instead of shamed or fearful, she felt cherished and impossibly safe.

He'd chosen her for the Season, and it was enough. It had to be.

*   *   *

Merriam took courage from Drake's studied nonchalance and did her best to draw from his strength and ignore the whispers and the sight of countless opera glasses pointed at their box. But this was worse than the park. The courage she had congratulated herself on at the house had abandoned her as they entered the opera house. A ride in public was still innocent enough to be misinterpreted, but there was no mistaking the meaning of the jewels at her throat and the way Drake kept a possessive arm draped over the back of her chair. She only hoped that after a time the performance would surpass the novelty of the Duke of Sussex and his new mistress.

"Drake," she whispered. "Everyone is staring at us!"

He smiled and then, to her chagrin, made a show of lifting her hand and kissing her fingertips. "It must be the necklace."

She struggled not to smile, trying not to encourage him as several more bejeweled opera glasses turned toward them. Merriam imagined what they must look like, their heads bent together, the intimate interest in Sotherton's eyes unmistakable at any distance. "Drake, please behave!"

He gently released her hand, his expression a mockery of contrition. "If you insist," he said, leaning back in his chair. "But I'm afraid I may have to punish you when we get home for being so cruel to me in public."

Merriam gasped at the erotic threat, her face flooding with heat. "You—"

The sound of an attendant at the door made her stop instantly, praying they hadn't been overheard. "Excuse me, Your Grace, but there is a Lord Colwick who would like a few minutes with you. He's downstairs in the gentlemen's lounge."

Drake's expression sobered instantly. "I'll go down. Wait for me outside the door." He turned to Merriam. "Forgive me, my dear. I'll return shortly." He kissed her cheek and followed the attendant out of the box.

Merriam risked a glance over the audience to see if the number of onlookers had decreased by some godsend. She dreaded the thought of sitting alone while a theater full of people gawked at her. A lifetime practicing how not to be noticed was no match for the torture of being openly studied and discussed by her peers. She knew nothing less than an emergency would have induced Drake to leave her unattended, but still . . .

She shifted nervously, doing her best to focus on the performers. She clenched her hands together and kept her expression neutral. Unfortunately, the Italian opera was hard to follow, and Merriam found herself wondering if the singers got headaches from all the screeching and wailing.

She heard the door open behind her and sighed in relief. Without turning she whispered, "I'm glad you're back. I think everyone in the theater was placing bets on how long it was before—"

"Mrs. Everett." Julian took the seat next to her, and Merriam almost jumped from her chair.

It was only her awareness of the people avidly watching her that held her still. Even so, she could hear the quiet wave of new interest created by the Earl of Westleigh's arrival at her side. Her hopes for the novelty wearing off died quickly. Julian had intentionally or unintentionally ensured that act two of her nightmare was well under way.

"Sir! Sotherton isn't here, and I hardly think this is an appropriate time or place to—"

"I deliberately waited until he'd left. It's difficult to find you alone. I meant to secure your forgiveness since I'd angered Sotherton when we met in the park. It wasn't my intention to draw you into the middle of an ancient quarrel."

"You're forgiven. Well, good evening then."

Julian's smile at her attempt to dismiss him from Sussex's box made her stomach flutter. His charm in such close quarters was almost too much to bear.

"Mrs. Everett, I probably deserved that."

"Deserved what?" Her brow furrowed with confusion. She kept glancing nervously toward the door, where Drake would appear at any moment. "Please, sir! If Dra—His Grace finds you here, he may misunderstand your intentions. I'm asking you to be merciful. I can handle only one scandal at a time, my lord."

Julian sighed as he noted the growing number of onlookers, then turned his attention back to her, unconcerned. "If you insist, Mrs. Everett. I'll go, but we must talk another time. It's extremely important." He took her gloved hand and kissed it gallantly.

Merriam pulled her hand back as if his touch burned her. "Please, just go." She tried to recover her composure, wondering how any woman could have landed in such an awkward position.

"You're in danger, Mrs. Everett."

His look was so intense, so serious that she was sure he'd meant from himself. It was as if he was about to lunge at her—or kiss her. "Then you should leave immediately."

He stood. "Not from me, Merriam." His whisper was so low it was like a caress down her spine. And then he was gone.

Merriam tried to control the trembling in her limbs. It had been one of the most unexpected and strange encounters of her life. Not from him? From whom then? Did he mean Drake?

The mouse inside her suddenly chimed in with a squeak.

Drake had said nearly the same thing.

Sotherton had said that first night that coming to him was dangerous. She'd thought he was teasing her because he'd spoken of her courage, and decided then that he was just trying to keep her off balance. But his conversations in the park and the way people reacted to him increased her anxiety as she added those elements to the puzzle.

Merriam gave herself a small shake. Her imagination was getting the better of her, and she forced herself to look back at the stage as a rather large woman in a pink toga started her solo while clinging to a wooden column. Merriam gripped the arms of the chair like a woman facing execution but kept her expression neutral.

She would ask Drake later.

And in the meantime, she was determined to sit there calmly, even if Beelzebub himself joined her and inquired about the opera.

"What is this about, Colwick?" Drake wasted no time, a part of him anxious at leaving Merriam alone and exposed in public. She'd made a great effort to hide her misgivings, but he knew his mistress was far from happy about all the attention she was receiving. "It isn't like you to pull a man out of a theatre for small talk."

"Sotherton, I'm not one to interfere. We've been friends a long time."

Drake's suspicions about this meeting surged. "Are you saying that something has changed? Since we're still friends as far as I know, I'm surmising that it's your policy on interference that has altered."

"Who is she, Drake?"

"What difference does that make?"

"It makes a difference. You'd sworn off women. I seem to recall endless speeches about their usury and deception. And now, over halfway through the Season, you suddenly have a mistress?" Alex didn't go on to say the obvious. That Drake had acquired not just a mistress but apparently a very unlikely mistress—a retiring and shy young widow about whom no one could recall much, but who had set the gossips on their ears trying to determine what would happen to the "poor lamb" next.

"A man can change his mind . . ."

"Who is this Mrs. Everett, Sotherton?"

"A lovely widow I've taken under my wing." Drake managed to keep his tone level and calm. "You're turning into quite the inquisitive gossip, Alex."

Alex's eyes narrowed; he was not at all put off by Drake's displeasure. "She's the one you were looking for at Lord Chaffordshire's that night, am I right? You sought her out, like the search for that magician's costume."

"Alex, I'm warning you." Drake didn't raise his voice.

"She's part of it somehow."

"And if she is?" Drake held his ground. "My business is my own."

"Sotherton, see reason before it's too late. Whatever you're doing for—"

"We've had this discussion before," Drake cut him off impatiently, "and if I recall correctly it ended badly. I have no desire to repeat the exchange. I don't want you involved in this, Alex."

His friend shook his head in disbelief. "All these years, and you don't trust me?"

"I trust that, as my friend, you won't approve." Drake ran a hand through his hair. "I trust you to stay clear and let me do what I must."

"Do you honestly think that Julian murdered her? Are you so sure, Drake? What won't you risk for revenge?"

Drake sighed, and then a chill settled into his eyes. "You're asking the wrong question, Colwick."

"Oh?" Alex asked, one eyebrow arched. "And what is the right question, Sotherton? Enlighten me."

"Ask me what I am willing to risk . . . ask me what I am willing to give to see him destroyed for murdering Lily."

"All right, I'll play. What will you risk? What will you give?"

Drake's smile sent a shiver down Alex's spine. "Everything, anything, and *anyone*. Last warning, Colwick. Stay out of this."

"You aren't the villain you aspire to be, Sotherton."

"We cannot all aspire to sainthood, Alex." Drake made a half bow and left without looking back.

Alex let him go and forced himself to wait a few moments to give the maelstrom of emotions roaring through him a chance to settle. Lily's brutal murder was an open wound, and no matter what Drake asserted, Alex wasn't convinced that a scheme for vengeance would yield anything except more tragedy.

But he also knew that any bid Sotherton made for a "new start" was tainted as long as his peers remained secretly convinced that the Duke of Sussex had gotten away with murder. Still, Alex was having trouble grasping the logic of his friend's secret plans, or how a woman like Mrs. Merriam Everett could possibly play a part in them.

He picked up his hat and cane and walked determinedly to the door. Drake wasn't the only one with the resources to seek information or the will to set things in motion. He would get to the bottom of things. And since Drake wasn't going to stop, he would do what he could to prevent the worst from happening.

Drake headed back up the staircase to his box, regretting that, once again, he'd been forced to risk his friendship with Colwick. But he'd meant what he said about being willing to sacrifice anything in order to achieve his goals. And he'd gone too far to turn back now.

He glanced up and saw Westleigh coming down the stairs. He knew that this was not a chance encounter when Julian's steps slowed as he saw who was coming toward him.

"Looking for me?" Drake offered.

"Not at all." Julian gave him a smug grin before trying to pass him.

Drake caught his arm. "Leave her alone, Clay."

Julian made no effort to pretend he didn't know what Drake was talking about or to deny that he had come from seeing Merriam. "The same old Sotherton, I see."

"She is mine, Julian." Drake tightened his hold. "And this time, you won't trespass."

"Still under the false impression that a woman is something you can possess and control?"

"Is that what this is? A lesson on the independence of women?" Drake let go of his arm. "Is that the lesson you think I need to learn?"

Julian brushed at his sleeve. "Among many, yes."

"You aren't the teacher here."

"Why not demonstrate that you've turned over a new leaf, Sotherton?" Julian gave him a wry look. "Unlike Lily, when she chooses me over you, why don't you let her live?"

Drake grabbed Julian's coat, slamming him into the carved paneling of the staircase. The move caught Westleigh off guard, knocking the wind out of him as Drake seized the upper hand. "Don't you dare speak her name to me!"

"Afraid of ghosts, Sotherton?" Something flickered in Julian's face. "I know I am."

Drake released him with a sound of disgust. "You have more cause to be."

Julian's eyes met his, raw with emotion. "When you first came back, I couldn't believe it. But now"——he straightened his evening coat and took a step back—— "I'm looking forward to besting you, Sotherton."

"This time, Julian, I won't turn my back. If you

want anything I have, you'll have to take it openly. And when you fail, I want you to remember that you never actually bested me, Julian. Never."

Julian's eyes narrowed at the threat. "Her blood is on your hands, Sotherton."

"And yours." Drake didn't move.

It was Julian who finally retreated, continuing down the stairs and outside.

Drake watched him go, wondering if Julian would turn back to see whether he was still there.

Had they meant Lily's blood? Or Merriam's?

Something in Drake's chest ached at the questions that echoed through him. Because, it occurred to him, he honestly didn't know. The only thing he knew was that the game had just turned more dangerous.

Twelve

When Drake had returned to their box, Merriam had been sure that his colder demeanor had everything to do with the visit Julian had paid her. But as the carriage moved through the dark streets of London, Drake had made no mention of it. Instead, the closer they drew to the sanctuary of his manse, the less tense he seemed to become. "Did you enjoy the opera, Merriam?" His tone held no threats, no sarcasm or hint of a trap.

"Not really," she admitted, testing him a bit with her honesty, the darkness giving her courage. "With everyone staring, it was hard not to feel like a disappointment." His hand found hers in the shadows against the seat cushions, squeezing her fingers in encouragement, and Merriam continued, heartened. "I think people were hoping you'd select a more glamorous woman for your paramour."

"You shouldn't care what people think."

"Oh, really." She couldn't help but smile. It was an easy thing for a man to say. Drake had already proclaimed his independence from the gossip of the Ton. But a woman, especially a plain one prone to shyness, walked a different path. Transformation or no, the mouse would always be a part of her. And a mouse knew better than to disregard a city full of cats.

"There is only one person's opinion that should sway you," he went on, lifting her hand gently to peel off her glove.

"Oh?" she asked, feigning ignorance, anticipating his reply. Typical man! He would say that his was the only one that counted and then pay her a compliment to soothe her bruised confidence.

"Oh, yes." Drake moved her palm up to his mouth and flicked his tongue over it before kissing it. "Your own. Yours is the only opinion that matters."

"Oh!" she exclaimed breathlessly. Before she could think of something more clever to add, the carriage pulled to a halt before his home.

Drake climbed out first, then helped her alight. He escorted her upstairs, and Merriam held his arm with trembling fingers. He was treating her like a delicate treasure, and the anxiety she'd experienced this evening began to melt away.

"I like this dress," he commented when they reached the sanctuary of the bedroom. He drew her toward the large bed they shared. "You look like a siren, a moonlit siren, in this dress."

Her body responded to his words, every fiber of her being longing to embody an alluring creature that could draw him to her. Moisture pooled between her thighs above the silken ties of her stockings, and her breasts swelled against the confines of her bodice.

She moved into his arms, lifting her face for his kiss, a slow, sweet invitation that she knew he would accept. His mouth lowered to capture hers, and it was like a first kiss. So reverent and tender she thought she would weep. The gentle friction of his lips against hers was the barest brush of fire, which wrenched a moan from deep within her.

Her tongue flicked out to dance along the ridges of his mouth, and his arms tightened around her, his tongue joining hers as their desires fed into each other.

Drake forced himself to end the kiss, his breathing fast and hard. "Tonight," he said, before he moved his lips against her forehead and temples, "I want to go slowly, Merriam. I want to linger and savor you, until I can't think anymore."

Her eyelids fluttered open at the sound of his voice, her gray-blue eyes glinting in the soft glow from the firelight as she absorbed the promise in his words. She simply nodded. "Yes, I want that too, Drake."

His smile was like slow lightning that worked through her, a sizzling arc of invisible energy that made her bones feel pliable and hollow.

"A new game, then," he said.

"Yes." Merriam smiled, her heart skipping a beat, excited by the prospect of his inventive loveplay. Her Merlin invented the most wonderful games, and she loved to learn of new ones that he seemed to create solely for her. "A slow game," she added, ignoring the eager pace of her desire. He'd said he wanted to linger and savor, and she wasn't about to forgo that torturous pleasure.

"Yes," he agreed. "A slow game."

Drake let go of her and took a step back, surveying her with eyes. "Stay there, Merriam."

He sat at the foot of the bed, his gaze never leaving hers. "The rules are that you do everything I command you to do. The rules are that you obey me without question and we'll both be rewarded."

She tried hard not to laugh. "Hardly a game, Drake!" Her hands found her hips, a mockery of saucy defiance that fooled neither of them.

He raised an eyebrow. "Sounds like a woman who is too frightened to play . . ."

"Not at all." Her eyes blazed with desire and interest, making his cock tighten. "Command me, Master. I am your willing familiar."

"Undress for me."

Merriam's breath paused for a moment at the words. She'd undressed for him a dozen times, and been undressed by him an equal number. Yet somehow, this was different. To stand before him and strip, his eyes on her, holding her, caressing her . . .

Merriam's hands trembled as she began to work on the tiny hooks at the bodice of her gown, unlatching the front, her fingertips brushing against the inner curves of her breasts. When she'd finished with her bodice, she made no move to push the material off her hardened crests. Instead, she turned her attention to the ties at her sleeves, letting him catch fleeting glimpses of the flesh that he hungered for, drawing out his anticipation.

She lifted one of her arms, turning to ensure that Drake would at least see the ripening outline of her breasts as she finished her "innocent" task. The sound of his sharp gasp was the reward that made her knees start to quiver.

She untied each sleeve and then, without a word, let the dress slide from her shoulders to the floor. Next she stepped out of her shoes, wickedly leaning down to undo the bows, her bared breasts suspended for his appraisal with her rose-hued nipples aching for his touch.

A part of her expected him to urge her to hurry, but Drake was silent. Allowing her to set the pace, ignoring the obvious tightening of his flesh, he was not to be rushed in his enjoyment.

She straightened, reaching behind her waist to work the ties of her petticoat. They gave easily, and she took one last steadying breath before dropping it to join her gown on the floor. She kicked them both away and then turned to face him, now wearing nothing but pale blue stockings tied with silver ribbons and a matching half corset that pushed up her bare breasts. Her dampened curls shadowed her sex from his gaze, and Merriam successfully dismissed the urge to cover herself with her hands.

"Go on," he pleaded gently.

"I . . . I need help with the laces," she admitted, wary of spoiling the game.

But as she drew close and offered him her back and pert derriere, he complied without complaint, loosening the laces of her half corset, his fingers avoiding her skin, before gently turning her around. "Finish it, Merriam."

She was closer to him, standing between his spread legs, and it was a command that she didn't need to hear twice. The corset slid over her hips with a small shimmy, her breasts bouncing slightly from the maneuver. She dropped the garment to the floor and hesitated, waiting to see if he would lean forward and capture one of her impertinent nipples in his mouth.

"The stockings too." Drake's eyes were locked on the last barrier between his hands and her skin, but he kept his hands on his knees.

That he hadn't reached for her was maddening. Her desire began to take on an edge of sweet, undeniably potent frustration. The game was to obey his every command. But how she obeyed him was entirely up to her. A mischievous smile flitted across her lips.

Merriam lifted her right leg onto the bed, her ankle against the outside of his thigh, her moist sex offered to him, as she undid the ribbon that held up her stocking. She could smell her own arousal and knew that it would work on his senses. When the ribbon was loosened, she rolled the silk off her leg, her fingers splayed to highlight the journey she wished him to take, the skin she burned to have him touch.

She dropped her right leg and repeated the process with her left, once again rewarded only with the approving look in his eyes and the sight of his now painful erection straining against his tailored breeches.

She dropped her leg reluctantly and stood before him, entirely naked except for the pearl and garnet necklace he had given her.

Her heart hammering against her rib cage, she waited expectantly for his next "command."

"Climb onto the bed, Merriam. Against the pillows."

A wave of relief coursed through her. She moved away from him and got onto the bed, shyly reclining against the pillows, then looked to him to undress and join her.

Drake stood, aware of her expectations but enjoying himself immeasurably. Still, he hardly wished to fight with his evening clothes later, when he planned on giving in to his desire to plunge into her body and lose himself inside her. He undressed at a leisurely pace, surprised at how much he enjoyed the way her eyes roamed over him, and the way she squirmed and moaned at the sight of his swollen cock jutting from his hips.

She held out her arms. "Drake, hurry."

He shook his head. "It is a slow game this time." He moved onto the bed but kept his distance, shifting to its center, toward the bottom of the down-filled mattress.

She bit her lip, rebellion warring with hunger as she stared at his erection. Finally, hunger won the field. "Very well." Her gaze released his hard sex and managed to meet his eyes. "What is your will, Merlin?"

"Spread your legs," he ordered her, his voice thick with lust.

Merriam eased her knees apart, her toes curling into the coverlet as she opened herself to his gaze. "Drake . . ."

"Wider."

After a second or two, she complied until her thighs were taut, the crimson, wet folds of her sensitive entrance entirely revealed. She was vulnerable and so incredibly lush and sexy. Drake couldn't imagine a more glorious sight than Merriam reclining against the pillows, naked and open to him.

But he wanted more. "Touch yourself."

"W-what?" Her eyelids fluttered in a shock that he considered endearing.

"I want to see you touch yourself, for me. I want to see you pleasure yourself. I want to watch you come."

Embarrassment fueled her mutiny against his command. "I-I can't . . . Drake, please, just come here," she cajoled with a pout that threatened to wrest control from him. She held out her arms to him again. "Let me feel you inside me."

He shook his head. "Obedience first, then rewards." He watched the heat rise over her breasts, the flush in her cheeks at this request making his own body surge even more. He raised himself onto his knees, his erection, jutting toward her. Merriam's eyes dropped to it, and he watched her legs shift, her muscles clenching in a primitive dance that begged him to mount her and ride her to release. "The slow game will go quicker, my dear, if you'll just do as I bid. Please, Merriam, imagine that your hands are my hands. Please."

His eyes were almost black with hunger, and she silently acknowledged that she didn't have the strength or the desire to fight him. She wanted this. His eyes emboldened her. With each passing second, her vulnerability transformed into power. She looked again at his luscious cock, *so ready just by looking at me,* a part of her marveled.

I want this.

Her hands began to move, and his moan of pleasure was the last encouragement she needed to abandon her reserve.

My hands are your hands, she repeated silently, the connection between them growing with each passing second. She cupped her breasts, holding them up, pressing them and rolling them with her fingers, until at last her palms grazed the darkening tips. She pulled her nails over each nipple, pinching them until her hips bucked at the pathways of heat that her rough touch had opened directly to her throbbing clit.

Drake stared, his expression full of wonder and molten lust, and Merriam understood that there was no way she could go too far. That no matter what, he wouldn't look away from her.

She dropped one of her hands and let it trail down her stomach, past the thick curls on her mons, until she reached the places she wanted to feel him. At first, she touched only her nether lips, so wet and silky soft that she lingered to adjust to the new sensation of her own hand against herself. But she wanted more. And it was clear that Drake did as well.

She released her breast, letting that hand follow the same path as her other. She used her fingers to spread her lips, to find the hardening bud above her slit. With one fingertip, she worried and caressed the tiny button, biting her lower lip as the tension between her hips began to mount in gyrating pulses that made a sheen cover her breasts and thighs. She quickly discovered the pressure and rhythm that marked the path which would take her over the edge.

"A slow game, Merriam." Drake's whisper sent an erotic shiver through her. "Remember?"

She nodded, alone against the pillows but so incredibly with him as the intimacy of her explorations

wove a spell around them both. She slowed the dance
of her fingers against her clit, writhing to lift her hips
high, ensuring that he could see everything she did—
and her body's every response.

Her eyes slid closed as she inserted a finger inside
herself, just around the rim but adding the friction of
this invasion to the intricate play of her other hand.
The delicious tension spiraled upward and Merriam
knew that her release couldn't be held off much
longer. She opened her eyes to focus on him, to convey her dilemma, but the blaze of understanding in his
face was the last push.

Of their own accord, her fingers again increased
their speed, and when Drake licked his lips, she was
helpless to stop the sumptuous slide into bliss as the
first wave of her climax seized her.

"Don't stop, Merriam," he encouraged, then moved
to grasp one of her feet, lifting it to his mouth.

This is insane, a part of her screamed, but nothing
seemed to induce her fingers to cease or the waves of
pleasure to stop ricocheting up and down her spine, as
Drake began to explore her for himself. He kissed her
instep, suckled her toes, and then worked his way up
the curve of her calf. He paused to nuzzle the back of
her knee, and another wave ripped through her with
even more force, making her cry out. "D-Drake,
please . . . n-no more . . . ."

He shook his head. "Yes, more. Much more."

He reached out to touch her wetness, and as her orgasm continued, he lifted his fingers to inhale the honey-sweet silk of her arousal. Then, as she watched, he dipped his fingers into her wetness again, this time touching the soaked fingertips against her nipples.

"Drake!"

He leaned forward to savor the taste of her on her own breasts, suckling her as if it were her clit, unrelenting in his torture. Then he shifted between her legs and ruthlessly but gently took over. His fingers took the place of hers, the rhythm and pressure a perfect match of her own. With his other hand, he easily caught both of her wrists to capture and hold them over her head. She was helpless now to fight the cascade of her release. She writhed underneath him, struggling more to absorb each new level of sensation than to free herself from his grip.

She was trapped in a triangle of erotic perfection. The surrender of her hands above her head, his mouth sucking on her breasts with a hunger that kept pace with the work of his fingers against the implosions inside her.

Her orgasm stretched out so long, its hold so powerful that she couldn't breathe, couldn't cry out, could do nothing but surrender to the bright wall of stars that seeped up from beneath her and swallowed her whole.

She lost consciousness for a few seconds, only to return on another wave of pleasure.

Drake pulled his hand from her clit, unable to hold back his own need for easement. He put a hand on himself to position his cock against the searing passage that his body was screaming to penetrate. He gripped himself, pulling down on the velvet skin around his hard core, mindlessly moving his fingers up and down its length. He'd waited too long. It was too much to ask.

He came against her clit, the release seizing him so hard and fast that he was sure he saw stars and light trails streaking across his line of vision. He came without thought, driving into her as his last spasm ground through his body's frame.

He left her asleep, prowling downstairs to his study and pouring himself a brandy.

You aren't the villain you aspire to be.

"Oh, you're wrong," he whispered to the empty room, answering the echoes of Colwick's accusation. For the first time since he'd begun this venture, he found himself struggling with his conscience. The memory of her writhing against the pillows, her eyes burning into his, so trusting as she climaxed for him, made him take another drink from his glass.

That she could affect him so completely sent a cold chill down his spine.

Bedding her was becoming an addictive activity. Drake realized that he had to get control of himself or his plans could fall apart.

The next day, as Drake waited in his study for his afternoon appointment, he continued to turn over the past and his current dilemma in his mind.

How had it all started?

He sat at his desk surveying the tidy piles of documents and innocuous looking accounting books that had become his weapons of choice. Lily had once jested that he was a man who thrived on order . . . but secretly fed off chaos.

How had the simple rivalry with Julian gone wrong?

Her blood is on your hands, Sotherton.

And yours.

They'd been best friends at one point. He'd known Julian for as long as he could remember. At university, they had brought out the best and the worst in each other. The perfect foils, the perfect rivals; two young men setting out to find their places among their peers, reckless of anything but the pleasure of the day and their own entertainment.

In a brothel when they were twenty-two, Drake had made an offhand comment about a test of endurance. Then he'd bedded one girl, enjoyed himself tremendously, and sat downstairs waiting as Julian took his words to heart and attempted to bed the entire third floor of the house. Later they'd laughed as Julian crowed his victory, only to have Drake point out that, while he was equally sated, it was Julian who had lost his purse for his troubles.

"There is always a price for victory!" his friend had countered, undaunted by the loss of a few coins.

But Drake had shaken his head. "The cost may be too high, my friend."

"Never," Julian had vowed, his eyes gleaming.

Drake had loved that gleam, had fed it and nurtured it, challenging Julian again and again, only to sit back and laugh at the outcome. Win or lose, the games had been generally innocent—at first.

But then, Julian had told him that there wasn't anything Drake possessed that he couldn't take from him if he desired to. They'd been drunk, and Drake had paid little attention until later, when Julian had started collecting Drake's lovers and then, later still, set his sights on Drake's new bride.

Jameson appeared in the doorway. "Your solicitor is here, Your Grace. Shall I show him in?"

"Yes, thank you, Jameson."

Drake stood to greet his lawyer, William Hughes, as the man arrived carrying his black leather satchel and sporting an impossibly neat appearance that warned against any hint of frivolity. "Good afternoon, Mr. Hughes. I thank you for your prompt appearance."

Hughes gave him a precise bow and moved forward with measured steps. "I pride myself on handling the matters of my most important clients with great immediacy, Your Grace."

"Please"—Drake indicated one of the chairs across from his desk—"let us begin then."

The solicitor sat down. "I took the liberty of presuming that this meeting was in regard to the matter we had previously discussed: your desire to accumulate specific 'opportunities' relating to a certain individual."

Drake nodded, appreciative of the man's straightforward style. "Any progress?"

Hughes smiled, his eyes lit with a touch of pride at his efforts. "The Earl of Westleigh has not been as discreet as one might have anticipated. Though it wasn't easy to compile,"—Mr. Hughes removed a few papers from his satchel and passed them to Drake—"here is a fairly complete list of his current debts and outstanding balances."

Drake surveyed the list of names and accounts. "And the symbol next to these?"

"Personal gambling chits and markers, Your Grace."

Drake let out a long, soft exhale as he surmised that well over half of the items on the list had the telltale stylized cross next to them. "I hadn't realized it was this high."

"His holdings are largely mortgaged, and it is clear, Your Grace, that he has extended himself beyond the limits of his resources."

Drake set the list down on his desk, feeling a twinge of sympathy that a man's life could be reduced to a tally sheet of losses and mistakes. But then he shoved the emotion back. He'd paid for his sins, both real and imaginary. It was Julian's turn to feel the vicious bite of a change of fortune.

"Proceed then." Drake leveled his gaze at Hughes. "By the end of the week, I want to own every marker against him. But as we discussed, I want it done without alerting Westleigh."

"As you wish, Your Grace." Hughes rose, an efficient man set to the task. "I'm sure his creditors will be relieved to see coin for their trouble."

The solicitor departed, and Drake stood with his list in hand. Something about the emotionless and bloodless method of this move against Julian managed to satisfy him but also made him feel restless.

It might be possible that this lever alone would see Westleigh exposed for the murderous slime that he was. Perhaps once he held a sizable piece of Julian's financial future in his hands, Drake would offer him mercy in exchange for a confession. No, he shrugged off the idea almost as quickly as it formed.

It was more likely that, once Julian realized who held the reins, he would panic and strike against Drake in any way he could.

His familiar could come into play.

Before, Drake had always assumed that Julian would simply try to replay the past, that he would try to take Merriam from him, even attempt to destroy her to punish Drake and best him. But now a new thought took root.

If Merriam was Julian's creature, if she was really his accomplice, as Drake had initially thought, then the blow might not come from Julian at all.

It would be Merriam who would strike at him. And it would be a blow to his back.

No, a grim voice inside him amended, because he wasn't foolish enough to turn his back on a cat with claws. No, he would pull the noose tighter and tighter around Julian's neck, and when the time came, he would be prepared for anything that his former friend threw at him.

Even if it was Mrs. Merriam Everett.

Julian stretched his legs beneath the elegant embossed card table, feigning indifference to the dwindling pile of chips in front of him. A high-stakes game of cards was probably not the wisest selection of amusements, but, there was the devil to be paid.

The cards in his hand held elusive potential, but Julian struggled with the distracting turn of his thoughts. How could Sotherton be so smug, so self-righteous? His earlier reference to forgiveness still galled Julian. It was the first time that Drake had thrown out the word, as if Julian would ever be the one to offer it to him.

No, he'd bested Drake all those years they'd been friends—and Lily.

Lily.

His throat closed as if her cold hand had come to rest on his shoulder. Drake had killed her only to ensure that Julian didn't win one last time.

"Your luck isn't improving, Westleigh." His opponent's eyes weren't nearly as sympathetic as his words indicated.

And suddenly, Julian was in no mood to pretend indifference. "Give me the chit to sign and be damned." He signed it ungraciously, his movements stiff and his signature uneven. He left the club without looking back and hailed a hired carriage.

"Where to, gov'ner?"

"The Crimson Belle," he barked and settled back into the cushions. He was a man in need of release, and the women of the Belle had always been accommodating.

Thirteen

"He'll be gone for the day, madam," Peg relayed, looking hopefully at her mistress for any signs that Merriam might take advantage of Sotherton's absence and escape. "I heard the chef say that dinner would be held for him."

Merriam didn't hide her disapproval. "I'm not sure that it's any of your concern, Peg."

The maid's gaze dropped. "Supper in your room, madam?"

Merriam bit her lip as an alternative idea struck her. "No, I'm going out to visit an old friend. The blue day gown should suit."

"I'll have Jameson arrange for the carriage," Peg countered more cheerfully.

"N-no." Merriam stood up from the vanity. "I'll take a hackney. I'll be back long before His Grace, and there's no need to disrupt—anything."

Peg nodded and ducked quickly into the wardrobe to fetch the dark blue dress. "You'll want a wrap. It's a mite cool and likely to rain."

"Yes, thank you, I'll take it then." Merriam pulled open a dresser drawer, seeking a scarf she'd placed there a few days ago. She would drape it over her hat to hide her face from any curious onlookers when she reached the Crimson Belle. She was a bit nervous as she rushed to get ready for her clandestine outing to see Madame DeBourcier. It was the first time that Drake had left for the day on business, and Merriam wasn't sure when her next chance would come. There was little time to waste.

As her hands moved through the silks and dainties, her fingers touched something familiar. Merriam pulled out her reticule, its dark embroidery and heavy fabric a reminder of her old life. She opened it to note that it still contained the large square of folded pound notes, the bribe she had once thought would purchase Sotherton's discretion, along with a few other little sundries she had considered vital.

She smiled, recalling how she had clutched at this little bag, desire and fear almost choking her. The notion that Sotherton had ever terrified her seemed ridiculous in retrospect.

Then Merriam's eyes caught on an unknown item in her bag, and she fished it out.

It was the calling card that he had so imperiously handed to her in the greenhouse. She stared at the or-

nate letters that had announced Sotherton's entrance
into her life, bent slightly from the tight grip with which
she'd held it that night. She could have sworn he'd
dropped it on the floor, but he must have later tucked it
back into her things. Smiling at the little talisman, she
decided she would carry it with her—for luck.

The hour worked to her advantage, and Merriam was
shown to the oasis of the young madam's private rooms
without crisis or delay. The lush and inviting room
soothed her nerves, and Merriam was glad she had
risked the journey.

"What a pleasant surprise, Mrs. Everett!" Madame
DeBourcier guided her toward the divan. Still dressed
for the morning in a flowing robe of rich emerald silks
over a purple gown, she looked like an exotic butterfly.
"If I'd known you were coming . . ."

"I should have sent a note first," Merriam explained
as she took her usual place amidst the embroidered
cushions, "but I'm afraid it was an impulsive decision to
see you today."

"In need of a quick tutoring session?" Jocelyn teased,
leaning forward to pull a tray of refreshments on the
table within easier reach of her visitor.

"No." Merriam smiled. "I just wished to see a friendly
face."

"You lack for them?" Jocelyn asked in mild surprise.
"Has something happened?"

Merriam managed to nod, suddenly unsure of where

one began an explanation of events that hardly seemed to make sense. She'd come for more than a friendly chat or female advice. She realized she'd come for validation. She'd come to hear a woman she trusted assure her that she hadn't destroyed her reputation for nothing. "You were right, about things changing. It seems . . ." Merriam took a deep breath to steady herself. "Things took a turn after the ball that I hadn't anticipated."

Jocelyn's focus became intense, that of a mother tiger bristling to protect a prized cub. "Your rake? Is he causing problems for you?"

Merriam stifled the urge to laugh. "Not exactly. It seems I seduced the wrong man—"

"Good heavens!"

Jocelyn's astonishment and shock were so unexpected that Merriam lost her battle and gave in to merriment. "But he was the right man, after all. I mean"—she shrugged—"it seems that I wanted passion more than I wanted revenge."

Jocelyn looked at her, her eyes shining with understanding, her expression almost one of envy. "And you found it."

"He swore to give me a decadent Season, one that I wouldn't ever forget," Merriam confessed in a rush, "and he is proving to be a man of his word."

"I am glad, Mrs. Everett." Jocelyn filled their sherry glasses. "I am glad for you, though I never would have guessed your news. You were so reluctant to let go of your reserve."

"Yes." Merriam colored at the admission, growing serious again. "But I can't think of the consequences." She rose from the divan, pacing as she openly wrestled with her choices. "I don't *want* to think of the consequences. And when I'm with him, when he looks at me or touches me, there is hardly room for thoughts of anything *but* him."

"I'm the last person who would want to impede your happiness. Just guard your heart if you can, Merriam."

"Well, yes, of course." Merriam's steps slowed, and she returned to sit next to her friend. "There's no risk of that. It's—it's only for the rest of the Season."

Jocelyn's eyebrows arched at the detail. "So, it is a formal arrangement then?"

"I am his . . ." Merriam swallowed hard, wishing her courage extended further so that the words didn't stick in her throat. "His mistress."

Jocelyn took a sip of her sherry. "It is such a public step."

"Yes." Merriam lifted her own glass and followed suit.

"He's married?"

Merriam sputtered, unprepared for the question. "N-no!"

"Anyone I may have heard of?" Jocelyn asked, her curiosity getting the better of her. "Another rake?"

"I would rather not say." Merriam did her best imitation of a prim dowager and made them both smile. "It's strange. I'd always dreaded the Season. And now . . ."

"And now?"

Merriam bit her lower lip. "It goes too quickly."

Jocelyn leaned forward to take one of her hands, a simple gesture of comfort. "Decadent Seasons generally do."

"You think me foolish?" Merriam asked softly.

"No, I think it unique to know in advance when you will exchange farewells," Jocelyn admitted honestly, her eyes flashing concern.

"All things come to an end." Merriam bristled defensively.

"True, and if you both prefer to set a predetermined date and time for your affair's demise..." Jocelyn trailed off gently.

"The rest of the Season—I...I will have this, Madame DeBourcier."

"Of course you will, Mrs. Everett." Jocelyn tucked her legs and skirts beneath her, gracefully relaxing as she warmed to her former pupil and the subject at hand. "Every woman should experience a grand affair, but not every woman is lucky enough—or courageous enough—to seek the chance."

"You must have many such chances."

The madam's mysterious smile gave nothing away as she took another sip of her sherry. "You must make the most of the chances you have, Merriam, and leave the rest of us to ours."

Merriam leaned back against the carriage cushions, grateful for the morning with Madame DeBourcier and the freedom to speak of her situation. It had been easy to lose track of time as they'd sat like innocent school friends, giggling about their likes and loves, and Merriam wondered that a young woman as elegant as Madame DeBourcier had seemed equally thrilled at the chance to visit and talk. Still, she hadn't expected to feel so protective of Drake's identity. In light of the speed and efficiency of London gossip, she knew it was probably a wasted gesture. But even as a "wanton mistress," she felt compelled to be as circumspect as possible. In the quiet confines of the coach, though, it occurred to her that, in guarding Sotherton, she had also been foolishly guarding the last remnants of her old life. After all, no matter what happened, the Season would draw to a close. Her time in Drake's arms, in his house, and in his bed, would end.

Her throat closed with emotions she didn't want to name. Madame DeBourcier had urged her to protect her heart, and Merriam knew it was no idle warning. It would have been easy to mistake the physical intimacy of her life with Drake for something else. A less practical creature could make that error, she lectured herself.

But I know better.

Don't I?

Sotherton was hardly a man prone to romantic attachments, and he'd made it clear that this arrangement suited him. He'd been honest about his desires from the outset.

And she had accepted his terms.

My heart has nothing to do with this, she told herself firmly.

The coach arrived at the house, and Merriam alighted calmly. Unhurried, she let Jameson take her wrap and made her way up the stairs. Lost in thought, she removed her scarf as she crossed the bedroom's threshold.

"Enjoy your outing, my familiar?"

Drake's voice was so unexpected that she cried out in surprise. "I-I . . ."

He rose from the chair, and her heart pounded at the sight of him, powerful and lean, the shadowed glint in his eyes sending a chill down her spine. "Was it a pleasurable assignation?"

Oh, dear. Does he know about Madame DeBourcier, or is he just toying with me?

"A social call to a friend," she replied, tossing her bonnet and scarf on top of the chest at the foot of the bed. "I am your mistress, Drake, not your prisoner."

Oh, God. Why did I say that? How did I dare?

The look in his eyes was almost predatory, and Merriam's mouth went dry at her own cheekiness. But her reluctance to reveal the madam's identity and the nature of their friendship was pure survival instinct. The truth was too telling. Whatever else he thought of her, his animosity toward the Earl of Westleigh was too great to be disregarded. Better to face his ire over an anonymous "friend" than the rage she anticipated if he learned about the extent of her previous interest in his rival and the lengths she'd gone to in seeking out the madam's help in the first place.

"No." His voice was like a caress. "You are not my prisoner." He drew closer, and Merriam had a fleeting thought that this must be what small birds felt like when they were hypnotized by cobras. She stood paralyzed. "My question was simply a polite inquiry."

"I didn't mean to be rude." She held her ground. "Y-you startled me. I was told you would be out until after dinner."

"My business concluded early, and I rushed home to be with you." His eyes studied her with unguarded intensity. "Aren't you touched?"

Merriam's cheeks flamed, echoing her internal debate about the detached nature of this arrangement and the very real emotions this man evoked coming to life.

"Well?"

"Are you deliberately trying to frighten me?" She made an effort at bravado, her chin rising a bit.

Drake smiled. "Merriam, it is never my desire to frighten you. Ever." He moved to the fireplace, giving her the precious illusion of the security of space between them. He turned back from the mantelpiece, a formidable opponent. "I want you to stay away from Julian Clay."

Merriam's mouth fell open in shock at the unexpected edict. "But I—"

He held up a hand, cutting her off in one elegant gesture. "Don't bother, Merriam. It is clear that he is interested in you."

"The Earl of Westleigh has no . . ." She faltered, wondering how she would substantiate the argument without revealing that, at one point, she had very much hoped the Earl of Westleigh would be interested.

Drake continued, "Every acquaintance I have who will still admit to knowing me felt compelled to guarantee that I was aware of his visit to our box at the opera the other night."

"He wasn't invited," Merriam asserted, determined to clear up the misunderstanding. "It's not as if I am seeking out this man." She regretted the words instantly, the contradiction between her past and her present streaking across her face in a blaze of color. "Drake, please . . ."

His wry look was infuriating.

She squelched the childish urge to stamp her foot in frustration. "I was *not* with Julian Clay this afternoon."

He didn't look at all convinced. "Nonetheless, you'll avoid him in the future."

She crossed her arms. "I will do as I please, but since it pleases me to avoid the man, you can congratulate yourself on a stunning, bloodless victory."

Drake smiled humorlessly, but his stance relaxed slightly at her admission of defeat. "How very generous of you, my dear."

Merriam's anger drained away without warning, and she suddenly longed for a truce. Her lover in all his moods was hard to resist, but at the sight of the latent fire in his hazel eyes, it struck her why some women deliberately tried to evoke jealousy in men. The possessive gleam warmed her to her toes. "Did you really rush home?"

She was rewarded by his low, rumbling chuckle which released the tension between them.

"Now who is incorrigible?" Drake walked toward her and pulled her into his arms. He ran his tongue down the side of her neck, and his fingers began skillfully to release her from her clothes.

It was only afterward that she realized he'd never asked what Julian had wanted that night at the opera and had never pressed for the details of their conversation. It was as if he already knew them.

Fourteen

The gathering was expected to be elegant. True to his word, after their meeting in Hyde Park, Lord Andrews's invitation to dinner had arrived, and Drake had sworn to take Merriam. He'd said he hoped the evening would serve as a peace offering, a more low-key social outing to make up for the turmoil of their night at the opera. His thoughtfulness had touched her. It was the closest he had come to admitting that he was aware of her struggles with her new situation.

Merriam was sure she would be the dullest woman in attendance, but Drake's eyes made her feel awash in feminine heat and power. He commanded her focus as he escorted her into the salon. He squeezed her hand. "You are beautiful, Merriam."

She averted her face and whispered, "I would feel more beautiful if we were alone, Drake."

In the confines of his house, she was protected from the consequences she was determined to ignore. It was easier to hide in his bed, in his arms, and lose herself in the luxurious touch of his body to hers. But Sotherton was insistent. A decadent Season meant going out.

"Time enough to hide later," he'd teased, nuzzling her neck.

Blasted man. She sighed. It was so inappropriate to have his lips against her throat in public, but it had been exactly what she'd craved. Still, she did her best to summon a disapproving look, only to be rewarded by Drake's wry smile. The duke was clearly not fooled.

"Ah, there you are, Sotherton!" Lord Andrews came forward to greet them. "I knew you wouldn't disappoint."

"You hoped, Elton," Drake corrected him with an affable air.

Lord Andrews took Merriam's gloved hands into his and made the gallant gesture of kissing one of them. "Well, at least I now know who to thank for this happy occasion. Good evening, my dear Mrs. Everett."

"I cannot take credit, Lord Andrews. You were so kind to include—"

"Ha!" Lord Andrews tucked one of her hands into the crook of his arm and made a grand show of stealing her from Drake's side. "What would society be without the allure of the witty company of beautiful women? Why, a bunch of male dullards moping about playing cards, I should think! Now come, Mrs. Everett, let me introduce you to my friends, and you can try to tell which of them is the most pleased to meet you!"

Merriam could only look back at Drake, hoping he would rescue her, but Lady Andrews, a robust woman who was determined to claim her own prize in the socially elusive Duke of Sussex, stepped to his arm. "Elton insisted you weren't coming, you naughty man! I told him that he was off. I asked him what could possibly frighten you away from such a grand gathering. Invitations are not to be squandered, I told him, and I see that you agree, sir."

"Well, any invitation from—"

"You are a prize, my dear Sotherton. A prize! And I knew Elton was wrong. For all the man dithers about things, it's a wonder anything is accomplished! Are men good for nothing but bluster and fuss?" Lady Andrews punctuated the question by slapping Drake's shoulder with a playful *snick* of her closed fan.

"As a man, I'm sure I am unqualified to defend my gender, madam." It was Drake's turn to cast a pleading look in Merriam's direction. But Lord Andrews had already pulled her beyond reach, and he was left to fend for himself.

"Of course you are! How insightful of you, my dear Sotherton!" Lady Andrews giggled with the enthusiasm of a child winning a game. "Now, come let me show you the portrait I just had commissioned of my darlings. It is so rare to find a man who can appreciate the finer things. Elton says that the artist made my pugs look like small chimpanzees, so I shall leave it to you to redeem the day. You do love dogs, do you not? Of course you do. I can see by your expression that you do . . ."

Each introduction blurred as Merriam did her best to ignore the curious looks from Lord Andrews's male acquaintances and the icy disregard from their wives. True to his reputation, he knew more gossip than anyone she had ever met, and he seemed to delight in sharing enough shocking details to make her blush again and again.

"There, you see that man?" Lord Andrews leaned forward conspiratorially. "I don't think the baron could tell you the color of his wife's eyes or recall her first name. Hasn't seen the creature in twelve years! She runs his houses in the north country. Of course, that suits his mistresses well enough."

"Lord Andrews!" she gasped. "What a thing to say!"

He chuckled merrily, his eyes flashing with benign pleasure. "What is a party without a few favors and surprises? Besides, the secrets that most require keeping never last long. It is a great service I provide to my acquaintances by ensuring that they will never fall prey to other unsavory characters."

"And how do you ensure that, Lord Andrews?" Merriam found herself smiling, drawn in by his enthusiasm and unrepentant attitude.

"Why, who could ever threaten them with exposure when I already know their secrets and make no false show of keeping quiet? I am a true friend, Mrs. Everett."

"Do you know everyone's secrets then, sir?"

"Not yours, Mrs. Everett." The twinkle in his eyes settled into a glittering focus that made her feel exposed and vulnerable. "For I swear, there seem to be none to be heard at present, besides the whispers that Sotherton must have kidnapped you from a cloistered nunnery for all that anyone has heard of you previously. Is it true that he was a business associate of your dead husband's and that you have become his mistress to clear an old gambling debt of Mr. Everett's?"

Merriam's jaw dropped in disbelief at the overt fabrication, a part of her bristling at the ploy to rile her into sharing personal details of her life. "I think I should return to Sotherton, sir."

"Oh, you mustn't mind me, Mrs. Everett!" He was the picture of jovial innocence again. "A man must have his hobbies. Here, come, keep your secrets for now. Let me show you the rest of the main floor and the wretched portrait halls. We'll look at boring, musty faces and I will play the perfect host and you'll forgive me entirely for trying to trick you into confidences."

It was hard to hold a grudge in the face of his humor and persuasive manners. Lord Andrews held out his arm, and Merriam took it shyly. "I am sure your portrait halls are hardly wretched, Lord Andrews. And the narrative you tend to provide will keep any sense of mustiness at bay."

"Ah, you are a generous and kind soul, my dear lady." True to his word, he escorted her from the main party and generously showed her the arts and treasures he had amassed, along with the liberal recasting of his ancestors' sins and past exploits. Faint strains of music caught his attention and slowed his steps. "Oh, dear. If you don't mind, Mrs. Everett, I want to make sure the musicians have their instructions regarding waltzes. Marie will descend to hysteria if her evening is mismanaged with scandalous tunes."

He left her without waiting for assurances, and Merriam could hardly blame him as she tried to picture his wife in a fit of hysterics. She stifled a giggle as it occurred to her that Sotherton could very well still be in Lady Andrews's clutches evaluating paintings of dogs.

Ah, that would be a sight. Her stoic and dashing Drake trapped between a dowager and her "darlings" in an old-fashioned temper tantrum. Hardly the grand outing he had planned, but a wickedly delicious memory of her decadent Season if it came to pass.

"Enjoying your evening?"

Merriam's breath caught in her throat at the question, the voice unmistakably familiar.

Julian materialized from the play of shadow and light against curtains and paintings that lined the hallway. She watched in numb surprise as he approached, handsome and graceful as any jungle cat. At last, her voice returned. "I-I did not realize you were also one of Lord Andrews's acquaintances. I'm not sure I would have agreed to come if I had."

"Please don't take this the wrong way, Mrs. Everett," he countered smoothly, "but I'm not sure you're in a position to discriminate. A woman who lives beyond the pale cannot play the repressed widow as convincingly as she once may have. Besides, I am hardly in pursuit of a liaison. We need to talk."

"*We* don't need to do anything, sir. We conversed at the opera house and I'm sure I've had my fill of your dire whispers."

His smile was pure sin to behold as he moved toward her. "You don't give a man that impression, Mrs. Everett. I haven't had a chance to—"

She stepped back. "No. There is some wrong between you and Drake, some history. I refuse to get in the middle of whatever quarrel it is." Merriam squared her shoulders. "I should return to the party before—"

"It won't wait, Merriam. And while I had hoped to earn your trust, and your friendship, before I told you the truth"—his eyes narrowed as he drew closer—"I can't live with the consequences of waiting."

"What consequences are you talking about?" She was impatient at his mysterious game, but curiosity kept her in place.

Julian glanced down the hallway toward the salon doors, then back. "Here, come this way. We must talk privately." He took her arm and began gently but relentlessly to lead her down the hall.

"N-no . . ." Merriam struggled to think of all the

logical reasons not to obey. He was the last man on earth she wanted to be caught with, but his tone was compelling. "Sotherton will be furious."

"Sotherton is exactly why we must talk."

Julian led her into a candlelit alcove before she could protest. A cushioned divan graced the small semicircle of stone and would have seemed inviting if not for the unwelcome company. The velvet curtains that he pulled for privacy reminded her too much of a similar alcove. The irony of at last being alone with her "rake" after all that had happened was hard to absorb. She dug in her heels. "I'm returning to the party. This is beyond—"

"He's going to kill you, Merriam."

Shock and protest pulsed through her. She sat on the divan. "You're insane . . ."

Julian lowered himself next to her. "I may be many things, dear lady, but fit for bedlam, I think not." He took a deep breath, then let it out slowly as if gathering his thoughts. "Against any other man I can see how the claim would seem unreasonable, but Mrs. Everett, I'm having trouble understanding your shock at hearing such a warning about the Deadly Duke."

"The what?"

"The Deadly Duke," he supplied easily, then arched one eyebrow in an expression of disbelief. "Is it possible that you aren't aware of his past?"

Merriam wasn't sure what was possible. Drake's own vague hints, the reactions of the few people she had encountered, all seemed to mean something more as the nickname that Julian had repeated echoed in her head.

Deadly Duke. There had once been whispers of a "Deadly Duke." She'd never been one to pay any attention to gossip, and it had been years since she'd heard the tales. *Oh, yes, a man of great wealth and power who had brutally murdered his* . . .

Merriam's eyes widened as a nightmare unfolded inside her thoughts.

Julian seized her hand. "Drake murdered his wife and then eluded justice when the authorities turned a blind eye to his crimes. He left England to avoid the social repercussions and has only recently returned, perhaps thinking that his money and title would be enough to regain his standing amidst his peers."

Her mouth fell open slightly as she struggled with astonishment. "N-no, he couldn't have done it. He wouldn't do such a thing!"

"Don't be naïve."

She stiffened at the admonishment and pulled her hand from his. "Why are you saying this? There were rumors but nothing more! If there had been proof against him, if he did this thing, nothing would have induced the authorities to turn a blind eye as you say. Who are you to speak to a man's grief or to determine how his wife died?"

Julian shook his head slowly. "Drake knows nothing of grief—or of love for that matter. And don't think for a single instant to delude yourself with some fantasy about her dying in her sleep with a fever or tripping on the stairs. Lily was brutally murdered, and Sotherton was responsible."

"That's a lie! Drake would never..." Merriam struggled for composure. "I may not remember all the gruesome details, but whatever rumors and lies you wish to foster, I'm sure I've heard enough."

"You haven't heard nearly enough. Perhaps it's the details you most need to hear." Julian captured her arms and prevented her escape, the tight grip of his hands matched by the intensity of his gaze. She was like a small bird in the clutches of a deadly predator.

"Release me this instant, Westleigh, or I will scream and bring the house running!" she hissed in panic. "I'll listen to nothing you have to say. Nothing! Do you hear me?"

"Drake's temper was always formidable, Merriam. I've known him for many years, and even I underestimated his rage. If I'd had any inkling, I would have stopped him." He pulled her closer to him, the gesture a mocking echo of a lover's embrace. "But that is my guilt to live with. Drake has apparently found a way to live with his."

"Y-you cannot be so sure, so confident in your suspicions! You speak of this as if you were there..."

"I was," he told her softly, "Drake and I have a history, as you've guessed, Merriam. We were friends once. We were all friends. Lily was a beautiful young woman, accomplished and confident. She was willful and independent, and impossible to tame. Drake loved her to distraction and began to see rivals and interlopers where none existed. He accused me, his best friend, of cuckolding him, and I just laughed. I thought to diffuse the situation. I had no idea of the tragedy I set in motion that fateful night."

Merriam's breath caught in her throat, reminding her that she had somehow forgotten to breathe, or blink, as Julian's tale began to unfold.

"He murdered her, Merriam. Make no mistake. Her body was found later that night. Beaten to death." He gave her a gentle shake. "You've seen how jealous and possessive he can be. Surely you can't deny what your own senses convey."

"If it is as clear as you say, then Drake would never have been allowed to leave England. He would simply have been arrested, tried, and executed." Merriam hated the trembling in her voice as she attempted to find the threads of logic that would save her heart from the chasm of suffering yawning open ahead of her.

"There were no witnesses who would agree to come forward. No one to protest when he proclaimed his innocence and played the heartbroken widower."

"No one but you." The accusation slipped past her lips, and Merriam braced for his anger.

But Julian's eyes held only sympathy. "Lily was a

friend, Merriam. You would rather I have stayed silent?"

"Silent? No, not silent, but . . . There were no witnesses. It could have been anyone. You were his friend, too, Julian. Isn't it possible that he deserved your loyalty?"

"Loyalty? Lily was almost unrecognizable from the force of the blows of that fireplace poker. This was a crime of passion, Merriam. Whoever struck at her wanted to do more than hurt her. He wanted to destroy her, to punish her, to ensure that nothing of her would remain. There in her own bedroom, he saw to it."

It was hard to respond past the lump in her throat. "Th-the servants heard no screams?"

"They'd been dismissed for the night—convenient, don't you think?"

"Hardly." Drake's voice was a sinister whip that made them both jump.

Merriam screamed and leapt up as Julian instantly released her. She was sure that no scene could have been staged to look more incriminating to Drake than the tableau she was frozen in. Her skin felt icy, but as Drake's eyes raked over her face, the fire of a guilty blush worked across her throat and cheeks. "Drake!"

Julian rose, his expression droll and unconcerned. "Your timing, as usual, is decidedly wretched, Sotherton."

Merriam gasped at the blatant lack of contrition

from Westleigh, but couldn't think of a thing to say after being caught in such an untenable position. *Oh, God. How much had he heard?*

Drake's eyes betrayed no emotion but seemed to convey a hint of an executioner's bloodlust. His focus centered on Westleigh, but he extended his hand to her. "My timing improves, while yours seems to deteriorate. Merriam, come."

She started at the cold command, hesitating a telltale instant before one satin-encased foot moved to obey him.

Still, Drake's eyes never left his nemesis as his fingers closed possessively over Merriam's arm.

Julian lifted an eyebrow in wry derision. "This is far from over, Sotherton."

Drake pulled back the drapes with a theatrical flourish as he began to leave with Merriam in tow. "The end is coming sooner than you think, Clay."

The drapes fell back as they moved through them, and Merriam was awash in misery at Drake's side. Julian's accusations had been like physical blows against her psyche, but to have Drake discover her in Julian's arms, whispering sordid tales . . . Hints of his temper had seemed inconsequential before. But now, her mind could think of nothing but endless gruesome consequences.

Should she refuse to leave with him and plead for her life and safety? Did she believe Julian? Was it possible that her life was in danger at the hands of the very man who had brought her to life? The questions came too quickly for answers, and Merriam stumbled at the bruising pace, her knees wobbling before Drake steadied her.

"Are you going to faint?" Drake stopped in the dimly lit corridor, the sconces on the wall casting light on his chiseled features as he looked down at her. Merriam wished she could retreat so that he couldn't see her expression.

"N-no," she managed, trying to settle her nerves. She tipped her head back to address him, newly aware of how tall and physically overwhelming he was. The realization that, even reeling from Clay's assertions about him, she still wanted him set off another flutter of raw panic and emotions. Was it a sign of his innocence, a flash of intuition that her body, at least, trusted and desired him still? Or was it an indication of just how far she had truly fallen?

He tilted his head, continuing his careful assessment of her state. He was clearly unconvinced. "You look pale, Merriam. Come." Drake's fingertips brushed over her jawline, the tender gesture adding to her confusion. "Let's get you home."

"Won't Lord Andrews be insulted if we depart before dinner?" She struggled to discern if his calm tone belied a hidden fury or if he even cared that the woman who shared his bed now internally debated whether it were possible that his past could hold such bloody terror.

He shrugged his broad shoulders casually, making her pulse race. "I doubt that he is easily put off. And frankly, this is one invitation I will risk squandering. I don't think I approve of his guest list."

He put an arm around her waist and began to sweep her toward the main hall, effectively sparing her a response. It was only as they reached the outer steps and his carriage drew forward that Merriam realized she'd left the house without a sign of distress or protest. She was paying no heed to Julian's incredible warnings.

Reality instead asserted a stronger hold. The reality of Drake's strong, warm hands assisting her into the sumptuous interior of his carriage; the reality of his weight settling into the seat next to her; and the warmth of his body when he shifted against her—her nerves thrummed as the carriage door was closed and latched, darkness and shadow enveloping them both.

They were alone.

She was alone with the Deadly Duke.

The carriage pulled away from the house, and Merriam impulsively decided that whatever happened, she would brazen her way through. Cowering in a corner would gain her nothing, and all that she knew of Drake prevented her from accepting Julian's words without a fight. But to ask him? How did one phrase such a question?

Pray, tell me, sir, did you murder your beloved wife in a jealous rage?

Drake's seductive growl interrupted the hysterical flow of her thoughts, one of his hands closing over hers as they twisted nervously in her lap. "Did you enjoy your evening, Merriam?"

"Hardly," she answered truthfully. "I think I have had enough of parties and gossip for a dozen decadent Seasons. Perhaps I will claim a headache the next time and escape the torture."

He slowly lifted one of her hands to his mouth, tracing the contours of the silk-enclosed tips of her fingers with his lips. "Parties and gossip—is that all you wish to escape, my familiar?"

Merriam bit her lower lip against the subtle onslaught of his touch and the unsubtle menace in his tone. "As you yourself pointed out, Sotherton, I am not your prisoner. And I-I am not afraid of you, sir."

It wasn't entirely a lie, but she prayed that he wouldn't hear the undercurrent of doubt or misread the nervous tremble that bloomed at the base of her spine. She wasn't sure what to believe, but alone in the dark with him, her body began to hunger for an end of debates and discussions.

Drake began to slide the tips of her gloves from her fingers, each tug triggering a ricochet of desire inside her. "No, and lucky for me that you say you are not."

The glove of her right hand surrendered its grip, sliding from her elbow in a caress that bared her skin to the cool air in the carriage. Velvet and shadows dueled as her senses reeled with desire and she lost the will to conquer. Here, as he kissed the palm of her hand and nibbled the racing pulse at her wrist, there was only the need to surrender.

He used the hand he had stripped to pull her against him, trapping her with a twist of his frame so that she couldn't lean away. He honed in on her sighs and found her mouth with his. He was past tender games of seduction, and Merriam absorbed each bruising kiss, heat radiating through her and gathering between her thighs.

His free hand wrenched her bodice lower, until her breasts were bared for him. The fabric of his waistcoat brushed against her nipples, making them pucker at the glorious friction. She squirmed to end the contact, learning just how little movement she was allowed. His attentions were fierce, and her body responded instantaneously.

Oh, God, she silently intoned. This was the moment she should push away, demand that they talk, that she banish the fear that even now she was making love to a murderer. But the moment was beyond words.

She moaned into his mouth, and Drake's mouth left hers, only to work with maddening brushes of his tongue and teeth along the taut contours of her neck. She arched against him, silently urging him on.

It was madness. He released the hand he had held behind her to keep her pinned, only so that he could lift her breasts to suckle and tease them. His fingertips pinched and rolled one rosy peak in a rhythm that matched the work of his mouth and teeth. She cried out in frustration, wanting more and, at the same time, overwhelmed with sensation, unsure if she could bear the intensity of his touch.

The sound of a passing carriage wrenched another cry from her lips. Merriam's eyes fluttered open. "We shouldn't . . . What if someone hears us?"

"How do you do it?" His breath fanned the flesh he had just made wet, making her nipples ache for contact. He growled as he lifted up, only to turn her roughly away from him. His hands around her waist, he gripped her tightly to resettle her on his lap. She gasped at the disorienting speed of the movement, and at the unmistakable press of his erection through the folds of her skirt. Her breasts jiggled with each movement of the carriage, and Merriam was all too aware that she may have pushed him too far.

"So prim and proper." His mouth worked against the sensitive skin of her neck and shoulder, and she shivered. "Even now . . . something holds and restrains you, but this"—he touched her through the barrier of her skirts and petticoats, unerringly finding the slick apex between her thighs—"this part of you doesn't lie, my familiar. This part of you doesn't care about what anyone thinks."

She gasped as he began to push her forward, yanking up her skirts and exposing her naked bottom to the evening air. She caught herself on the vacant seat across from them, to avoid falling. Her cheeks flamed at the alien position of balancing in a carriage, curtains drawn against the night air, on a busy street in London, with her bottom hovering near Sotherton's face. "D-Drake!"

His hands gripped her hips, his fingers splayed over the ripe curves of her bottom. "Tremble and play the helpless innocent, but your sweet, tight slit knows better." He pulled her backward against his mouth for just a few seconds, tasting her but not to savor or tease. Merriam tensed, crying out at the wave of fire that coursed up her spine, her thighs damp with her own juices.

Even as she wantonly shifted to give his mouth access, to ride the sweet invasion of his tongue, he pushed her forward again without warning. Merriam's knees began to buckle at the loss of erotic contact as she braced herself against the seat cushions. Before she could give voice to a new protest or recover to stand, he was at her back, guiding her onto her knees. He'd freed his cock, and she felt the fiery, swollen head of him pressing against her in a fierce, silent onslaught, notching inside the hot grip of her folds.

He drove into her in one merciless stroke, not waiting for sighed invitations or the gradual yielding of her flesh. She felt molten inside, but at the entry of his hard cock, it was as if that liquid core solidified around him, gripping and claiming him to become part of her. She stifled a cry at the pleasure-pain of the sudden change, involuntarily pushing back to spare no part of her from this invasion. It was as if he meant to punish her with his body, but Merriam felt the climax inside her gathering momentum. She whimpered as he pulled out almost his entire length before slamming into her again. The friction was so sweet, she could taste it.

Faster and harder, he pumped into her as she helplessly knelt against the carriage seat. Her face buried in the velvet upholstery, her fingers clawing the cushions for purchase to push back against the ecstasy of his body pushing into hers. She cried out as the first edge of her orgasm finally washed out beyond her control, cascading into an explosion that made her shudder and spasm. On and on, mercilessly he drew out the moment, his movements gaining speed until she felt him tense. Drake groaned behind her, and hot jets of heavy liquid soothed the throbbing flesh inside her.

His body covered hers, their ragged breathing the only exchange between them as they slowly regained their composure and the sounds of the London night began to seep in through the carriage.

Gingerly, he lifted himself off her, then began to help her back onto the seat. In the dark, silently, he found his handkerchief and pressed it into her hands. Merriam instinctively shifted from him, wiping the silk square over her tender flesh. The intimate act seemed so strange and so simple after the primal savagery of their coupling. She finished straightening her skirts and folded the silk into a deep pocket. Out of habit, she reached up to check the disarray of her curls, horrified to realize that they'd managed it all without her losing a single hairpin.

Something like that . . . it should show afterwards, shouldn't it?

"You're in danger," the mouse tried to remind her. Oh, yes. She was sure of it now. But how and why and even if the monster she feared really existed was lost in the fog of her thoughts. Drake. Drake, who desired her and made her feel vibrant. Drake, who could summon her to impossible feats of wanton release. Drake, who admired her courage and made her laugh. He couldn't be a villain.

Could he?

There was no answer. He spoke not a word the remainder of the ride home, his hand resting politely on hers. When the glow of a lamp slipped past the curtains, she caught faint glimpses of Drake as he watched her in the dark shadows, a jungle cat waiting to see which way the mouse would run.

Fifteen

Peg added more scented oils to the steaming hot water of the bath, careful to shield any splashes from Merriam's face with a towel she held in her left hand. "There now, that should do for a while yet."

Merriam sighed at the soothing swirl of scented water around her and closed her eyes, sinking down, stretching out her limbs in the beautiful enamel tub. It was bliss. She wanted to steam out the memories of the previous evening. Once they'd arrived at the duke's house, he'd retired to his study and left her to her own devices. It had been a long, sleepless night alone, wrestling with the lingering effects of Julian's version of the past alongside Drake's ruthless passion on the ride home and apparent withdrawal afterward.

He'd denied nothing, but then, if she were honest, she hadn't worked up the courage to ask the question.

Had he meant to convince her of his innocence by making love to her? Was it his own frustration that had made him take her so roughly, or his guilt at deceiving her for so long? A million questions churned in her head, and it was all she could do just to be still and allow the warm morning bath to work its magic.

"He's rough with you." Peg's voice came from the doorway, where she'd withdrawn to give her mistress privacy.

Merriam sat up with a startled splash, sputtering as she was rewarded with a face full of bathwater. "N-no!" She reached for a towel, sure that if she weren't hip deep in water she'd have burst into flames at the embarrassing comment. "Don't be impertinent, Peg."

The maid stood, undisturbed by her denials. Blue eyes watched without betraying her thoughts. "Bruises tell the tale, my mother used to say. It's not my place, but there it is."

Merriam wasn't sure what was worse. Having a maid point out intimate marks on her body, or having her identify the origin of those marks as if by long experience. Would she have seen similar marks on her late mistress? Merriam stood from the water, pulling the towel around her to end the maid's inspection. "There is no tale, Peg, and it . . . it isn't your place."

Peg bobbed a curtsy, her curls bouncing in concert, but her china blue eyes never dropped. "No tales then. I'll make a salve and leave it on the dresser."

"Oh!" The concerned gesture made Merriam feel

even worse. The girl was just trying to be kind. "Thank you, Peg. I . . . I appreciate your concern."

The curtsy was repeated, this time with smiles. "I'll take care of you, mistress. You needn't worry." Peg turned, pitcher in hand, and Merriam was left alone to finish her toilette. Glancing at her body in the full-length mirror in the corner, she bit her lip at the tale it retold. Pale skin made the marks more pronounced, but Merriam blushed as she noted the faint bruises on her hips and throat. They hurt only when she pressed against the mottled flesh, and she blushed to think that the part of her that felt the most tender was completely out of view.

Toweled dry, she wrapped up in the lavender dressing gown she'd used since her first morning under the duke's roof. Leaving the luxurious marbled bathroom, she returned to the room she shared with Drake. Curling up on the chair in front of the fireplace, Merriam began combing out her hair.

With the late morning light streaming through the windows, it was hard to believe that her world could feel so unbalanced and strange. She abandoned the chore of working the tortoiseshell comb through her tangles and crossed to her dressing table. Setting the comb down, her eye caught on the table's contents. There, in undiminished, glittering beauty, were the necklace and earrings that Drake had given to her the night they'd attended the opera. His generosity belied a darker nature, she was sure. Tragedy had struck, and Drake had lost his wife in a stranger's brutal act of violence. If Clay had once been a great friend to him, then Merriam considered that his accusations must be even more painful for Drake to hear.

Remembering their strange tea after Lady Sedgewold's appearance, Merriam wondered if the topic of friendship had been the reason Drake had become so withdrawn. Even without a friend's betrayal, surely a murdered wife was excuse enough for a man to suffer moods. Wasn't the past something they both wished to be free from? Merriam sighed, fingering the silver filigree with its pearls and garnets.

Or was she once again playing the role of accommodating mouse? She'd never pressed him for answers to the dreadful questions Julian had raised. She'd given in to passion when a more practical woman would have refused him. She'd let him order her about and yielded to his wants. And yet . . .

He made her feel like a cat.

"Am I interrupting?" Drake came up behind her, the stealth of his gait making her jump slightly. He gave her a cynical look. "Pardon me. I didn't mean to frighten you—again."

Without thinking, she struck him playfully on his chest. "You didn't frighten me! And stop trying to, like some oversized bully." She bit her lower lip, a bit shocked at her own cheek. "You should, however, apologize for abandoning me last night . . . without a word."

He took a step back, his stance wary. "I didn't think I

was very good company last night, considering my mood. But I will apologize. On the next occasion when I am acting like an oversized bully, I'll hand you the reins."

When he said reins, Merriam had the unexpected fleeting image of an erotic ride with Drake between her thighs, which dispersed the speech she had been composing. The man had a talent for leading her thoughts down a decidedly hedonistic path. "Drake, we should—"

"Finish seeing to you, I would think," he interrupted, his shoulders relaxing as if all critical matters had suddenly been settled. He held out the chair in front of the dressing table with all the gallantry of a man at a royal dinner party. "Madam?"

She took the seat with a swish of her dressing gown. "What are you up to, Sotherton?"

He picked up the comb, his gaze meeting hers in the mirror's reflection. "Since I was a roaring success as a footman, I thought lady's maid might have some delightful rewards."

"Oh, no, you don't! I'll ring for Peg, and when she's finished putting me into some semblance of myself—"

"We've talked enough." He moved behind her, his touch gentle on her shoulders.

"I'll have those reins now, sir." She held out her hand for the comb, doing her best impression of a firm nanny who was not going to be charmed by a handsome little boy.

"You have them already, madam." He leaned over

and kissed her. Tenderly this time, Drake savored her lips until he drank in the little sighs and hiccups of her growing desires. "See?"

"You're incorrigible," she intoned, wondering if she could ever truly win any battle with this wickedly seductive man.

With the comb, he began a slow campaign against the tangles of her long, wet hair. At any excuse, he touched her neck and scalp with his fingertips, adding as much pleasure for her as he could to the tedious task. Her hair was darker when damp, and he studied the muted tones of earth and pewter as he worked.

He'd been inexcusably rough in the carriage last night, blind with his own needs and the struggle with his emotions. Andrews had done as he'd requested. He'd invited Julian and made it all too easy for him to be alone with Merriam. To Clay, it would have appeared to be a favor from his gambling partner. The plan had simply come together far earlier in the evening than expected. But instead of a conspiratorial exchange, Drake had walked in on some sort of warped retelling of that fateful night. He had always assumed that Merriam had been playing coy when it came to his past. Julian was doing nothing to shield his lover from fear, casting Drake as the Deadly Duke of old. He'd heard only the last moments. Clay wished to play the hero and rescue the damsel from the dragon's lair. He'd expected it, but the sight of Merriam so close to Julian in that alcove had hit him harder than he wanted to admit.

By possessing her, he'd hoped to draw Julian out. The simple fact that Clay had magically appeared after he'd taken Merriam into his bed confirmed that his plan had merit. As far as Drake could surmise, the two seemed to be acting in accord. Now it was just a question of what Julian would do next: either replay the past or set Drake up for an even greater fall. Either way, there should be no surprises. Except Merriam. She'd looked so guilty when he'd drawn back the curtain, and then trembled at his side as he'd escorted her from the party; Drake had almost lost his nerve. No matter what her deceptive role, he was using her for his own purposes, and a guilty conscience was beginning to gnaw at him.

In the carriage, he'd once again felt compelled to drive Julian from her mind, every instinct within him wanting to keep her close, to guard her and at the same time punish her for taking Clay's side and keeping her secrets from him. If she'd fought him or left him, it would have been a relief. She'd been afraid of him, but for all the wrong reasons. His hunger for her never seemed to lessen, and even when his blood raged to possess her, she managed to keep some part of herself innocent and out of his reach.

She leaned her head trustingly against his hands, and Drake smiled at the gesture. She was like a cat in many ways, sensually pushing against pleasure, continuously questing for satisfaction.

But time was growing short. The confrontation last night had shown him that, even after eight years of discipline, he wasn't a patient man. And worse, despite all his efforts, he'd become dangerously attached to his familiar. The end of the game must be achieved . . . at any price.

"By the way, I've decided to host a grand party here next week."

Merriam's eyes widened, her reaction distinct horror. "A . . . a party? Here?!"

"Yes, I've decided to prove to you that you can be a dazzling hostess after all." He continued to work the comb carefully through her hair, effectively keeping her captive in the chair as he glibly went on with his happy announcement. "Tomorrow I'll send for the dressmaker to come with her latest designs. Something appropriate for my beautiful familiar to show off in."

"But . . . I have so many gowns . . . a week is—"

"The Season is almost over, and I want to give you a night that you will never forget." He watched the color fade from her cheeks and wondered how much she'd intuited.

The Season is almost over.

Merriam heard the words as if they had been spoken far off, the echo more powerful than the initial sound. The social season was brief, but she'd never considered the quick pace of her days and nights while under Sotherton's roof. As distracting as the terror that hostessing Drake's affair was, something in her managed to recall the threads that had brought her to this point. Drake was the Deadly Duke.

She deliberately freed herself from his hands and pushed away from the chair to stand and face him. "Drake, we must talk."

He set the comb down. "If you wish."

"Drake, please," she entreated. "Tell me about Lily."

Though he didn't appear to move, she felt the tension whip through his body. "No."

"I realize it is a painful subject," she tried again, "but I need to understand why—"

"What is there to understand?" His eyes darkened with icy disdain.

"All those oblique references to your reputation"— her voice was choked with emotion—"I thought it was because of . . ." Her fingers touched her lips, as if to stop the shocked flow of her words.

"Because of what?" Drake leaned forward, his attention engaged completely.

"Because you were a rogue!" she blurted out. "I imagined you'd broken a few hearts or gambled. I never thought . . . And now, you refuse to say anything of your wife."

"And why should I substantiate the lies of a man like Julian Clay? And why, for one moment, would I believe that you didn't already know? That your protests of ignorance and feigned naïveté weren't just a polite deflection from an unpleasant topic? Isn't that what lonely young widows do? Sit around and gossip about other people's sordid and far more interesting lives?" Too late, he saw the sting of his words was more painful than he'd intended. She stood pale and trembling before him.

"Yes, that's it. How could I have resisted you otherwise?" Her laugh was hollow. "How, without the mystique of being a murderous bastard, could you possibly have lured me into your bed? Relying on your charming personality would hardly have been failsafe."

He bowed his head. "I am not a murderer."

For an instant, she knew she should respond without hesitation and reassure him that she believed him. But the lurid details of Julian's warning were too fresh in her mind, and Merriam struggled to think of what one was supposed to say.

"Ah, don't rush to agree, my familiar." He leaned back against the table, stretching his long, muscular legs, deliberately taking the pose of a man unaffected by the topic at hand. "Obviously, Clay's chilling tales have wormed their way into your heart. But you needn't wait until he has the chance to add another chapter to the sordid fiction he's created. I'm sure there are others at the ready. Or do you prefer his version?"

"I prefer the truth." She wasn't retreating. "Tell me, Sotherton. Tell me again, why am I here?"

A moment passed, and then another as the silence stretched out between them.

"Because I want you here." The words almost choked him as he swallowed against the bittersweet admission. A part of him railed to let her go, insisted that the risk to her life wasn't worth any justice that might be left in the world. But he'd come too far. He couldn't tell her about

Julian, his theories of how Clay had accomplished the murder, his own plans for vengeance. She would simply tell her precious Julian, and all would be lost.

"Tell me the truth."

He folded his arms across his chest. "Not good enough? Well then, let's try another theory. If you believe Mr. Clay, apparently you are here so that I can satisfy my bloodlust and see to your inevitable and gruesome demise. I imagine he told you that I will have to be a bit more creative this time to deflect a turn at the gallows. Perhaps if you simply disappeared . . ."

She hated the cold that blossomed in her chest and wrapped its tendrils around her heart. "What an inhuman thing to say!"

"Aren't you afraid of me, Merriam? Am I not portraying the monster Julian described?"

"No! I'm not afraid of you, and I-I want nothing of this cruel game! Do you wish me to be afraid of you? Is that it? You say nothing of your wife and then speak in twisted lies and half-truths and insist that no one is wronged but you. How is that possible, Drake?"

For a fleeting moment, she read a softening regret in his eyes, but it was gone before she could acknowledge it. "None of my past seems possible to me, Merriam. It is a painful tangle that I will not discuss with you—not now and not ever."

"Where is your heart, Drake?"

He propelled himself toward her, pulling her against the hard wall of his chest. "Leave it!"

"Y-you are not an inhuman monster." She looked up at him, her eyes a soulful gray in the morning light, her body, warmed by the bath, pressed along his. "But you cannot just leave these things unexamined. Please, Drake, if you're haunted by the past . . ."

"Merriam—"

"What can I do? You say you want me, but then . . . it's as if you shut me out. 'Leave it,' you demand, but I feel so lost in all of this. Whatever your dispute with Julian, whatever happened eight years ago, why can you not tell me the truth?" Tears filled her eyes, and Drake lessened his hold, drawing her more gently against him. He smoothed his hands over her damp curls and held her protectively against his chest.

"Stay." He supplied an answer at last, watching himself with a cool detachment in the mirror behind them, his tone purposefully warmer. "I just wanted a few weeks untouched by the past. An oasis from endless years of agony, Merriam. You didn't know or didn't care about the sordid lies in my past, and I desired you all the more for it." He kissed the top of her head, inhaling her scent to send a soft shiver of contentment down her spine. "Please, my Cat. Leave it for now. I promise . . . one day, I shall relive it all and answer every question, but for now, let me have this."

Merriam acquiesced by nuzzling his bare throat. "For now . . ."

Sixteen

Since the opera, not a word from you, but then I'll admit, it was I who trespassed. In all the years I've known you, you have been a professed wretch when it comes to social niceties. Whatever venture you are on, it is not my place to interfere. As your friend, I shall do all I can on your behalf.

The Season is almost over. My estates in the country are open to you. A hunting party away from the parties and dances you loathe should sound tempting enough. I will not press. But the invitation stands open and at the ready should you need it.

> *Your esteemed and holy friend,*
> *Saint Alex*

Drake dropped the note onto his desk, shaking his head in disbelief. Only Alex would be so tenacious and at the same time so forgiving. His offer of an escape from London was tempting. For a second, Drake imagined taking Merriam into the beautiful countryside and seeing it through her eyes. Making love to her isolated in their rooms, and playing the carefree hero, putting jewels into her hair and making her laugh . . .

But the daydream faded quickly.

One way or another, she would be gone from his life. He would do what he could to protect her from harm, but once Julian made his move, it would all end.

A knock on the door interrupted the painful spiral of his thoughts. Jameson stepped inside when hailed. "Peers has returned, Your Grace. Will you see him here, or should I ask him to wait in the library?"

"Bring him up, but by the back stairs. If Mrs. Everett is still in the solarium with her tea, I don't want her to be disturbed."

"As you wish, Your Grace," Jameson said as he withdrew.

Drake doubted that when the detective had been investigating the meek and beautiful widow, she'd ever caught a glimpse of him, but things were too close to completion to risk her seeing him now.

Peers entered, bowing without polish, but Drake hadn't hired him for his social graces. "Good day, Yer Grace, though it's a bit damp and cheerless out there in this weather."

"I shall assume that the weather report won't be an additional charge, Peers. Unless that is all the news you have brought today?"

"No, sir. I'd not waste your time . . . or mine."

Drake waited, his fingers tapping impatiently on the desk.

"You'd sent word asking about the other gentleman, the Earl of Westleigh, and if I could discover any ties between him and the widow." Peers made an effort to get to the meat of things. "Nothing scandalous. If he's the secret beau, he's been the soul of discretion. A couple of public meetings, but no word of him coming near the house, according to her servants. Lord Westleigh is said to have no current mistress, though he's a bit of a regular at the Crescent and the Crimson Belle."

"Nothing then . . ." Drake wasn't disappointed. The Earl of Westleigh had always been discreet, and he knew firsthand that Julian could be remarkably clever. Still, a solid piece of evidence would have quieted some of the doubts that continued to plague him. "What sorts of 'public meetings'?"

"Parties and the like, same guest lists, but then"— Peers lifted an eyebrow—"the gentry do quite a bit of that. You know, all attending the same parties and balls and soirees till you'd think you'd all seen enough of each other. If that's a sign, then I'll have to start looking at every gentleman stumbling through the streets."

"No, you're right." Drake let the matter drop. "And the unexplained 'lecture series'?"

"I was unable to determine it, sir. Whatever appointments she kept on those days, no one seems to know."

"Anything else?"

"Um, well, there's an unrelated matter . . ." Peers rocked back, uncomfortable with his next announcement. "You'd asked me to keep an ear for gossip, amidst a few key households . . . the local whispers and all that."

"Let's have it."

"Seems you have a reputation for being a jealous man and keeping your new mistress on a tight leash. Word has it, you're afraid Westleigh is about to steal her out from under your nose and that's why you've taken such care to keep her to the house. Seems the instant he shows up at a party or when you're out, you turn tail and carry her off without so much as a by your leave." Peers's complexion grew redder and redder as he spoke. "Somethin' about a scene at the Royal Opera House . . . and a dinner party at a Lord Andrews's home."

Drake made no effort to hide his pleasure. "Any chance the earl has heard the same?"

"Without a doubt." Peers nodded, "If the rumor of a book being opened at White's is true, I wouldn't be surprised if his name was at the top."

"Unbelievable." Drake stood to come around his desk and shake Peers's hand. "As the subject of the stories, I hadn't realized they'd developed so soon. But I'm not displeased." He pulled a few sovereigns from his waistcoat pocket. "Here, for your troubles."

"A-am I discharged then?"

"No. I want her followed. There should be enough there to hire another man or two if you need. If she leaves the house, I want no mysteries about her whereabouts."

Peers gave him a look that conveyed a bit of doubt.

"For her protection," Drake added firmly. "She is free to come and go as she wishes."

"As you say, Your Grace." The detective made a quick half bow, pocketing the coins. "I'll come by with the next word then."

"No." Drake returned to his chair. "Just send your report. No need to alarm the household again with a call in person."

"As you wish." Peers bowed again and withdrew from the room.

Drake glanced at Colwick's note. Alex had invited him to a hunting party to distract him from the "delights" of London society. The only delight he enjoyed was Merriam. As long as there was time, he had no intentions of relinquishing a single opportunity for that delight. But when it was finished . . .

I'll go, he decided. *If I survive . . .*

"Such short notice before the party, madam," the dressmaker clucked as she tugged at the bustle to pin it into place. "But I'm sure I will have it done in time. It will be a miracle, but for the duke, even the impossible seems manageable. He is . . . most impressive, is he not?"

Merriam managed a weak smile. *Impressive* was a diplomatic word choice for the bribery and intimidation he had undoubtedly used to secure the masterpiece that floated around her figure. She guessed that another patron had just had her prize stolen away after weeks of waiting, for there was nothing ready-made about the gown. Endless hours had gone into its creation. Muted copper threads embroidered a dark red satin, the intricate pattern matched by hand-stitched twists and inlaid amber beads along the sleeve and bodice edges. Even the hem gleamed with the treatment of copper embroidery and glowing beads. The red was earthy and decadent, and it took her breath away with each shimmering turn she made.

"I . . . perhaps I am too pale for this color," she protested, fingering the delicate strands at one shoulder. "Something more modest?"

"Not at all!" The modiste shook her head, dismay clear in her eyes. "You are a diamond in this! A gem. It is a burgundy, very understated. And the trim makes your eyes shine. Besides, look at the lines, dear lady! Your waist is so tiny, and the bust! It is a dream, yes?"

Dream, nightmare, Merriam wasn't sure she could explain the difference. The gown was a triumph, but she didn't feel victorious in it. The party loomed like a date with an executioner. It was one thing to think of brazenly taking Drake's arm at a ball, or ignoring people's stares in the park or at a simple social gathering. But to act as his hostess! Recalling names and greeting guests, overseeing the evening, anticipating any subtle shifts toward conflicts or public scenes, and somehow being expected to provide clever responses and keep her wits about her, all the while disguising pure terror as vivacious energy—it would be torture. Merriam's stomach churned at the avalanche of duties that Drake would expect her to fulfill. In the past, dinner parties of more than ten had undone her. Drake had sent out invitations for over two hundred guests. It was insane.

She'd told him she would stay, and he'd carried her to his bed, where she had set all her doubts and fears aside. Deliberately giving in to the sanctuary of his arms, she'd refused to think of anything beyond him, beyond his admission that he needed her and that the truth would come in time. But if her presence was an oasis for him, she wished he would cry off from inviting all of London to their private sanctuary. Whether he meant to end speculation about his past or shock his peers past forgiveness, he hadn't shared his thoughts. If she pressed, he became evasive or ended her queries with a seductive skill that continued to leave her breathless. It was impossible.

He'd asked her to stay and allow him just to enjoy the time they shared. Was it so great a thing to request? Merriam stared at her reflection, wondering if the dressmaker saw what she saw, a woman trying on costumes and masks for another charade. Only this time, instead of deceiving one man, she would attempt to fool hundreds into thinking she was worthy of her decadent Season and her seductive duke.

Peg came in with a vase of flowers for the side table, her gaze assessing the dressmaker's handiwork. "You're a vision in that dress, my lady."

Merriam gave her a grateful look. "His Grace chose it."

"He has a wonderful eye," the dressmaker added with a pleased huff. "Now if you will simply turn and stand still."

Peg stepped away as Merriam obeyed the modiste's commands, wishing her knees didn't ache from holding each position in what seemed to stretch out to hours. She'd always hated the process of pins and adjustments. Standing at the center of another woman's critical gaze was hardly comfortable under any circumstances. She glanced toward the top of the woman's head as she worked around the back hem. "Will it be much longer?"

"Patience, my dear lady," the dressmaker mumbled from the floor. "Perfection is no small thing."

"Shall I bring up a restorative, my lady?" Peg offered gently from her usual retreat into the doorway. "Something to help you keep your feet?"

"That sounds wonderful, Peg." Merriam watched the maid leave for the task, wishing she had the freedom to make so quick an escape.

"A bit to the left," the dressmaker requested, and Merriam obliged as best she could, a dull throb behind her eyes providing some distraction from the ache in her back. At least she could console herself with the singularity of the evening and the need for only one gown.

Drake could just as easily have chosen another half dozen, and there would have been no stopping him. Protests about economy or restraint meant nothing to the man. She'd spent years learning how to get the most out of a single bolt of fabric, recutting and redyeing it to suit, without much care for what fashion might dictate. But Sotherton didn't value her practical side, preferring to see that she was indulged at every turn and spoiled beyond reason "for her own good."

By the time the dressmaker had completed the fitting and packed up the dress, Merriam's headache had turned ugly. Peg returned with a restorative to help her. "Here my lady, this will help. It's the mint that soothes."

Merriam nodded, "Thank you. I'm . . . feeling unsettled, Peg. A bad headache, I'm afraid."

"I'll let His Grace know you're under the weather." Peg finished pulling out her hairpins, keeping a close eye on Merriam. "Let's get you to bed, even if it's just to close your eyes for a bit."

Merriam agreed, the pain too sharp for any show of false constitution. These headaches had plagued her since she'd been a girl of fifteen, and she dreaded them. Merriam knew that ahead of her lay long hours when only dark and quiet offered any solace. Peg took over, undressing her with quick, gentle hands and helping her into a nightgown. She pulled the drapes tightly closed and dimmed the lights, extinguishing most of them until only the glow from the fireplace was left.

Then she brought over the small, dark green bottle and tiny glass on a matching tray. Peg poured a draft with steady hands, managing it even in the enforced gloom. "Here, this will see that you rest and have no worries of a headache."

Merriam took the glass, sniffing it cautiously, only to wince at the acrid smell of mint and licorice.

The maid shook her head. "No smelling it first. Just a deep breath and down it goes . . . You'll see."

Merriam sighed. The stabbing pain through the center of her skull made childish complaints about the wretched taste of a tonic beyond useless. She would drink the foulest substance known to man if it would give her some relief. Without protest, she did as Peg advised and downed the tonic in one great swallow.

The burning sensation in her throat almost made her gag, but Merriam forced herself to swallow until the heat had subsided. "Oh, my!"

"That's it, my lady," Peg soothed, taking the empty glass from her and removing the tray. "You'll feel better soon."

Warmth trailed through her body like so many invisible waterways, and Merriam sank back against the pillows. The throb in her head was still there, but within minutes the tonic's effects made the pain a bit distant and less important. The world seemed to slide away, and her limbs seemed weighted down and impossible to move.

Peg's fingertips grazed over her forehead and cheeks.

"See?" she whispered. "Just sleep and let it all just float away."

She was wearing her costume, the black silk velvet and red satin caressing her sensitive skin, and she was the Cat again. But instead of the familiar masquerade, or the alcove where she would draw her Merlin into her arms, she was at the opera. It was odd, but alone in the box, she was perched like royalty overseeing entertainments provided just for her. Music drifted in from somewhere, though there was no orchestra, no singers, and no performers. She stood to look down into the theater and realized that no one else had come for the show. She would have turned to go, but the lights flickered to indicate that the intermission was over and the next act would begin.

She sat down on silk cushions, and when the lights dimmed, anticipation burst through her frame.

"I had to see you."

He wore a costume as well, a black cape, and she could see magical symbols embroidered into the fabric. He was a dark wizard wearing the night sky, and she was dazzled by it. But also by him. He wore a mask of folded black velvet with stars, and she knew that she had wanted him for a long time. Tonight, she would have her Merlin.

This . . .

This was familiar ground. In an alcove of shadows, she had planned this.

A sweet ache bloomed between her legs, and she squirmed on the cushions. "I waited for you." She glanced around the small room, noticing that the opera house had disappeared. "Kiss me."

He complied, her willing, beautiful slave, and she clung to his shoulders, drawing him down to the cushions. The kiss was languid and soft, and he tasted like cloves and cinnamon. His hands moved across her bare arms and her shoulders, to the tops of her breasts, teasing her from her bodice with light, feathery strokes.

"Like this?"

"Oh, yes," she sighed. "Kisses like that."

"And this?" His hands tugged at the laces, and his palms suddenly encompassed the ripe orbs, lifting them from the confines of her bodice as the rough pads of his thumbs circled her taut nipples. He fingered them, the pressure increasing until she jerked and spasmed with the pleasure-pain of it. Arcs of sensation from the relentless contact shivered to her core, and she bucked and whimpered for more of him.

He pushed up her skirts, gathering them above her thighs so that she was bared for him, her legs parted without shame. She made no play at shyness, spreading her legs and writhing so that he would see how aroused she was.

He loomed over her, and she felt his hand spread across her belly, his fingertips splayed to the width of her hip bones. His hand was large and strong, and he let her register just how much of her he could touch, could reach . . . the potential made her even wetter.

"Hurry, Merlin."

He complied again, and she marveled at her power. He was hers to command.

Hers.

His fingers were a sorcery of movement and friction, sweet and steady. She was open for him, and he worked her body to a fevered pitch, teasing her entrance with shallow strokes that grazed her sensitive walls. Another finger rested against the pucker of her bottom, and when another managed to rock against her hardened clit, she threw back her head and abandoned herself to the building waves of her release. She came hard and fast, and his hand only increased its play.

Wave after wave rippled out and in and through her until her thighs trembled and she was sure she could take no more.

"More?" she heard him ask, then before she could answer, he was pushing her over, onto her knees and she knew that "more" was exactly what she wanted.

She tipped her hips down, pushing into him, using her hands to add force to the movement, sliding over him and taking him inside her in one greedy shift of her body. Her muscles clenched around him, a new orgasm starting to build, and she groaned at the taut fit of his scalding erection to her slick channel.

"More?" he whispered.

She nodded, unable to answer, unable to move now, as his hands gripped her hips and seized control. He rammed into her, the impact of his cock a dull shock that made her cry out. He pulled out slowly, and she struggled to catch her breath, anticipation and desire spiraling. Again, he drove home, and now she moved against him, extending

*his invasion, prolonging his retreat. Again and again, it be-
came a brutal dance highlighted by the slap of their bod-
ies and her screams.*

*"More!" She could orgasm again, and she wanted it, the
impossibly magical release that eluded her now ....
"More!"*

*"Oh, yes." She heard him from behind her. "And you
should have what you want, my familiar."*

*"Oh, yes," another male voice echoed. "You should have
everything you want."*

*She lifted her head, and he was there too. But not in dark
robes of midnight skies. This Merlin wore a green so lush she
could drink it. His robes had the same symbols, but his mask
was made of leaves and golden threads. He pulled aside his
robe, and she could see his erection. It was a massive stalk
with a ripe, almost purple head. It bobbed and strained
against gravity, defiantly seeking her mouth and the sweet
plunder of her tongue.*

*She opened her lips and tasted him, her eyes held by her
Green Merlin even as her Dark Merlin reinitiated his
dance, taking her from behind, slower, but harder and
deeper. The rhythm of them both began to work a spell that
drowned her in the taste and feel and smell of his cock.
Whose? She didn't know ... didn't care ... they were one
and the same, and desires were fulfilled that she couldn't
speak aloud.*

*The release came, all at once. She tasted the jets of
molten, silky sex in her mouth just as wet fire pumped inside her and her own spasms blended beyond her control. It*

*was a long, seemingly endless explosion, and everything
begin to fade . . .*

*"No," she mumbled, losing her hold on the Green, and
then, before she could protest again, the Dark Merlin had
withdrawn as well. "No."*

*She looked up with a lazy smile, only to watch curiously
as both Merlins began to remove their masks.*

Drake . . .

Julian . . .

No, God, no.

In the early light, the room was a ghostly gray fog. Merriam sat up, her cheeks burning at the memory of her
dream. She reached across the sheets and realized that
she was alone. She must have fallen asleep in the afternoon and slept through the night. She pushed her way
out of the bed, scalded by the touch of the silk sheets
against her bare thighs.

It hadn't happened. It was a terrible dream brought
on by the tonic for her headache, but the effects were
harder to dismiss. Could her body contain such illicit desires and unspeakable wants? The chill that followed on
the heels of the heat of the images that leapt back into
her mind's eye was too much. It was such an alien sensation to realize that she might have no control at all.

After all, hadn't her secret and intemperate nature
gotten her this far? What else was she capable of? It
was horrifying to consider the loss of control that her
dream might herald.

Suddenly, she had to go. She raced to the wardrobe on unsteady legs, searching the back to find one of her own gowns. The feel of the sturdy, dark cloth gave her a surge of comfort; the familiarity of it, so long hated, now made her feel solid again. It was anonymity, the armor of a mouse, and Merriam was grateful to have it.

She dressed herself, each layer bringing an illusion of strength.

I can do this.

She would seek Madame DeBourcier for advice, one last time. She would get away from his house so that she could gain some perspective and see the path again. Merriam was sure that, if she could just get away, her head would clear and she would know what to do.

In a rush, she grabbed a reticule from a drawer and watched as a square of worn paper floated and flittered to land at her feet. It was his card. She'd been carrying it like a token of luck or affection.

Merriam started to put it back into the embroidered bag in her hand but then hesitated.

There was no logic to taking it . . . only an instinct to leave it behind. To protect his name, she thought without reason. Then whispered, "No." She walked over to the mantelpiece and laid it flat on the marble. It would wait for her return.

"Shall I have the carriage brought 'round, madam?" Jameson offered, clearly disconcerted at her unexpected change in routine and early departure. "Will you need a footman to carry your purchases?"

"No, Jameson." Merriam pulled on her gloves, ignoring his attempt to determine her purpose and praying that her unsettled nerves were not evident. "Hail a hackney and I'll . . . I'll return shortly."

"I'm sure His Grace would wish you to ride more comfortably in—"

"I've no desire to take the duke's carriage. Now, please hail a hackney, or open the door so that I might do so." She summoned a touch of Lady Sedgewold's style of intimidation, allowing her tone to insinuate that the issue seemed to be his capability in service and not the impropriety of her hasty departure.

"Yes, of course, m'lady." Jameson jumped to repair the damage to his reputation, and within a minute, he was assisting her into a hired coach.

"Where to?" the driver called out as Jameson shut the door, lingering to see her off safely.

Without looking at the butler, Merriam replied firmly, "I'll give you the address once we're away. Go on, driver."

And with that, she left an astonished Jameson at the curb and made good on her afternoon's escape.

Seventeen

Jocelyn practically purred over her small cup of hot chocolate. Curled up in her study in a modest silk day gown, she was convinced it was the simple pleasures that gave life its sweetness. She wondered what her enemies and rivals would make of the Crimson Belle's young madam if they saw her private chambers and discovered her secrets.

It was a daydream she rarely played out, a part of her stubbornly believing that imagining the worst generally invited it into your parlor. A scholar at heart, Jocelyn had given careful study to her choices and was not the kind of person to give in to impulse—or fear.

Her tiny study was separated from her bedroom and sitting room by a woven tapestry that hid it from view. Here, she felt like a sinful monk amidst leather-bound volumes and journals in her odd collection. In this room, which was hardly larger than a closet, she'd installed a comfortable little sofa and gas lamp so that she could read and work. It was here she sometimes pretended that the Belle didn't exist. Alone, in the world of her making, all things were possible.

Normally on such a morning she would be reviewing the week's accounts and noting down any items that might be needed for the week to come. A glance at the appointment book would yield critical clues for her shopping list. A certain baron seemed to enjoy rare French wines along with other delicacies he delighted in sampling off of his selected lady's thighs. Another regular guest would expect expensive oils; yet another demanded silk sheets that no human body had yet touched. Some professional houses would have cheated, cutting corners or using alcohol to fog a client's recollection, but not the Crimson Belle. Jocelyn guarded the reputation of her business and saw to it that her clients were, above all, loyal and satisfied.

The indulgence of a cup of steaming dark chocolate seemed a safe relaxation in her usual routines. This morning she had been too restless to face the dreary columns and practical tallies of profit and loss in the primal human exchanges of the Belle.

Ramis's ebony hand pulled back the tapestry as he cleared his throat, ending her reverie. "The mistress has a visitor."

She gripped her cup guiltily. "I'm not expecting anyone."

With an enigmatic smile, he continued, "It is a gentleman."

She sat up, immediately alert and wary. "Did he offer his name?" she asked without much hope. Her clients were rarely happy to use the common protocols of calling cards in such a place, preferring to come and go as anonymously as possible. "Is he a client?" she asked, setting her chocolate down with a twinge of regret. It would mean a scramble to change into more appropriate clothes.

"I have never seen him before, but the mistress should know he is most insistent that he speak to the madam of the house." Ramis shrugged, "Shall I tell him that you are not receiving guests?"

She bit her lower lip to think. "No. Better to address whatever problem he brings directly. It is a bit early for appointments, but see that Amelia and Jez are up and ready, just in case he simply wishes to clarify his expectations before selecting a partner."

"As you wish," Ramis bowed, the soul of discretion.

"Give me a few minutes to prepare, then bring him to the blue salon." She glanced down at the cooling liquid sitting in her favorite porcelain cup, then lifted her head to give Ramis a smile. "Time enough to laze another day."

"The mistress is hardly lazy," he countered, defending her with the easy grace of an old friend. "And the gentleman can be made to wait."

Jocelyn laughed. "Not today. If he's already insistent,

his mood may not improve with a lesson in patience. Just a few minutes, Ramis." She walked past him through the archway into her bedroom and rang for her maid. "Madame DeBourcier will be honored to receive him."

Ramis withdrew, letting the tapestry fall to hide the small, book-lined nook and to leaving her to her preparations. She was a master at transformation, and it never failed to fascinate him that the mistress's powers belied her age. Even he forgot sometimes.

He returned to the drawing room, noting that the gentleman was not entirely comfortable in his surroundings. He had paced to study some of the artwork on the walls. Rather than signal his return, Ramis waited for the man to finish his appraisal and notice his presence. It was a simple trick, to unsettle the man and let him know that, in this house, he was not entirely in control.

English gentlemen could be hazardously arrogant, and Ramis tolerated them only as required. Their money was a necessity, but it was Ramis's primary duty to see that their erotic requirements imposed no harm on the ladies of the house. Rank and title meant nothing to him.

For now, Ramis simply watched and wondered how well behaved this one would be.

Alex studied the painting, surprised at the understated subject matter. He'd been in a few brothels in his day and recalled that the themes generally had to do with inspiring visitors to head more quickly upstairs with the nearest, most fetching partner. But instead of succulent nudes lolling about on fainting couches, or Greek-style panoplies of sensual pursuits, he was looking at an astonishing painting of a wintry forest. He didn't recognize the artist, and there was no signature. The stark scene was blurred, as if by a storm, but the snowfall beckoned, whereas common sense dictated it should have seemed forbidding.

It was several minutes before he sensed that he wasn't alone.

Alex turned, startled at the silent presence of the enormous man he'd contended with earlier. His first impression was renewed at the servant's return. With a height that must have neared seven feet, he was a striking, ebony-skinned man in an impeccable black silk coat. Alex was sure that peace and order reigned at the brothel under this man's inscrutable gaze. The madam must prize him for it.

"I didn't realize you were there." It was an uncanny talent for a man of his size to move so silently, Alex thought.

"The gentleman was looking at the painting. I didn't want to interrupt."

Alex let the matter drop, aware that no apologies about breaches in etiquette were forthcoming. He was a caller in a brothel at an unfashionably early hour. He was hardly in a position to lodge complaints.

"Is the mistress of this house prepared to see me?"

"Madame DeBourcier will receive you, sir." The mountain didn't move. "Would you like some refreshments? A hot beverage on such a cool morning, or something stronger, perhaps?"

"No. My business is urgent. Will she be joining me here?"

The black man smiled, unruffled. "She will see you in the blue salon." Again, he did not move.

Alex's gaze narrowed; he wished he had Drake's talent for glaring men into submission. "Well, then. Lead the way."

"As you wish." He gave him a half bow, then straightened. "Please follow."

At last, Alex growled to himself. *I could've gotten audience with the queen with less drama.*

From the parlor, he was led farther into the heart of the house, catching only a glimpse of the ostentatious decorations and fantastic comforts that awaited the Crimson Belle's guests. A few paintings reflected the more common expectations of expansive, creamy flesh and scantily clad figures in the throes of passion, but here and there, quality pieces shone, and he became more and more curious about the owner's tastes. Among the men and women he'd met briefly in "the trade," greed was the common thread. Decorations were usually gilt and attractive paste, a proclamation of flash and show that hid a brothel's true wealth. A madam was more likely to sleep on her treasure like some fat, deadly dragon than to spend her money on a work of fine art.

He'd anticipated Madame DeBourcier and brought enough coin to ensure his success. She'd protest and make a fuss about sharing confidential information, but he knew that once the gleam of gold met her eyes, the old biddy would fold.

Through an ornate door in the upper hall, Alex was led up a staircase in what he surmised was an older part of the house. He kept a close eye on the man's back, disliking the sensation that he could get lost in the twists of the Belle. "Quiet this morning?"

The servant led him out onto the top landing. Without knocking the man opened a large door and stood back for Alex. "The mistress likes the quiet, sir."

Alex dismissed the comment and turned his focus on the interview to come. He squared his shoulders and walked through the open door. The room was rich with color and textures. Nothing was overdone or overwrought. Instead, it was a warm and inviting small room in elegant blues and soft ivory. Faint exotic touches like the scent of incense and perfume added to an undertone of decadence, but the furniture was tasteful and looked comfortable, piled high with embroidered pillows and tasseled throws. It was a relaxing sanctuary, and he wondered how many privileged visitors enjoyed its private comforts. Or was his hostess long past her prime and enjoyed this room as a buffer against the lack of paying partners?

"Madam?" he inquired, turning sharply as the door

closed firmly behind him. A jolt of nervousness hit him. He felt trapped, reminded that he'd told no one of his whereabouts or his intentions.

"I apologize for the wait, sir."

Alex turned again, back toward the center of the room, at the sound of her voice. She was stepping out from behind a folding screen in the corner, and his reply caught in his throat at the sight of her. She was nothing like the creature he'd imagined. Young, too young, he amended, taking in the vibrant red hair and arresting colors of a gown that set off her jade green eyes and porcelain skin to perfection. She was small, but perfectly proportioned. Lush curves were highlighted but not bared, the mystery more enticing. Her features were delicate, hinting at good breeding. This was no coarse overseer. She was like an elegant bird of paradise lost in the grim grays of London's back streets. Everything about her bespoke sensual confidence and supreme control, and Alex wondered how he'd missed word of her.

"Would you care to take a seat?" She gestured gracefully to the divan, positioning herself at one end near a low table and tray. "Can I offer you something to drink?"

He moved to take the proffered seat. "No, thank you. Your manservant already extended the offer."

"Ramis is most reliable." She smiled, conveying the understatement of it with little effort. "Well." She poured herself a small glass of sherry, as relaxed as if they were old and dear friends and his arrival expected.

She sat back, shocking him as her feet lifted from the floor and tucked underneath her skirts. She perched like a cat on the cushions, eyeing him with open curiosity. "You must tell me what brings you to the Crimson Belle and with such insistence on an interview."

"I'm sure you have your guesses." He stalled, trying to get his bearings. The sight of a sexy sultana studying him over the rim of her glass was more than he'd anticipated, and his body tightened in distraction, ignoring his mission.

"Of course," she agreed merrily, taking a small sip from the crystal. "Though I'm inevitably wrong." She shrugged. "Ramis indicated you were in a bit of a rush, so I thought you'd want to forgo the guessing games. Still . . ." She tilted her head, as if attempting to read him. "You don't have the look of a man interested in games. So, I'm guessing that you have a very specific purpose. Important enough and complicated enough that you've come in person rather than send a messenger or even a message. And since you are not currently a client, and this is not the hour of day when men generally apply for appointments, I'll guess that you're here regarding something or someone else."

He nodded, unable to hide his amusement at the facile turns of her mind. "As you say."

She took another small sip, then set down her glass. "And since you aren't scowling about some imagined complaint against my establishment, and haven't the desperate look of a man in some romantic entanglement, I'm going to guess that you want information."

"Well, that was too easy." Alex shifted, trying not to get too comfortable in her presence but finding it impossible. "A regular client or friend of the Crimson Belle. I was hoping you could tell me if—"

"No." She cut him off softly, without force or menace in her tone.

"I'm willing to pay a great deal for this information, Madame DeBourcier."

"And your name, sir?"

His jaw clenched, not entirely pleased at the way things were turning about. "I'm sure it's not relevant."

"I see." She sighed, disappointment flashing in her eyes. "And you are simply sitting on my cushions. An innocent act, don't you think? Imagine what a man who enjoys the Belle's services might feel if his identity were bandied about." She shook her head, clucking matronly disapproval. "I would be in business scant days if I were as indiscreet as you seem to hope."

"I'm not after another man's bedroom habits or the erotic details of his appointments. I simply need to confirm that he comes here . . . that you know him. Perhaps you have noted a change in him recently or can give me some insight into his character." Alex took a deep breath, aware that he wasn't making the best sense.

Her expression chilled. "Oh, is that all?"

"I'm looking for a murderer, Madame DeBourcier. I would hate to think of you or one of the women in your employ being in any danger."

Her demeanor changed instantly, her legs sweeping to find the floor, her eyes narrowing. "You're serious."

"Most definitely."

She stood, crossing her arms as she considered his words carefully. "I've heard no word of this. Your friend enjoys murdering prostitutes, does he?" Concern and fear, but also a wary measurement of his credibility, laced through her tone.

"No," Alex admitted, trying not to lose ground with her but unready with the truth. "Not that I'm aware of . . . but years ago . . . There are some suspicions, and I am attempting to find out if there is any chance or if the matter can be put to rest. Speculation can be an endless trap. But a man with his guard down . . . If Westleigh has made comment, said anything odd about certain events, I need to know."

"Westleigh?" Her expression gave away nothing.

"Julian Clay, the Earl of Westleigh."

The name resonated in the still morning air, and she stood facing him with steady resolve. "I cannot help you."

"Cannot or will not?" he pressed, also standing to put them on equal ground.

"Cannot," she repeated, clearly unintimidated as he towered over her petite stance. "And will not."

"You're deliberately protecting him?"

"Hardly." She shrugged. "Client or not, it makes no difference. What you ask is impossible."

"Not impossible. I'm asking you to help me end this.

If he is a favorite of yours or you think him innocent, I'm trusting you to reassure me. But if he's capable of such a thing, perhaps you can—"

"Suspicion and speculation are not what we sell here. I am not in the habit of encouraging confessions from our guests or making notes of their pillow talk. The only purpose would be blackmail, and no matter what your opinion of my character, I prefer a more honest living."

"A more honest living?" Alex was astonished.

Her chin came up in defiance. "You heard me."

"I will not be lectured on ethics by a professed whore. I'm simply looking to discover—"

Her sharp intake of breath at the word whore heralded the interruption. The door opened, and Ramis filled the frame. "The mistress wishes you to go now."

Alex froze, absorbing that the man must have been hovering outside the entire time, eavesdropping for her safety. "Madam, if I've offended you, I apologize."

"Ramis will show you out." Her voice was softer, the polite dismissal highlighting the fleeting glimpse of pain in her eyes. "I'm afraid we have no open appointments for you at this time. I'm sure the girls will be disappointed, but you will have to find your information and your pleasures elsewhere."

Alex bowed, reluctantly accepting his defeat at the hands of a miniature tigress. "I will bid you good day, then."

He withdrew without a struggle, shrugging off

Ramis's hand on his shoulder once they'd entered the hallway. "No harm done, sir," he said.

Ramis was unconvinced, his look chilling. The route they took out was much more direct, down a different set of stairs to the back entrance near the kitchens, and Alex's spine stiffened at the humiliation of it. He'd trespassed before, but had never in his life been literally "shown the back door."

The shock of having someone else enter, of the unexpected glimpse as the woman removed her hat and scarf, clearly believing that once inside the house she had no further use of the disguise . . . His steps came to an abrupt halt to avoid colliding with Mrs. Merriam Everett. He recognized her instantly from the Royal Opera House.

"Oh." Her exclamation was quiet and distressed, but he saw no matching recognition in her eyes before Ramis put a large hand at his back and pushed him past her.

Before he could protest, he was jettisoned beyond the doorway and barely caught his balance before momentum carried him down three short steps to the street. His visit to the Belle was over, but apparently, he'd just learned something after all.

Ramis slowly let out his breath, then addressed the miserable lady standing in his hall. He knew her from her meetings with the mistress, but for now it didn't matter.

"Oh, my," she moaned again, her eyes locked on the closed door, imagining the man on the other side of it.

Ramis read her fears easily enough. "I can barely see you in this light, m'lady. I think you worry over nothing."

"He seemed shocked to see me," she whispered, as if concerned the man might overhear her.

"For his own sake, I am sure. I was showing him out."

"Who was he?" she asked, still unsure.

"I do not know. But then, I do not have your name, so you see? All is well. If he were to try to inquire here, none but the mistress have your name and she would never give it. Never."

Her shoulders relaxed at that, and Ramis continued, "You have come to see the mistress?"

"Yes . . . I would have sent word, but . . ."

"I will see if she is receiving." He gave her a half bow. "Will you wait?"

Merriam nodded and watched Ramis go until he was up the stairs and out of sight. The wall coverings were marred with the smoke of the kitchens, and as time slowed she berated herself silently for not planning better. If she'd sent word first, the delay would have ended her flight. Facing Drake after that wretched dream, or trying to choke out an appropriate lie to get away . . . it was unthinkable.

Still, if she'd sent warning to Madame DeBourcier of her arrival, they'd have expected her and she wouldn't have been allowed to run into some gentleman departing after an early morning's appointment. Or a long night, she amended. He'd looked vaguely familiar, but she was sure they'd never been introduced. And it was no secret that she was Drake's mistress. Why should her appearance here do any more damage than had already been inflicted? Why did she feel as if a cold, dark weight were pressing down on her?

Anxiety came in waves, and at the sound of footsteps she looked up in relief. But it wasn't the striking butler who had come into the hall. A woman, about her own age, dressed in a gown that left nothing to the imagination gave her a cheerful smile. Her breasts were bare above a tightly laced corset over opaque pantalets that accented her naked legs and the dark triangle of her sex. "Here for another lesson, love?"

Merriam's mouth opened and closed, like that of a fish out of water. She was suffocating in a flood of shame. The betrayal. Had she been so transparent? Did they all laugh and share tales? Did they know about pathetic widows and stupid games of masquerade?

It was too much. Tears threatened, and Merriam tasted bitter defeat. She'd come for the sanctuary of Madame DeBourcier's company and advice, but here was no safe haven. Without a word, she fled the Crimson Belle as if all the demon cats in hell had decided that mouse would make a lovely breakfast.

Eighteen

The clock on the table provided an impartial count of the deadening seconds as they passed. The muffled *thik-thunk* testified to the eternal workings that would never be lost to her. Merriam had returned to her own house. To the small rooms and austere atmosphere so familiar to her.

The staff had been shocked by her unexpected arrival. But if they were curious about her long visit to an unnamed sick friend, they made no inquiries. Celia said nothing of her lack of trunks, or of any whispers they might have heard that the shy Mrs. Everett had made an extremely bold public show. They'd asked only if she wanted tea, and then they'd withdrawn to leave her to her thoughts.

Withdrawn, to make sure there was coal and to continue just as they had while she'd been gone. As if her presence made no difference to the days. They'd cleaned and polished and gone on without her.

She was alone, like a ghost in her own world. She wandered through her dead husband's study, fingering his books and wondered if Grenville had ever dropped by the house after she'd buried him and encountered the same sensation. She imagined his portly spirit gloating a bit that she hadn't bothered to move his things, disturb his cigars or bottles, or disrupt his "perfected systems." He'd have lingered and found no changes at all.

He'd made her feel so insubstantial through the years of their marriage. Even on his deathbed, she'd felt unnecessary. He'd ignored her presence at his side and looked at the doctor to deliver his parting words. He'd mumbled something about being thirsty and wishing he'd bothered to have a dog. "A real companion would have been a comfort."

She winced at the memory. He'd have happily replaced her with a beagle.

Merriam deliberately pushed one of the stacks of books off the desk, satisfied at the sound of them hitting the carpet and the sight of them in a heap. He was dead. Let him come and pick them up if he was bothered by their fall.

She climbed the stairs to her bedroom, the contrast of stark whites jarring after weeks living in the comfort of Drake's, more luxurious surroundings. In her closet, a few of her summer dresses and oversized coats remained. As she glanced through the drab grays and dark hues in her wardrobe, it was hard not to ask the question that hovered in her thoughts.

When did I die?

Before Grenville, she suspected. Long before. She'd been a ghost for a long time. The mouse who kept quiet and let the routines and requirements of her life keep her safe. Ignored and forgotten.

But something in her hadn't died. Even now, she couldn't regret her choices. This was the house that she would return to after the Season. But not as a ghost or a woman with her head bowed in shame.

"Madam," Celia interrupted. "There's a Mr. Sotherton to see you."

Merriam held her breath, a surge of longing and fear overtaking her. She released it in an effort to steady herself. He'd come for her. "I'll . . . I'll be right down."

Coming down the narrow stairs, she smoothed out the black fabric of her skirts. She found him in the downstairs drawing room, his broad shoulders and height overwhelming the space. He was far too substantial to risk the delicate and uncomfortable carved chairs, and was eyeing them like a man studying a potential trap.

"They're antiques," she explained, blushing. "I wouldn't trust them if I were you."

He turned to give her a wry look. "I'm trying to

picture Lady Sedgewold's vast bottom gracing one of these and am wondering how the old bat managed."

"Drake!" she chided him in a gasp, before a giggle overtook her shock. "She . . . she preferred the settee, if you must know."

He let the moment pass, his eyes dropping to take in her choice in clothes and her pale features. "Have you left me then?"

She froze, wanting to run into his arms, but something held her in place. "N-no. So much has happened, and I just needed to catch my breath. To see the house and assure myself that . . . If I'd had fears of bursting into flames when I crossed the threshold, I must have been mistaken."

He took a step closer to her, relief working into his eyes. "I could have assured you on that account. I cross into honorable homes all the time, and I've never seen so much as a wisp of smoke."

Merriam smiled at the whimsical image of Drake trailing a bit of soot behind him. "You admit you look for it then?"

It was his turn to laugh. "I can't be too careful in my position."

She drew nearer, meeting him in the center of the small room, thrilled at the sight and scent of him. The dreary space was vibrant because he was in it, and a hunger for him overtook her. "In your position?"

He nodded solemnly. "I am the Deadly Duke, Merriam."

"But are you a murderer?"

"No."

Oh, God, she realized in a rush of emotion, she didn't care.

She'd done precisely what she'd sworn wasn't possible. She'd given herself to this man and somewhere along the way lost track of her heart. Madame De-Bourcier's words of caution had been meaningless. Her own practical self-assurances that she'd known the risks and accepted the temporary nature of their arrangement were empty and hollow lies. She'd deceived no one but herself. As she looked into his eyes, she knew that she believed him utterly and that there was no hope of fighting or denying it.

I'm in love with this man. He might be the worst of all men, but I love him . . . and I don't think his answer would have touched that. If he'd confessed to it, just then, Merriam knew in her core she would still be standing there, every fiber of her begging for his touch.

It was impossible. Unthinkable. And true.

She'd never dreamed of love, only passion. She'd thought desire was the prize. She had longed for color and adventure, but love—love was for foreign tales and braver souls. Love was for fearless people who knew nothing of consequences and didn't worry about every twist and turn in the journey. Yet here she was, in love at last.

Merriam reached up to touch his face, brushing her

fingertips over the beautiful and forbidding beauty of him. "Drake."

"Yes, my familiar?" His eyes darkened as he looked at her. The intensity of his gaze and the questions she saw there made her want to laugh and dance and cry all at once.

"We should go."

He pulled her to him with a triumphant growl, and his mouth descended to taste hers. She opened her mouth, eager for him, her tongue lapping at his and escalating the kiss. She wanted him to taste her need and know how much he affected her. She arched into him, her hands seeking purchase, gripping his coat as the room began to spin and fall away.

He lifted his head, freeing her for only a moment. "We should go." He dipped down to tease a trail of kisses up her neck, his breath grazing her ear. "Unless you'd like to christen this drawing room."

She laughed and gently pushed him away. Her servants weren't as jaded as his, and she eyed the room warily. "I foresee disaster and a few bruises when the furniture gives way."

"A good thing my carriage is waiting outside." His smile made her aware of every inch of her own skin.

She nodded, her voice abandoning her briefly. It took seconds to locate her wrap and reticule, and she followed him out the door without a word to the servants. She was a refugee between the two worlds, dressed in her widow's weeds for what she realized would be the last time. It was no longer an effective disguise. Drake had seen past it, and at last, she did too.

Inside the warmth of the carriage, she stretched out against him in a slow melding, their eyes held in silent promises and sensual study. There seemed to be no urge to hurry for either of them, and Merriam's heart pounded with anticipation.

She touched his face again, then smoothed her palm and fingertips down over the pulse in his neck to the top of his shoulder. She slid her other hand inside his coat and across his shirtfront, exploring the heat that emanated from him, the cloth no barrier to her touch. He held still for her, in check only temporarily. His eyes blazed with desire, never leaving her face. The temptation to free the buttons of his collar and shirt was too great. Not since Milbank's had she felt so bold. But now, it was love and not vengeance that spurred her on.

With steady hands, she tugged at the fastenings of his collar, taking her time and purposefully letting the backs of her fingers tease his skin as she achieved her purpose. "I will taste only what I bare for myself," she whispered, thrilling at his gasp of pleasure.

"And when do I receive the honor of returning the favor?" he ground out, openly distracted as she moved on to the buttons of his shirt.

Merriam pushed back his coat and continued her sensual labors. "When we reach your bedroom, Your Grace . . . and not an instant before."

"Such a long wait," he teased, his expression warming with the challenge of the pace she was setting. "Are you sure?"

She answered him by planting a kiss at the sensitive juncture between his collarbone and his neck. Her tongue flicked against the rhythm of his life's blood before she grazed him gently with her teeth to make him shiver in reaction. He sighed his surrender, leaning his head back to give her the access she craved.

Light kisses marked each claim she would make, letting him anticipate the work of her tongue and the warm, wet heat of her mouth against his flesh. She kissed his chest, shifting the fabric away from the broad, firm expanse so nothing inhibited her view, then moved to each taut brown peak in turn. His nipples were as sensitive as hers, she knew, and she deliberately hovered over one crest, washing him in her breath. Hot exhales and cooling inhales made him writhe, and Merriam waited until his flesh was pebble hard and he was groaning in frustration before her mouth encircled him. She suckled him, tasting and taunting, before giving his other nipple an equally lavish show of affection.

"Merriam," he growled softly. "Hurry."

She laughed, refusing to show mercy. "I am in no rush, Your Grace. Perhaps when it is your turn at the house, you will feel differently . . ."

His reply was lost in the sweep of her hands over his skin, the baring of his stomach to her touch. His breath caught in his throat as she eased off the cushions to kneel between his legs, wedging herself between the seats so that the sway and jolt of the carriage wouldn't affect her. She teased the muscular workings of his stomach, dipping her tongue into each hollow and riding each ridge with little sighs and kisses. Her fingers splayed over his hip bones and across the tightening press of his trousers. She could feel his cock leap against her hand, as if it was fighting to reach her with the same hunger she felt for him. She spared one mischievous look up at Drake's face and was rewarded with the sight of him completely at her mercy, his eyes half-lidded with lust.

She began to free him and found no resistance from the buttons already taut from the pressure of his body. Merriam tickled his hips with her mouth and worked the fabric down from his thighs before leaning back to admire her handiwork.

"My sweet Merlin." She sighed. Erect and beautiful, freed from his trousers, the head of his cock was so swollen that the skin gleamed like polished mahogany. His flesh was like silk there, an enticing velvet that would cushion the force behind it. His shaft was textured with sinew and veins straining with need, and she marveled at the latent power and sheer primal beauty of it. The length of it pushed up, his hips bucking involuntarily against her hands, and Merriam licked her lips, eager to taste and hold him. A single drop of thick liquid welled in the tiny slit at the crest of him, and without hesitation, she stretched out her tongue to taste it, a cat stealing a drop of crème. The molten flavor of his ripened head made her fingers dig into his thighs with pleasure. His hips jerked again when she held her mouth still, savoring only the very tip of him, dipping the firm point of her tongue in and out of the tiny slit.

"Damn it, Merriam," he whispered, choking on the sensations she evoked.

In and out, she increased the speed; the light flicker and the heated circle of her enclosed over him was wonderfully maddening. Then, just as he was about to use force to take control, she pulled the entire head of his cock into her mouth, her tongue pressing against the sensitive juncture, the vacuum of her lips eliciting pure ecstasy. Her hands gripped his shaft and stroked him in opposing directions, and Drake was sure he was beyond all rational thought.

Gradually, ever so gradually, she increased the speed of her ministrations, until she was just about to achieve the pace and pressure that would give him the release he now desperately needed.

But she relinquished him instead, as he struggled to focus and understand what was happening, he realized that the carriage was slowing, that they'd reached his home.

"You cannot be serious, Merriam. I'll tell the driver to circle the park for a while." He started to lean forward to tap on the front wall of the carriage, but she stopped him.

"We've reached the house, Your Grace." She leaned forward to kiss him. "Which means it is your turn. But only when we're inside, yes?"

The carriage slowed to a stop, and Drake began to dress as hastily as he could. "Oh, yes. My turn."

Merriam gave him a wicked grin as she primly checked her hair, expertly smoothed out her skirts, and when the door opened, alighted from the carriage with the light step of a woman who hadn't a care in the world. Jameson was waiting on the front steps, and Drake was forced to take a moment.

"Are you all right, Your Grace?" the butler inquired, unaware that his master was incapable of standing without tearing out the front buttons of his trousers. Drake closed his eyes and smiled. She'd pay for this, his delicious temptress, and well she knew it. Hell, she was relying on it.

He took a long, deep breath and exhaled to the count of five. Thoughts of the ways he wanted to "punish" her for her naughty behavior weren't helping him regain enough control to climb out of the carriage.

"Your Grace?"

Drake opened his eyes and gave Jameson a cutting look. He suspected there was no escaping an awkward stride no matter how long he sat in his carriage in an attempt to cool his blood. "Stand aside. I'm not an invalid. I was just . . . collecting my thoughts."

Drake climbed out of the carriage with a lack of co-ordination he knew Jameson wouldn't miss. And he realized Merriam was still standing in the doorway of the house, waiting and watching. Then he forgot everything. He forgot games and vengeance and jests about punishing her. He forgot it all but her.

He moved up the stairs with a speed that betrayed his excitement, and she held out her hand to lead him inside. It struck Drake that he'd carried her up the stairs, and led her up the stairs, more than a dozen times. But this would be the first time she was in the lead. His body stiffened even more at the revelation, the ache bordering pain and pleasure.

The urge to rush left him. Whatever else he managed, Drake wished to go at the pace she set. Whatever pace it happened to be. Primal frenzy or lazy rogering, she would have it, and he wanted no more than to allow this sweet balance of power to sustain and keep them from the outside world for a time.

Inside the doorway of their bedroom, they undressed in a graceless ease, openly enjoying the sight of every inch of flesh bared for the other. Her breasts were firm and taut with her arousal, her nipples jutting out pertly, defying and teasing him in turn. The lines of her were lean curves, not perfect or so balanced that a man would wonder at the artificial shape of her corsets. But she was beautiful to him, and he couldn't think of how another woman could move him more.

She didn't blush or try to cover herself; instead, she looked at him with equal appreciation, and Drake felt his stomach tighten, his erection lengthen and swell. Her gaze made him feel like the most attractive man in the world, and he enjoyed the sensation of the illusion.

"Well?" she asked, stretching like a cat and moving toward the bed. "What is your will, Merlin?"

"Let's see." He moved to overtake her, carrying her against his bare chest the last few steps before tenderly placing her at the bed's center. "I believe I will start . . . here." He made her laugh by taking her right hand into his and beginning with a very formal kiss on its back.

"Oh, my." She sighed. "What a gentleman . . ."

But the kiss became more, and he lost himself to her. He kissed each fingertip and then her palm, working the sensitive pads of her flesh in a massage that made her squeak with pleasure. Up her arm, he trailed kisses and tasted the inside of her elbow before moving on. He found himself kissing her from head to toe. The journey was made with small spurts of speed when they both had trouble restraining themselves or when Drake realized that his familiar was ticklish in an unexpected place.

At last, she was spread beneath him, a siren he had no desire to fight. If her song meant death, then at that moment, he would have learned the words and joined in for the choruses. She was delectable, and he didn't want to think about anything but the taste and feel of her.

He'd kissed her everywhere except within the ripe petals of her sex and the distended nub of her clit. He said nothing, bending over her to inhale the sweet musk that made him feel drunk with lust. His tongue dipped inside the well, and he sampled her arousal with a shudder of pleasure. She arched against him, and he moved to explore her, tasting each soft texture and plump curve. But he avoided that tiny bud until she was crying out, writhing against his mouth and pushing into him. She ruled him and was ruled by him, and Drake gave in to them both.

He kissed the firm, tiny button, licking it and worshiping it with just enough pressure to bring the sensitive crest to full arousal. He'd intended to draw things out, but Merriam shuddered against him and cried as the taste of her climax filled his senses.

He drank her orgasm, milking it from her reverently but to fuel his own. When he couldn't hold back any longer, he lifted himself, his hips between her thighs, his cock pressing against the pure, fiery, liquid satin of her. "My turn," he whispered, before he drove home in one hard stroke.

She wrapped around him, and Drake winced at the heavenly feel of his cock inside her, the grip of her muscles capturing and keeping him. He surrendered the last of his control, burying himself in each thrust, faster and faster, giving only what she could take, but then he couldn't say where he ended and she began.

"Drake! Now!"

And he came, his climax exploding from the base of his spine and stealing his breath with its force and totality. He cried out, a long moan torn from his lips, pleasure drowning his nerves and bones so that he gripped her hips to keep himself from being lost in the currents. The sensations extended into echoes and aftershocks, and Drake kept moving until his cock was too sensitive to allow the indulgence of it. He'd spent himself entirely and, at last, allowed himself to rest on top of her while he waited for his senses to right themselves. She wriggled beneath him, and he kissed her to keep her still.

"Now who is incorrigible?" he teased as his lips suckled the lush curves of hers, and he was rewarded with her contented laughter.

Afterward, they lay in a damp tangle of limbs, neither one willing to let go. Merriam put her cheek against his chest, absorbing the sounds of his heartbeat and the fierce rush of air in and out of his lungs. Even in repose, he was a magnificent panther, strong and restless. Passion tamed him, but nothing would change his nature. She accepted that much of the truth.

"I'm terrified of this party, Drake. If I end up hiding in the garden, you must promise to send Peg out with some punch and sandwiches so that I can survive the siege." She made light of it, but the confession was heartfelt. "I don't want to disappoint you."

He held her more tightly for an instant, then relaxed his grip to reach up and brush a lock of damp hair from her face. "You won't. Besides, what is there to be so afraid of? It's just a party. I'm fairly sure that I'll do something inadvertently scandalous so that, next to me, you will seem the sweetest goddess. And everyone will wonder how you have survived and think you the bravest soul no matter where you hide in the house."

"You're not . . . planning anything, are you?" Merriam couldn't imagine what Drake considered scandalous and wasn't sure that she wanted to find out amidst a crowd of strangers.

"Of course not," he replied. "But since people are coming in the hopes of it, it seems cruel not at least to consider it."

She pinched him lightly. "You're incorrigible!"

"Perhaps." He retaliated by kissing her on the forehead and trapping her offending hand in his. "But then, if you're hiding in the garden, you'll miss it. A shame you can't keep watch. I mean, if you were there, I might behave to try to please you."

"I won't hide," she conceded, reveling in his gentle teasing.

"Good." He kissed her again. "Now let a man sleep and regain his strength."

Merriam smiled and closed her eyes while his

breathing evened out and he drifted off to sleep. The day after tomorrow was the party, and she would face her fears. But then, after all she'd faced already, perhaps Sotherton had the right of it. It was just a party, a gathering of people keenly interested in socializing with the Deadly Duke and living vicariously in his notoriety.

He'd called her a goddess, and Merriam felt like purring at the delicious blasphemy of it. She felt powerful when she was with him, a seductress. His familiar. At the party, draped in that rich red dress with copper in her hair, it would be easy to feel like a pagan goddess. There would be no hiding. It was the bold steps that won the best rewards. Hadn't she learned that lesson? Cowering and silently wishing had earned her nothing but years of invisibility and dull misery. But when she'd actively sought her heart's desire, she'd gotten it.

And what do I desire now?

His heart, the mouse crowed. *His love.*

And it came to her.

At the party. She would win his heart. She would be a goddess, and he would see her victory over fear. He would see her efforts and realize that time didn't have to end their happiness. She would prove to him that it was all within his reach. She would tell him her hopes, and even if he wasn't ready to shed the past and still loved his wife, he would treasure her for her strength and come to love her over time.

It was a wonderful fantasy that made her smile but also threatened tears.

For the Season. She sighed at the echo of their agreement. Merriam kept her eyes closed, burying her face in the warmth of his shoulder. She would win him, or have a finish to her glorious and decadent affair.

Nineteen

"**M**ore coffee, Your Grace?"

"No, Jameson, thank you." Drake surveyed his desk and the uncharacteristic clutter that had accumulated in recent days. Orders and invoices for the grand party the following evening, letters begging for admittance, and a stack of acceptances that threatened to slide over at any moment. He'd followed the general rule about inviting a third more than he expected to attend, but the nobility in London for this year's social season didn't seem to be following the rules. He'd no sign of anyone's regrets or a single note explaining that other plans would be taking precedence over his invitation. His mansion would be bursting at the seams by the late evening hours, and Jameson was concerned that there'd be no room for the musicians they'd hired.

"The deliveries have already begun, Your Grace. But we're managing, and I'm sure you'll be pleased with the results."

"I have complete faith in you," Drake intoned sincerely. "Please see to it that Mrs. Everett is troubled as little as possible with these matters. She has no love of large gatherings, so I wish to make this pleasant and easy for her."

"Of course." The butler began to withdraw, then stopped with a halfbow. "Will you be having luncheon here in your study?"

Drake shook his head and managed not to roll his eyes. So long as he had Jameson, starvation was not a possibility. "I believe I'll wait and see if the lady prefers a picnic in the arboretum this afternoon."

"As you wish, Your Grace." Jameson left to make the arrangements and attend to his duties.

Drake sat at his desk, grimly determined to make some order out of the chaos. A firm knock interrupted, and one of the footmen entered with a large brown envelope. "This just came, Your Grace. The messenger said to see it directly into your hands."

"Thank you." Drake took it and waved the man out. He knew what it was before he read the address. It was a report from Peers. He set it down on the stack of invoices without opening it.

It wasn't like him to play games of avoidance. But Drake's stomach tightened at the sight of the report, so neatly bound and sealed. It was a discreet item without any remarkable physical qualities, but he was having trouble not looking at it. He felt like a schoolboy faced with the dilemma of reading someone's private journal.

Surely there was nothing there he didn't already know or hadn't already surmised. It was probably some new drivel on Julian, or a meaningless update on Merriam's last shopping trip.

Merriam. He'd found his card, worn and ragged, on the mantel and had feared the worst. She'd left him. The speed of her departure, the lack of confrontation had rattled him. There'd been no discussion, no exchange to dissuade her or allow him to brace himself. He'd gone into her dressing room to assure himself that her gowns were still there, that she hadn't packed all her things, but he knew it was a meaningless sign. If she'd panicked about the party . . . or about him for whatever reason, she wouldn't have lingered to pack.

He hadn't even bothered to check with Peers or the man who would have followed her as he'd ordered. The list of potential sanctuaries for his shy cat was very short. The home she had shared with Mr. Grenville Everett was his first choice. The hunt had been brief; and she had been exactly where he'd hoped she would be.

In his carriage outside, he'd actually contemplated letting her go. His instincts told him that things were only going to get more dangerous with Julian and that there was more to fear at the party than a few wagging-tongued gossips. But he'd balked at the idea of relinquishing her.

As he'd waited in that wretched little drawing room with its crocheted doilies and fading wall coverings, he'd realized how far he'd come to pursue this "distracting widow." Weeks ago he'd convinced himself that, once he'd had her, he could put this all aside and attend to his need for revenge. But oh, so much had changed.

Everything teetered so close to completion, or disaster. He was past asking her for the truth. It was too late. He glanced at the unopened report on his desk.

I could stuff it into the coal grate without reading it. It would be ashes in minutes, and with one note to Peers, I could dismiss the business and let the battle between Clay and myself just play out. What would it be like to trust again? To let himself love her? What did it matter what was in that package?

It mattered only because he'd already come to care for her. She'd agreed to turn her back on his past, to let things go. Could he do the same? After all, he could destroy Julian without this secondary game involving Merriam as bait. Whatever her initial ties to the earl, whatever their previous arrangements, hadn't she proven that she was his now?

Another knock on the door, and Drake closed his eyes against the spike of annoyance that tore through him. *Damn it, I never thought I'd miss the quiet existence of being the Deadly Duke.* "Yes."

"Excuse the interruption, Your Grace. But Lord Colwick has come to see you."

His annoyance was gone instantly. "Send him in."

Drake came around the desk to shake his friend's hand warmly. "I'd foolishly assumed you were at your country estates."

Alex shook his head. "I take it that's why you omitted extending me an invitation to this private party of yours tomorrow night."

"Nonsense," Drake countered with a smile. "God must have stolen it from your mailbox to keep his favorite saint out of my hands."

"Enough already." Alex held up his hands in a gesture of surrender. "I'm hardly the one to beg invites, and besides . . ." His expression sobered, reluctance and regret warring in his eyes. "I came to apologize."

"To apologize?"

"You wished me out of your business, and as your friend, I simply couldn't leave well enough alone."

Drake's arms crossed in front of him, his eyes studying his friend warily. "Is this for past sins, or have you done something I'm not aware of?"

Alex sighed, shifting his weight to his heels as he composed his answer. "I always thought you had a dark view of the world, old friend. Even before things took such a tragic turn. And when you returned and admitted there was something afoot—a part of me hoped that you were wrong to be so suspicious of everyone around you."

"Go on." Drake deliberately kept his tone low, unsure of which direction this confession might take.

"Particularly in regard to Mrs. Everett." Alex cleared his throat before continuing. "My intentions were to diffuse the situation and provide some clue or piece of information that might offer you relief."

"Relief?" Drake's confusion was apparent.

"Instead of revenge. I'd hoped to learn enough to divert you from whatever mysterious plan you had come up with."

"Does it seem so dire from your position, Alex?"

"You've practically shouted me down on two occasions when I attempted to find out. What do you think?"

Drake conceded the point. "Very well. You've stuck your nose in again in an effort to save me from myself, subsequently apologized and confessed. I'm at a loss as to why you're looking like a man in charge of an execution."

"I attempted to dig into Julian's background and uncover some information."

"What?" Drake's spine stiffened in shock. It was so unexpected to think of Colwick even considering a covert action of any kind, much less initiating one. That Drake had paid Peers to do the same was irrelevant.

"I had little to go on, but I'd heard rumors that he'd frequently been spotted at a very fashionable and discreet brothel called the Crimson Belle." Alex's face reddened at the admission. "So I went there yesterday morning, thinking to pay for insight into Clay's character. It was a weak attempt, and I was stupid to think the authorities would have missed a man mumbling in his cups about murdering women."

Drake's jaw clenched. "If it were that easy, Alex, don't you think I'd have gotten the man roaring drunk within the last eight years?"

"Damn it, I'm new at this!" Colwick shifted his weight again, defensively.

"All right, then"—Drake ran a hand through his hair—"the damage is minimal. Clay knows I'm digging, and even if he hears that—"

"I saw her there."

The world came to an instant halt for Drake as Alex's words sank in. "You saw . . ."

"Mrs. Everett coming into the Crimson Belle," his friend continued, his tone weighted with dread. "I saw her in your box at the opera that night, and I recognized her as she came through the back door."

Drake began to shake his head, unable to voice a denial or think of a logical reason why his Cat would be there.

"I waited in the alley and managed to follow her. From there, she went to her town home off Bellingham Square." Alex took a deep breath. "It seems that the Belle . . . is where they must have met, or . . ."

Drake swallowed hard, unwilling to let his friend suspect how this news had hit him. He turned his back and walked to the windows, looking out over the front of the house and onto the street beyond. Finally he turned back, his expression neutral. "I'd always known that there was more to Mrs. Everett than met the eye, Alex. Please don't trouble yourself on my account. We have an understanding, she and I. And as for my dreadful plans . . ."

"If I can help—"

"Trust me," Drake cut him off, "I have things well in hand."

Alex nodded, turned to go, but then hesitated at the door. "I'm sorry, Drake."

He was gone before his old friend could reply.

Well, then . . . Drake returned to his desk with slow, heavy steps.

He opened Peers's report, a glance solidifying the ice in his chest. The detective had followed her from the house. He reiterated that the brothel was one regularly frequented by the Earl of Westleigh and that Mrs. Everett had gained admittance through a lesser known back entrance, apparently with the ease of someone familiar with the premises. She'd stayed only briefly on this occasion, but by the early hour of her arrival and use of a hired hackney, Peers's professional instincts deduced that the Crimson Belle was the destination for Mrs. Everett's mysterious "lecture series."

I always knew.

But he hadn't really. He'd suspected and fumed and

schemed and assumed so much. He'd had scenarios in his head about the two of them walking in gardens or Clay recruiting her to his cause to entangle the Deadly Duke. Jealous fantasies had never yielded anything close to the simple, painful truth.

Mrs. Merriam Everett had been a whore for Julian Clay all along.

"Another favor?" Lord Andrews leaned back against the soft leather chair, dropping his jovial mask. "I believe you owe me for too much as it stands."

Julian didn't wince. "If you are heavy-handedly referring to my outstanding debts at the tables—"

"Not at all." Andrews cut him off, surprising Julian. It was a rare thing to see the Earl of Westleigh look confused, and Elton relished it for a moment. Whatever the tangle between Sotherton and Clay, it promised to be a good show. He'd collected on his marker with interest, though of course, Clay wasn't to know that. It was like a hand of cards, and Lord Andrews was too experienced not to hedge his bets. "I meant the dinner party at my house. I allowed you to attend even though I suspected it was Sussex you were interested in, and not my dear wife's wit."

Julian gave him a look of pure cynicism. "I'm not aware I'd made any attempt to disguise my goals. As for your wife"—he lifted his glass in a mock toast—"you're hardly interested. Why on earth would I be?"

Andrews chuckled, letting the gibe at his annoying bride pass. "Ah, but it wasn't the duke you wished to confront."

"Your assumption. It didn't seem polite to correct you. Besides, we exchanged words. The result is the same."

"And Mrs. Everett?"

Julian shrugged, the gleam in his eyes taking on a more heated focus. "What a sweet and biddable creature . . . I believe there is more to her than one might initially suspect. An instance where first impressions can be misleading."

Andrews kept his gaze steady. "I take it you had a more pleasant confrontation with Mrs. Everett then?"

"A gentleman doesn't share the details."

"Ah, but it is the details that make life fascinating, and in my opinion, it is the only currency that holds its value in this world." Andrews didn't hesitate to seek Clay's soft underbelly. "You were his best friend once, weren't you?"

Julian shook his head in cool amazement. "You really are a whore for gossip, old man."

Lord Andrews rewarded him with an enigmatic smile. "You have no idea."

Julian stretched out his legs, bored with the posturing and pretense. Andrews could play the buffoon or sit over a hand of cards with the visage of a deadly viper, depending on his mood or how deep he was into his cups. As an ally, he was hardly reliable. But in this instance, he had something that Julian wasn't willing to go without. And since gossip was the only coin he had to pay in . . .

"I need your help. I need to get into Sotherton's little soiree tomorrow night."

Andrews pulled air through his clenched teeth, making a great show of his reluctance. "Well . . . that may not be wise. The last time he caught scent of you near his mistress, he stormed out of my house in a clear snit. His reputation precedes him, Julian. You play with fire."

"His reputation is well earned."

"So you keep telling me." Andrews shrugged. "But it occurs to me that you are a primary source of that reputation—even now, am I right? You were the first to cry foul, and I cannot help but wonder at your insistence in this matter."

"Veer off." Julian waved his hand dismissively. "For a man who lives for the latest news, you have a remarkably poor memory." He sat up in one fluid movement and set down his scotch. "Will you help me or won't you?"

"I'm not in charge of the invitation list."

"I said I needed help getting in, Andrews. I didn't ask for an invitation." Julian's gaze never left his friend's. Endless hours as adversaries over cards had taught him that, if for nothing else, Elton would play just for the thrill—and a chance to get a juicy piece of new gossip.

Andrews nodded slowly. "Very well. I'm not sure I

recall the specifics of the house. I was there only once or twice, and it's been quite a few years."

Julian rewarded him with a wicked smile. "And for me . . . but the specifics of that house are something I will never forget."

Andrews leaned forward to watch Julian sketch out the floor plan on the back of a menu card. The entire time, he forced himself to swallow the giddy feeling of knowing far more than he should.

Oh, yes. This promised to be a very good show. A show that Lord Andrews had no intention of missing.

Twenty

Before dawn, Drake walked alone through the house. In a sea of gray shadows and chilled rooms, he noted the final preparations that would transform the first floor of his home into a winter fantasy of sparkling crystal and gold.

He'd always been reluctant to host events, yielding only when his first wife had pouted and raged for weeks. The inspiration for this grand party was hard to place. He'd wanted to make a show of his happiness, a great splash that would propel Julian into a furious frenzy. He'd hoped for something—a public scene in which Julian would reveal too much or, even better, a display of Julian's dangerous jealousies that would strip him of his defenses.

Now the scenarios all seemed beyond foolish to Drake. None of it was necessary.

He steeled himself to avoid all thoughts of the luscious vixen who slumbered so innocently in his bed upstairs. She had been a distraction, and a costly mistake, but all that would end soon.

He entered his study and lit the gas lamps. Then took his place at the ornately carved desk to complete a letter intended for Hughes. It took very little time. He reread the note, concise and without any betrayal of emotion, that called in all of the Earl of Westleigh's markers simultaneously for immediate payment in full.

His solicitor had assured him that everything was in place. All he had to do was pull the trigger. It was vengeance without a hint of drama or flair, but it would bring total devastation to the earl's door and might prove unsurvivable. In one move, Drake would end the game and utterly destroy Julian Clay.

Once Merriam learned of her lover's state, Drake would let her know that he was aware of her true loyalties. He would throw her from his house and leave her for a bankrupt Clay to care for. A messier twist, but it couldn't be helped.

He'd dreamt for years of defeating his nemesis and putting ghosts to rest. In his convoluted schemes, he had been willing to risk anything . . . or anyone. He hadn't realized he would be risking his own heart. He'd thought of himself as disconnected, sure that he wasn't capable of feeling anything after Lily. But he had been wrong.

He hadn't realized that there are levels of loss, of

pain he'd never known. Merriam had drawn him in, and he'd forgotten . . . everything.

He wrote Hughes's address on the outside of the letter, folded and sealed it. And then Drake dispatched it before the rest of the household had even stirred.

Noise spiraled through the house, a merry chase of music and laughter, conversations and applause. The bejeweled gathering glittered in lit halls and luxurious rooms, the crush of the attendance keeping them to a slow promenade as they enjoyed all the sights and sounds. The solarium was like a paradise, with crystal lanterns strung in the trees and plants, and the music gallery was awash in midnight blue bunting and gold panels. After almost a decade of disregard for society's pleasures, the Deadly Duke was throwing the grandest party of the Season.

As Jameson had feared, the musicians had been crowded out of their corner in the salon, but their retreat into the jungle of the solarium was an improvement as far as the guests were concerned. Their invisibility made the entertainment more exotic, as the music drifted out from unseen hands behind a screen of palms.

"A triumph! A veritable triumph!" Lady Andrews gushed before she kissed Merriam on the cheek. "You must be thrilled. You are the absolute envy of every woman drawing breath in England tonight!"

"You are too kind," Merriam demurred, sure that if flattery and exaggeration were competitive events, Lady Andrews would have no equal. "It is . . . well attended, I think." Merriam smiled at her own deliberate understatement. If Drake's notorious past was keeping anyone away, there was no sign of it.

"Well attended! My goodness, I think I've caught sight of at least four recluses and one or two people who appear to have returned from the dead not to miss this party! You are too sweet a soul to stand there and not think to boast about this remarkable gathering." Lady Andrews released her hand at last, her attention drifting toward the salon. "Now if you'll excuse me, I must ask Mrs. Phelps about her dogs."

Merriam nodded. "Of course. Please enjoy your evening." Trapped in the entryway, she stood a few feet away from Drake as they performed their official duty as host and hostess. The nerves she had expected to battle were banished, and Merriam felt almost giddy at her liberation. She tried to catch Drake's eye when she could, but he was invariably busy with yet another arrival vying for his attention. A private word with him would have to wait.

"What a delightful surprise!" Lord Milbank appeared before her, a jolly gnome openly staring at the house and decorations. "I love it when people come out of hiding and throw grand affairs. Of course, none as grand as mine, but how could I miss yours?"

"I . . . We're so glad that you didn't." She tried to gather her wits. "Have you met—"

Drake was suddenly at her elbow. "Lord Milbank, an honor. Though I wasn't aware I was hiding."

"No." Milbank's smile lost a bit of its energy. "Nothing to hide. I just wanted a chance to see the happy couple for myself. I mean . . . It was such a—"

"Enjoy yourself," Drake cut him off, and Merriam's mouth fell open a bit at his rudeness. She had the feeling that there was something else going on between them, and while she had no wish to highlight her nefarious debut at Milbank's masque ball, Drake's reaction was more extreme.

He's protecting me, she realized with a warm jolt. He must have worried that his guest would say something indiscreet, though she was confident that only Drake had seen past her disguise that night. But that he would fear for her, and intervene—it made her hope. As Milbank withdrew, Drake glanced at her, and Merriam caught his arm to give him a smile. "I'm sure he meant well."

Drake's arm stiffened at her touch, but he didn't withdraw. "I seem to be more out of practice than I thought."

She cocked her head, studying this new Drake, so restrained and oddly moody. He'd been so involved in the last-minute preparations for the party, she'd barely seen him the day before, and last night he'd slept in his study. She hoped he hadn't exhausted himself. "Is it possible you're more nervous than I was? Is that why you're acting so strangely?"

A muscle in his jaw ticked, but then he smiled and she wasn't sure what his mood was. "This is me making an effort to behave myself," he countered, lifting her hand to kiss her gloved fingertips. "Aren't you pleased?"

The gesture was distracting, and before she could respond, he stepped back and another small group of arrivals ended their exchange.

It was a whirlwind afterward. More and more guests arrived, and Merriam shook hands and welcomed people until it was a blurred experience she was sure she wouldn't later recall. Everyone seemed very excited and pleased to be there, and it was clear that the reclusive duke's reluctance to throw parties had created a bit of a mystique. Dozens assured her that they had never before seen his house or gardens and were thrilled at the chance.

By the time most of the invitations had been collected, Merriam was convinced that half of London was pressed into the rooms. She looked to Drake to see if he was ready to leave the footmen to manage any stragglers.

And she caught him looking at her, as if he'd never seen her before, his expression strange.

"Is-is everything all right?" Merriam reached a hand up to the copper coiled in her hair in a nervous reflex. "Have I wilted entirely?"

"Everything is just as it should be." Drake offered her his arm. "I meant to tell you how beautiful you looked before things became too hectic."

She blushed, happy to take his arm. "Thank you. Are you ready to enjoy your Grand Party, Your Grace?"

"Yes." He began to guide her into the salon. "Let's see what kind of triumph we've managed."

Merriam was sure she was positively glowing by the time they'd reached the music room. Walking through the crowd, instead of fear, she experienced only pleasure at the feel of his arm under her fingertips, and an honest pride in being the woman at his side. Everyone had come to gawk and gossip, and none of it touched her. Women fawned and men flirted, they drank heavily and happily debated public policies, and none of it touched her. She was beautiful and desirable in his eyes, and as she stood next to the man she loved and exchanged pleasantries with their guests, Merriam was truly happy.

The mouse was forever banished, and tonight she would tell him that she loved him.

"Oh, my!" a woman Merriam was not acquainted with interjected. "How clever of you to hide the musicians in the garden room. I thought I was hearing fairies!"

Merriam laughed. "Sotherton's charms can be substantial, but I'm fairly sure Queen Titania refused his request to borrow her orchestra for the evening."

"Do you hear fairies often, Lady Meeks?" Drake added, the subtle mockery in his tone difficult to miss.

Lady Meeks giggled, an amazing feat for a woman of her size and stature. "I just might, you rogue!"

Behind them, Merriam caught sight of Lady Andrews and braced for the inevitable chatter to come. She glanced to Drake and then realized that the musicians might be her magical saviors after all. "Your Grace, perhaps we should dance and set a good example for our guests?"

Lady Andrews reached them with a huff of relief, thrilled to offer her expert opinion on the matter. "Oh, he'll not dance, my dear. It has never been seen."

"Never?" Merriam asked, not entirely surprised. "Not even once?"

"Never," Lady Meeks and Lady Andrews both chimed in on cue.

Drake played along, "What is it about dancing that appeals?"

Merriam could think of one advantage, but with the ladies standing so close by, she could hardly point out the reward of a polite escape from a looming discussion of fairies. "And what part of it do you fear?"

One dark eyebrow raised at the challenge.

Merriam leaned over, boldly teasing his earlobe before whispering, "You promised never to ignore me, Merlin."

"Or underestimate you," he added, his tone hard to interpret.

Merriam straightened, her cheeks flushed. "Then prove it and dance with me."

She thought for a fleeting instant he would refuse, but then he yielded. "I will not warrant the safety of your toes, Mrs. Everett."

"I will not hold you accountable." Merriam gave the

ladies a quick smile. "If you'll excuse us. His Grace has offered a dance."

He pulled her away, leaving the ladies to stare at the rare and wonderful sight of the Duke of Sussex headed toward a crowded dance floor.

For a man who had spent a lifetime avoiding this very activity, Drake moved her into position and entered the flow of the other partners with relative ease. The waltz was made more challenging by the traffic, but Drake's arms and piercing gaze distracted Merriam from the effort. She was sure that heaven must offer a waltz or two, as the spins and turns made her feel light and graceful.

"Are people staring?" she asked softly, teasing him a bit.

He managed to scan the room over her head. "Not as much as you're hoping."

"I wasn't hoping!" She stifled a giggle. "Besides, you should be pleased. This is what you wanted, wasn't it?"

"What I wanted . . . ," he echoed, his focus lost before his eyes met hers.

"This party. A chance to show everyone that you aren't—"

"Deadly?" he asked. A tension snapped in his gaze and Merriam wondered at it.

"I meant to say 'antisocial.'" She watched the storm in his eyes, curious and praying that he would share whatever was troubling him. "You're sure there's nothing wrong? I don't mean to press, it's just that I have a sense your mind is miles from here."

"Not miles." He denied it, looking away over her shoulder to navigate the next turn. "I apologize if I seem distracted. I can't remember this many people in the house."

"A triumph, according to Lady Andrews."

"So far." Drake spun her, a deliberate move that made her laugh.

"I think it's safe enough to relax. Unless, of course, you have scandalous plans for drunken sack races later . . ."

"You're incorrigible," he whispered, the jest tempered with a flash of pain in his eyes.

"Drake—"

He took another brisk turn, then released her just as the music ended. As he bowed, she felt compelled to curtsy, to hold the tumble of questions plaguing her until they could withdraw from the floor. Without the music to shield their conversation from being overheard, Merriam knew it wasn't the time to push. He was clearly distressed about something. Could it be that he had begun to dread the end of the Season? Did he regret their plan to end things so soon? Merriam swallowed hard as a surge of hope filled her.

In the hall, he was hailed almost instantly. Merriam tried to hold him back for a moment. "Drake, we should talk."

He nodded, a distant and chilling expression in his eyes. "Later."

And with that, he turned and left her in the milling crowd.

* * *

Andrews watched anxiously, keeping a close eye on the entranceway from the south garden. It had been no small feat to wander out inconspicuously and unlock the garden gate entrance in the back wall. Finding the door had reinforced his instincts that Julian was a bit too familiar with the workings of the Duke of Sussex's home. Unless he had the memory of a prodigy, which after years of watching the poor boy play cards, Andrews was sure he did not, Julian had been in and out of this house more often than most. He doubted Drake himself could have described the location of the ancient wooden door in that wall or coached him on how to unlock it with a simple piece of bent metal.

The Earl of Westleigh was an unlikely burglar. But more likely to have dallied with another man's wife. Even so, the currency was sweet and plentiful, and Andrews was sure tonight would provide entertainments yet undreamt of.

But there was no sign of Clay . . .

He ignored all the lesser drama that on another night or in another place would have kept him happy. No, tonight was the saga of the Deadly Duke, and if he'd played his cards correctly, Sotherton was going to live up to his name.

But hours passed. His wife had begun to fade, her whining requests to depart grating on his nerves. Where in the hell was Clay?

And, for that matter, where in the hell was Sotherton?

*   *   *

Drake had retreated upstairs for a brief escape. If he could just clear his head and remember why he was there. He should have felt some measure of satisfaction, shouldn't he? He'd wanted revenge, and he was getting it. This time, he was the one who had taken someone from Julian. He'd taken Merriam, though it galled him to consider that the challenge was an illusion with the two of them in league together. Everything with her was an illusion. He'd forgotten it and was already limping in anticipation of the pain. But she would never know it, and Julian wouldn't have the satisfaction.

No. Whatever damage he'd incurred by becoming emotionally attached to her, it was an injury he would nurse in secret. To hell with her.

Today, he'd destroyed the man she loved. Clay would face financial ruin, and Drake would have the satisfaction of knowing that, in some small way, Lily's death was avenged. The balance would be paid, and she would cease to haunt him.

Damn it, he should have felt something besides this icy remorse. It was paralyzing. All night long, he'd tried to keep Peers's report fresh in his mind, but Merriam had undone him at every turn. A vision in that red dress that made her skin glow and her eyes shine. She'd laughed and smiled and come to life in front of his eyes, conquering her shyness and mastering a room full of the most intimidating sots he could have gathered. She'd jested about hiding in the garden, but he'd been the one fighting the desire to flee all night.

He hated it all. The leering faces and curious gazes of his peers, all drinking in as much of the house as they could manage, perhaps hoping to catch a glimpse of mementos of his dead wife, or clues. Instead of driving Julian to ground, it was self-inflicted torture to smile and respond to their insipid comments. All the while, watching his familiar and knowing he'd already lost her.

She was killing him with every tender touch.

She didn't know yet the calculated horrors he'd inflicted on Clay. And he couldn't bring himself to gloat and tell her.

All he could do was wait for the ax to fall. And he found that even this small task was proving a bit too much for the Deadly Duke.

He walked to the mantel, leaning against it to absorb some of the fire's warmth. But instead, his fingers found the card she'd put there just two days before. He'd left it there, like some kind of talisman.

I came to give you your card back.

It was enough. He didn't need to be here. He needed to gather his strength for the storm to come. He needed to go.

He tucked the card into his coat pocket and made his way down the servants' back stairs. He'd had enough of vengeance for one night. He didn't want to see her face when she learned just how "deadly" he could be.

"A perfect evening!" yet another dowager reassured her, and Merriam did her best to focus on the praise and not the knot in her stomach.

She hadn't seen Drake since he'd withdrawn after their dance. As she'd been pulled into conversations, or even cajoled into another dance with a prominent guest, Merriam had endlessly scanned the rooms for a glimpse of him.

She'd thought that she had experienced every mood the man was capable of—but this was beyond her experience.

The evening had been going so well. Until their dance. But she clung to his assurance that they would talk later. It was long overdue, and Merriam surmised that if he were preparing some heartfelt admissions regarding his past—and, she hoped, his future—that might be the source of his odd actions.

But speculations frustrated her, and she politely disengaged from a small group of ladies to make another circuit of the rooms. She smiled at the reversal of roles. Though she highly doubted he was cowering in some corner, afraid to face the public. It seemed more likely that he'd simply been distracted in a private conversation somewhere and lost track of the time.

"Mrs. Everett!"

She turned at the call, summoning a polite smile.

"Ah, Lord Meeks, I had the pleasure of speaking to your wife earlier. I . . . I believe she is in the dining room if you've lost her."

"Yes, yes," Meeks readily agreed. "For I heard you are serving little cream canapés, and my Violet is sure to stand guard nearby."

Merriam blushed, wishing the men of England had a better regard for their wives. Grenville had had a similar style, and it rankled her. "Out of boredom, perhaps, since you appear to have abandoned her to the crowd. She has a lively wit, and I found her most charming."

A look of respect entered his eyes. "Yes, she does. I should have kept pace but was distracted by some of my racing cronies." He shifted his weight, an awkward moment before he recalled his original purpose in achieving her attention. "An acquaintance of mine indicated he'd met you, and I thought you would wish to welcome him, despite his flatteringly late arrival."

"Oh, yes, of course." Merriam was relieved at the practical request, though she wasn't certain who he was referring to. Of Drake's invitations, she was sure she knew only a fraction and had already greeted the faces she recognized.

He led her through the arched doors to the entryway, and toward a gentleman who, at first, looked only vaguely familiar.

"I believe you've met Lord Colwick, my dear. He indicated he had had the pleasure."

"Oh." She extended her hand, shock undercutting the rote polite gesture as she recalled where she had seen him. "P-perhaps not formally, but Sotherton speaks very highly of you, my lord."

"He is a great friend." He bowed over her hand, cutting quite a figure with piercing brown eyes. "A dance, Mrs. Everett?"

"Oh, well . . . I really shouldn't—"

Before she could think of a reasonable protest, he'd whisked her past a flabbergasted Meeks, and out into the music room, and onto the dance floor. There were fewer dancers, and Merriam noted miserably that there was, as a result, almost no way to pull away or refuse him without the scene being noticed.

"L-Lord Colwick."

"Mrs. Everett," he countered, bowing to begin the dance. She curtsied and stepped into position, worrying her lower lip with her teeth and bracing herself for whatever he might say.

"I am his good friend, you know," he began, his tone neutral and not threatening.

"He . . . he speaks highly of a Lord Colwick. You mean a great deal to him, I suspect."

"Drake is usually careful about who he allows to get close."

"Usually?" she asked, hating the defensive edge in her voice and the nervous flutter in her hands. "If you imply that he has made a mistake—"

"I said nothing," he answered, his voice lower to cue

her that she hadn't been as discreet as she might have wished.

"W-what do you want?" Her spine stiffened as they moved across the floor. "I will not be bullied."

He smiled, surprise crossing his face before his expression grew more serious. "I sincerely just wanted you to tell me . . . that you mean him no harm."

"Of course not!" Anger and horror snapped into her eyes. "How could you think such a thing?"

A cynical twist of his lips reminded her that he'd seen her in the worst possible context.

She blushed furiously, then whispered in a tight, low voice, "It wasn't . . . I cannot tell you my business at . . ." She glanced over his shoulder to ensure that no one was near enough to overhear them. "At that establishment." Merriam took a deep breath, steadying herself against her worst fear of scandal and exposure. She looked up at him, praying that he would see the sincerity there. "I . . . care for Drake beyond words. I realize that by visiting . . . It looks highly irregular. A woman in my position would hardly think to . . ."

Her eyes dropped as the miserable composition of her words unraveled against her will. She couldn't tell a total stranger about her quest, about finding wisdom and solace and a true female friend in the form of a London madam. Not without exposing her prurient nature to his examination and judgment. It was unthinkable.

Lord Colwick intervened, giving her a brief reprieve. "Drake accuses me of being naïve and not seeing the deceptive nature of most people. I am hardly the saint he insists I am, but then I suppose he is right in that I do not seek a dark nature in everyone I meet."

"My intentions were not dishonorable," she said and caught her lower lip in her teeth. "It is a private matter, but please know that I . . . I am the last one who would wish him harm. "

He gave her a puzzled look, then sighed as if the issue were suddenly settled. "Drake was right. I have no talent for schemes and subterfuge. If I've erred—"

"I don't understand." He wasn't making any sense that she could see. What schemes?

"I swore to him I would stay out of his business, but I seem unable to keep that promise. I've taken these moments just to try to reassure myself that it was truly you I saw there that morning."

"Please." It was as if a cold hand were squeezing her throat closed. "Please say nothing of it to Drake. I . . . I had planned to tell him everything tonight . . ."

His expression grew distant, his brown eyes filling with icy disregard. The music ended, and he released her.

She'd pressed him too far, and she knew it. Her chin lifted defiantly. "No matter what you think of me, the truth is my own. Tell him if it pleases you. I don't expect you to go against your conscience on my behalf. Nor should I have begged you to. If I've committed any wrongdoing, it was in that act alone."

She spun on her heels, a swirl of copper and burgundy accenting the firm public cut as she turned her back on him and walked away with her head held high.

Alex shook his head, unwillingly admiring her fiery spirit, surprised by the stern admonishment and her sincere indignation. If he'd falsely accused her . . .

But he sighed. It was past that now. The path was set, and the Fates themselves wouldn't be able to change things. Feminine bluster and protests of innocence wouldn't help. If Clay was her secret champion, then Alex prayed he'd defend his own. Once Drake made up his mind, it was hard to dissuade him. Whatever his plans for Clay, whatever his intentions, Alex had a sinking feeling that Drake was determined to embrace his reputation.

The last guests were ushered out well after midnight, and Merriam was exhausted, both physically and emotionally. "Have you seen His Grace?" she asked Jameson anxiously.

"I believe he went upstairs earlier, but I haven't seen him since."

Merriam climbed the stairs, her legs heavy with dread. If Colwick had already said something to him, it might explain his odd mood and the strange looks. *Oh,*

God, she prayed, *how will I right this?* If he'd misunderstood her actions, then anything was possible. Still, he hadn't seem enraged or completely put off, so she bolstered her spirits with the hope that he might still listen to what she had to say.

There was a chance. After all their intimacies, all their shared moments, she knew she could trust Drake alone with the secret of her lessons—her desire to learn to be braver. He would understand when no one else could. He'd been a part of helping her lose the shame that had held her trapped for so many years. He would see the path that had led her to such an unconventional tutor. After all, where else did one ask the unspeakable and express a longing that, before she'd met Madame DeBourcier, she could hardly have named? If he wanted, she would offer for him to meet the young madam. She would confirm all—

Even the identity of the original object of her affections.

Even that.

There was the rub that had pushed her to such lengths of deception. A confession would have been a simple matter but for that. If only Drake didn't hold such hatred for Clay. But he did, and she knew it was the point on which her case might perish. He might not wish to hear of her love if he knew she'd first been attracted to Clay.

But she hadn't known Drake then. She hoped he would see it as the cruel coincidence that it was.

She pushed open the bedroom door. "Drake? Are you here?"

The silhouette of a man unfolded from one of the chairs by the dying fire, and she took one step toward him, then hesitated, suddenly unsure of herself. "Drake! Are you well?"

"I'm not Drake, Merriam. And I am not well."

Merriam gasped as she realized that it was Julian Clay.

Twenty-one

"What are you doing here?" she barely managed to choke in a terrified whisper, torn between an urge to scream for the entire staff to come to her rescue and the unspeakable fear of what Drake would think when he found Julian Clay in their bedroom alone with her.

"Where is he, Merriam?" Julian's tone brooked no argument. "Where the hell is Drake?"

"I . . . was just looking for him." She retreated a single step, "I'm sure I don't know, but you should go—"

Julian leaned against the chair in casual defiance. "I don't think so. You see, Drake and I have some unfinished business. And while I unfortunately missed the party due to"—his hands shook as he ran a hand through the loose golden curls on his head—"a financial misunderstanding, it is a matter of life and death that I see him."

"Why don't I ring for refreshments? Perhaps you'd like a brandy or some port . . ." Merriam moved over to the bell pull as she spoke.

"Don't."

One word, and she froze. There was something so cold, so frightening in his voice, she obeyed instantly. "Sit."

She shuddered but made her way to the small chair at her vanity. It was the farthest seat from him, and a part of her wondered whether she could spot a makeshift weapon if needed. "This is most rude of you. Whatever your complaint, you won't make things better by appearing here—like this. With me," she added in a whisper, fear choking her.

"Are you afraid of me, Merriam?" he asked, keeping his distance.

She nodded.

"Are you afraid of him?" Julian moved closer.

She shook her head, "No . . . not really. He isn't . . ."

He shook his head, pity softening his features. "I failed to convince you, and now, somehow, I am cast as the master villain. This will not do, Mrs. Everett."

"Then leave."

"No." He settled onto the bed, sitting on its edge as if it were the most natural thing in the world to lurk in someone else's bedroom and await them in the middle of the night. "You'll see. He'll return, and then, you'll see what he is and isn't. I, for one, have no intention of allowing him to slink away. Not this time."

"Th-this makes no sense. You're mad." Tears threatened, but she gripped the table's edge for strength. "Drake . . . isn't a murderer."

"Are you sure?"

She started to nod, but then he asked again, his voice so soft, hypnotic, and frightening. "Are you entirely sure of that?"

Oh, God. No, she wasn't, but she'd made her choice. He'd denied it, and she'd believed him. And now . . . now she didn't know who to fear or what to think.

"Please . . ."

"Am I interrupting a tender scene, or should I just wait in the hallway while you finish?" Drake's voice was like a whip slicing through the tension in the room, and Merriam squeaked in surprise.

"Drake! Thank goodness, you're here. Mr. Clay was just . . ."

He never even glanced in her direction; his eyes locked on to Julian with a hatred that made his expression seem demonic. "When I didn't see you at the party, I should have surmised you might try something less public and a bit more dramatic, Julian."

"You bastard. You timed it all and walked around toasting our acquaintances, all the while letting your solicitor do your dirty work. What was it, Sotherton? Couldn't face me directly? You couldn't fight the truth, so you decided to destroy your accuser and silence me by sending me packing to the poorhouse?" He nearly spat at Drake. "You're a coward, old friend. You always were."

Drake launched at him, bare-handed, with a howl of anger. Julian caught him with a blow to his stomach, and both men tumbled over the bed and onto the floor on the other side. Merriam leapt from her chair, only to watch them begin to struggle in earnest. Drake had somehow regained the upper hand, and receiving a vicious punch to his face, Julian reeled and stumbled back. But Drake gave no quarter; he followed, striking Julian with each step he took. The sound of his bare fists striking was nauseating to her, and Merriam screamed, "Stop! Drake, please, you're killing him!"

But her lover was deaf in the grip of his rage. As Julian fell to the floor, Drake went down with him, beating him without mercy. "You killed Lily, you son of a bitch, and you'll pay!"

"Drake, no!"

As if in a nightmare, she watched Julian's hand stretch to reach the fireplace poker near the grate. His fingers gripped it, and before she could scream a warning to Drake, the weapon came up and barely missed his skull. The momentum of it threw him off Julian, as he was forced to defend himself.

"Drake, please! Enough of this!"

Julian gained his feet, the poker pointed toward Drake as he gave his attacker a lopsided grin. "It seems your mistress is more concerned with my safety than yours. But then, we're not surprised, are we, Drake?"

Drake made a blind move, impossible to predict. He dropped a shoulder and drove into Julian in an attempt to disarm him by simply tackling him. Merriam averted her face, her hands over her eyes, unable to watch any more of it.

But at the odd sound, like a grunt from Drake, she risked a peek.

All the color from the room faded away at the sight of Drake leaning against the chair with the fireplace poker jutting from his side, its tip planted just under his ribs. His expression was one of surprise, and Merriam knew that she would never forget it as long as she lived. It was a scene beyond dread.

Julian stood, battling his own pain, his eyes wide at his handiwork. "Th-that's what you used to kill her, wasn't it? Ironic, don't you agree?"

Drake pulled the poker out and dropped it to the floor. "I wouldn't know, Julian. I wasn't there."

"Liar," Julian accused him, more softly but with a desperate edge.

"Oh, God," she whispered, watching the bloom of crimson at Drake's side.

"I wasn't there, but you were."

"You're dying, old man," Julian managed to grind out, his own legs starting to give way.

"Hardly." Drake put a hand against the wound.

Merriam ran forward. "Damn it, stop, both of you!"

She grabbed Drake's arm, trying to pull him toward the bed, tears blinding her. But Drake wanted none of it and pulled away from her grip with a sharp tug. Unprepared for his strength, she fell backward catching her foot on the edge of the rug, and struck the back of her head against the table's edge.

The room spun, and she wasn't sure how she'd managed to find herself looking at the beautiful cutwork ceiling from the floor. For a fleeting moment, she forgot about the men entirely, a wave of gray pain clouding her thoughts.

"My lady, are you all right?" Peg was at her side, and Merriam tried to tell her that she was only stunned, that the wind had been knocked out of her—and then she saw the gun.

"P-Peg?" Merriam sat up slowly, sure this was a dream. The men's ragged breathing was the sole sound in the sudden stillness, and Merriam could only wait for the surreal moment to unfold.

"I hate this room," the maid declared, backing away so that all of them were forced to hold still, within her sight. "But not at first."

Drake spoke gently. "Peg, we . . . meant no harm to Merriam. This matter is between Julian and me. Now, put the gun away."

The maid shook her head, her expression calm and unruffled. "No, you never get it right. Neither of you did, and I'm tired of waiting."

"Waiting?" Julian asked, trying to mirror her calm.

But his charms were hindered by the condition of his face, wrecked from Drake's pummeling. "Whatever for?"

"She was the most beautiful woman I ever saw, like an angel. And I loved her." Peg's voice was compelling. "But you didn't." She pointed the gun at Drake. "She married you for your title and your money, but you didn't stop it. You never really cared one way or the other."

Drake's jaw clenched in pain, but he kept his silence.

Peg went on relentlessly. "You knew about her lovers and said nothing. And I hated you for that. She tupped your best friend to try to get your attention. And I hated you for that too."

She turned to Julian, her look openly contemptuous. "You used her, and then you just left her. I saw it all. You lorded it about and rode her till you both were covered in sweat, but you didn't care. She wasn't a whore!"

"No." Julian shook his head, shaken now. "She wasn't."

"I remembered all the wonderful things she'd said. That I had soft hands and that my hair was almost the same color as hers—and I loved her and I wanted her to know it. She was upset and crying after you left. I finally worked up the courage to tell her. I knew it would make her feel better, and she'd see that I'd been there all along. But she laughed in my face. She was drunk—upset. Sh-she opened her gown and spread her legs and said I could have a 'free taste' if I wanted. I-I just wanted her to love me. But she . . ."

Peg's grip on the pistol was terrifying. Merriam saw it was too steady, the look in the maid's eyes cold and disconnected. If only she would waver, but the deadly calm held them all in place. "I killed her, and I waited for someone to come for me. But no one ever did."

Merriam's throat closed; she had just gained a new understanding of Peg's pain. To be so invisible that you could love without being seen. And then to commit the worst crime and have no one even look in your direction for absolution. It would be like a living death. "Peg . . ." She began to reach out, instinctively seeking to comfort her. But as the maid's gaze met hers, Merriam realized her mistake.

Drake spoke, his face pale from shock and blood loss as he struggled to stay upright. "Why didn't you say anything? Why didn't you tell the authorities that Julian had been the man in my house that night? That you'd killed her?"

"Because you both should pay for what you did to her. Because I wanted to see you punished—for having her and each looking away." She turned again toward Merriam. "You've been so sweet, m'lady. But he doesn't love you." She nodded toward Julian. "Old tricks. Like a dog who turns on things just because they're weak or in pain."

"Peg, please . . ." Merriam tried again, her eyes filling with bitter tears at the dead look in the young woman's eyes.

"And His Grace"—Peg cut her eyes to him for a

moment—"he doesn't care. I heard about the arrangement. And now the Season is over, and he'll throw you out in the gutter. He made you a whore." She looked back to Merriam. "Sometimes you kill people because you love them. Sometimes"—she raised the pistol and leveled it at Merriam's chest—"you do it to save them."

Drake roared, but it was Julian who got there first. He pushed Merriam out of the way as Peg pulled the trigger and the gun exploded. The maid lowered the weapon to shoot him again as he fell, but Drake managed to strike her hand upward so that the second shot found the ceiling as its victim.

Then it was pure chaos. Jameson and two footmen rushed into the room to envelop Peg, ripping the gun from her hand before she could fire it again. She was screaming uncontrollably. "No! No! They'll just hurt her! They'll just hurt her like before! I loved her! I loved her!"

Jameson barked out orders. "A surgeon! We need a surgeon! Run for the watch and send for help!"

The footmen dragged the maid out kicking and screaming, moving quickly to subdue her but also to get aid for the injured. Drake looked on helplessly as Merriam moved toward a fallen and unmoving Julian Clay.

"H-he's been shot." Merriam knelt next to him, then looked to Drake, tears streaming down her face. "She shot him."

Drake could do nothing but struggle to sit on the

bed, waving off Jameson's clumsy attempts at assistance.

"Please, Your Grace, just let me see. Did she stab you, sir?"

He nodded, unwilling to accuse his potentially dead rival of any more crimes. He could do nothing. Drake sat awash in the pain of watching Merriam weeping and attending to her beloved Julian and absorbed just how much he'd lost.

He'd been wrong about so many things. But about his dear familiar and Clay . . .

It was an insurmountable blow, and he knew his heart wouldn't recover this time.

She cried, and all he could do was watch.

Twenty-two

He turned the card over and over in his hand. It was a ragged, pathetic thing now, stained and bloody. It was an odd little memento and something he couldn't bring himself to destroy. It would be easy to toss it into the fire, but something held him back.

I came to give you your card back.

Gone. She was gone. She'd left, taking none of the clothes or jewels he'd bought for her. A more pragmatic woman would have stripped the room of anything of value for the hell he'd put her through, and he felt small-minded even to think of it now. No, she'd taken only her widow's weeds of practical weave and weight, draped in accents of crepe and dreary black buttons, and that ugly black reticule. She'd marched from the house into a rainstorm and refused even Jameson's offer of a carriage home.

She'd wanted nothing that was his, and nothing of him. Drake was sure of it.

It had been weeks since that night. Weeks of physical healing, initially at Colwick's country estate to escape the endless inquiries that had rained down. Then he'd returned to town to save face. He wouldn't play the coward and hide ever again.

The papers had enjoyed the story with salacious fervor, and if there had been any consolation, it was the loss of his nickname. Poor Peg had taken the brunt of it, though his relationship with a certain widow was mentioned on a regular basis to keep the journalism spiced. Drake had also helplessly learned that the universe enjoys a dry sense of humor. Julian was touted as the brave hero who had stepped in to save his "old friend," and news of his miraculous recovery was followed in grinding, gory detail. The irony of once again appearing to be a bit of a villain next to Julian's uncanny gift for maintaining a spotless reputation wasn't lost on Drake. Even with the temporary loss of his fortune, the Earl of Westleigh looked to be a social darling and could well emerge the winner.

Drake sighed. It was a battle not worth fighting.

He turned the card over and over.

A part of him wished he'd retained Peers. Then he would know if Merriam had gone to Julian—if it was too late. But he hadn't kept his spies and could only guess at what she thought of him after the confrontation with Clay, after Peg's incredible confession.

I came to give you your card back.

Drake wondered how much courage it had taken her to do that. To come to him and hold out that card, knowing it was an excuse.

Well, perhaps it was time for him to find out firsthand.

Merriam reread the passage on Indian festivals and finally set the book aside. The distraction of exotic locales wasn't as effective today. She was becoming an expert on distraction or, more often, on things that failed to draw her attention, but it wasn't to be helped. She'd redecorated her sitting room and ordered new fabrics for the rest of the downstairs. The musty, dull tone of the house was being overthrown in gradual rebellion. Merriam had decided that, while her kingdom was relatively small, it was hers to rule as she wished.

She'd busied herself with a new wardrobe full of colors, though decidedly more practical and modest than the gowns she'd left behind at Sotherton's. All her black gowns and drab mourning ensembles had been donated or burned.

Merriam hadn't gone back to her old life. Instead, she had begun a new one.

"I brought you a tray, m'lady," Celia offered, entering shyly. "You didn't touch your breakfast, and Cook's more than a little worried."

"Thank you, Celia. Assure her I'm fine and let me know when the fabric samples for the bedroom are delivered." Merriam shifted the book to her lap and began to pour her own tea.

"So many changes," Celia commented.

Merriam gave her a questioning look. "You disapprove?"

"Oh, no! I think it's wonderful . . . to brighten things around here. If you don't mind me saying." The maid curtsied and left as Merriam worked hard at not giggling. A lifetime trying to please, and she still couldn't stop herself from asking her maid if all was well.

She sighed. Another point to be accepted. No matter how much changed, a great deal would always be the same.

She heard the faint ringing of a bell but paid no attention. The neighbor's bell often jingled merrily in the afternoons with callers. Of course, no one called at her door anymore. Not that she'd ever received a flood of social visitors. As Drake had insightfully guessed, a few aging friends of her dead husband's, a committee member or two, and on occasion, women making calls for their favorite charities had constituted the bulk of her guests. As he'd also guessed, she couldn't lie and say she truly missed them very much.

So, she'd resolutely embraced her exile. After all, on a practical note, her kitchen staff wasn't bothered with surprise requests for tea and cucumber sandwiches. She had more time for reading and writing in her journals. She'd taken to long walks in the park and begun to stop wondering if anyone recognized her from her "deca-dent Season."

There was a certain independence to being an out-cast. But the loneliness that came with the new solitude of her days and nights was the most difficult element. The rest of her fears just never seemed to take shape. The shame never arrived. She regretted almost nothing.

Almost.

But it would pass.

And if it didn't? The cat in her pressed. If the burning and longing for him never ceased? If she was forced to accept the vast emptiness that his absence had created? Of biting the pillow at night to muffle her cries as she rode her own hands and thought only of Drake?

But there was nothing to be done.

It had been so ugly, that last terrible scene. Julian's blood everywhere, Peg's screams, and Drake standing there wounded, his look unreadable. She'd packed her things and fled in the aftermath, the authorities insist-ing on interviews and Drake repeating that she should be allowed to go, that she didn't belong there.

She'd expected him to follow her at first, to protest her departure, but it never happened. And she didn't blame him. The trauma had been overwhelming, and he was probably still reeling from the painful collision of his past and present. She would only remind him now of that night. He deserved to be happy and to free himself from the nightmarish tangle of their affair. Though most of it had been a beautiful dream to her, she'd known the Season she'd agreed to was irrevocably over.

"M'lady—" Celia interrupted her thoughts with a small server, a calling card at its center. "You have a visitor."

Merriam glanced at the tray; the card was all too familiar. Stained and bloody, it was his card. It was *the* card.

"Show him in."

She stood to prepare herself, her hands nervously smoothing out the lightly patterned lavender folds of her skirt with its jade trim, then touching her hair. He'd come at last, but whether to gloat or just to see that she'd survived Merriam refused to guess.

He came in with a hurried bow, and her breath caught in her chest at the sight of him. He was more handsome than she'd allowed herself to recall, filling the room with his elegant power and making her new furniture look dainty and diminished.

"W-would you . . . like some tea?" She gestured for him to take a seat, unsure of how to conduct polite conversation with a man who had once made her lose consciousness from the force of her climaxes. It was like a farce, only she didn't have a script. "Or some brandy?"

He lifted an eyebrow at the last offer, his humor still intact. "Perhaps later. Thank you for the kind offer."

He took the seat she indicated, and Merriam perched across from him, prim and nervous but determined to hold her own. "I . . . I hope you're recovered. I'd heard that you'd left to heal at Lord Colwick's estate, but there was no word. I'd have sent—"

"Merriam," he interrupted, his gaze too intense to allow for delays. "I'm afraid I just have to tell you— what I came to say, or I won't get through it."

"Oh, well." She bit her lower lip. "As you wish then."

He took a long deep, inhale, then began slowly. "There was a great deal I'd wanted to tell you. But after Peg's rendition came so horribly close to the bone, I wasn't ready, and I convinced myself you probably didn't wish to hear it anyway. But it's that sort of assumption that can leave one isolated and beyond redemption. I should know. I seem to be an expert at wrong conclusions and even worse actions."

Drake unfolded from the chair and paced in the small confines of the room, a caged panther describing the jungles of his memory. "I didn't love Lily . . . at first. I married for the reasons most men of title do. Out of duty and a sense of family honor, and the hope of an heir; it was simply fulfilling a requirement. I needed a wife, and Lily had seemed a more than suitable choice. She was a beauty with fortune and good breeding, and I never looked further. I never considered that there was more to the spoiled and lovely little creature I'd selected as the Duchess of Sussex."

He absentmindedly picked up a carved box from a side table, examining it without seeing it. "She drove me mad with her coy games and erratic sexual appetites. I was in constant heat, and she tortured me endlessly." He shrugged and returned the box to the table. "A year into the marriage, I confessed that I loved her. And that was when it all fell apart. Her attitude changed completely. It was a subtle shift at first. Then it was more obvious. She became disinterested—bored, really. She actually tried to insist on separate rooms. But as I had no heir, I refused to relent. Still, she had other means of retreat. She began openly to encourage me to spend more time at my business enterprises, at the club, anywhere but in her presence."

"Oh, my." Merriam's heart ached at the wounding of it. She knew what it was to feel so disregarded, but by someone you loved . . . it was unimaginable.

"Lily didn't want to be loved, Merriam. She wanted to be pursued." He moved back across the carpet in tight lines. "I never suspected Julian until afterwards. When he was the first to proclaim that I must be her killer, when he seemed the most distraught of our friends, a part of me started to accept it.

"And then it was so obvious, I couldn't believe I'd missed it. After all, Julian was the ultimate hunter. Lily lived for the chase. How could they not have found each other?"

"I can think of nothing worse," Merriam whispered, unable to hold back.

He laughed without humor and shook his head. "Oh, I can. There are things much worse. The worst thing is that I failed her. I failed to really fight for her. I'd known what she desired most, but out of hurt and wounded pride, I'd deliberately not pursued her. When she made it clear that she didn't want me, I did everything I could to punish her, to teach her that I was stronger and could live without her readily enough. I would exist happily just beyond her reach until she begged forgiveness and pleaded for my affections. And then she was dead." He sat back down on the settee, spent.

"Why were you never formally accused?"

"I had an alibi . . . one that they couldn't defeat." He took a deep breath. "I was halfway across England on business and had been gone for the month. Julian made it clear that he was sure I'd hired someone . . . or managed a secret journey back to London to discover that my wife had been unfaithful."

"He knew she'd been unfaithful—"

"Because he'd been with her that very night," Drake supplied, his eyes meeting hers, not trying to hide his anguish. "Julian slept with my wife because he enjoys taking things from me. Lily was just a pawn in a game, and ironically, he hurt her the same way she had hurt me. A part of me may have known what he was up to, what would happen between them. But I let it happen."

His shoulders dropped, the admission draining his strength. "That's why I left England. I was sure that I had stood by and quietly let her be destroyed. I'd imagined a lovers' quarrel over his inevitable departure, and I was sure that I had a part in his guilt."

"But you seemed so angry . . ."

"The rage came later," he admitted with a bitter smile. "I conveniently chose to forget the rest."

"Why are you telling me this?"

"Because I was a coward, before. Because it's easy to just turn your back on these things. And when I did that with Lily's murder, I just fed it and gave it the power to rule me all these years." He leaned closer, diminishing the space between them, and captured her hands in his. "Because I don't want to run this time. You love Julian, and my schemes and blindness might have taken him from you. A better man would come to give you his blessings. But we shared something, you and I. And I'm not turning my back on that. I'm going to fight to win you, to keep you, and to deserve you."

"Oh, my!" Merriam's mouth fell open in shock.

"But there is one thing I still don't understand. And I'm hoping you'll explain."

She waited, dread and hope twisting inside her.

"What was your connection to the Crimson Belle?"

"I . . . I went there for lessons." Merriam's hands gripped her skirts. "M-Madame DeBourcier was very . . . informative."

"To a brothel?"

"Where else? My marriage had yielded almost no experience I wished to relive or recall. I could hardly inquire at the Ladies' Botanical Society meetings. Can you picture Lady Corbett-Walsham expounding on the sensitive parts of a man's anatomy, or better yet, explaining how to masturbate?"

He smiled in spite of himself. "Their membership numbers would undoubtedly improve."

"Drake!" she exclaimed. "It isn't amusing."

"You're the one who mentioned the old dragon, not I."

Merriam bit her lower lip nervously. "I overheard some men talking about the Belle and the infamous Madame DeBourcier. So I secretly sought her out and begged her for help. We became good friends, and I wanted to be discreet to protect us both. I even went to see her after agreeing to our Season, but only to have someone else to confide in. I know her profession is . . . immoral, but I care for her as a contemporary and an equal."

Drake sighed. "As you may. I shudder to think of where else you might have sought guidance and should probably be grateful."

"But you see the dilemma?"

"I see it." He took another deep breath before going on. "I'm still not sure that I see how Westleigh entered into all of this. Was he . . ." Drake steeled himself, his shoulders straightening as if to pick up a heavy burden. "Was he simply for practice? Madame DeBourcier's visual example . . . for your lessons?"

Her eyes widened in shock at the novel and naughty idea. "N-no! I . . . he was at Lord Sinclair's ball. It was . . ." She steadied herself, the moment of truth at hand. "I thought he was handsome. He seemed so . . . worldly. And I overheard him saying something cutting, and I realized that I was the pasty creature he'd denounced to a friend. I was insulted and crushed and—furious."

"He called you a whey-faced widow?"

"Yes, and I swore right then that I was done with being ignored. All of my life, I was the mouse."

"The mouse?"

"Merriam the Mouse. My father used it because I was so plain and brown and quiet. I hated it! I was invisible and nothing, and when Grenville repeated it after we were married—I hated him for it. I . . ." She paced, loathing how childish it all sounded now. "When the Earl of Westleigh made me feel so insignificant, I was seized with a determination to prove that I could be something else. That I could break the rules and at last be the one in control."

"So you transformed yourself." He sat down, giving her room to move. "Into a cat."

"With Madame DeBourcier's help. I set out to torment him and tease him. I planned to make Clay desire me, and then I was going to leave . . . before . . ."

"Before consummation," he supplied, a bit in awe.

"I wanted him to know that he was nothing to me!"

"But there was confusion, and a matter of mistaken identities . . ."

"Yes. Instead of Westleigh, I found you. And, as you well know, the plan didn't exactly hold up against . . ." She sighed more dreamily this time, her skin flushing at the memory. "It was magic."

He held his breath at that, letting it all sink in. "Then you and Julian never . . ."

She smiled. "In one word, no. When you introduced us in the park, the only reason he recalled me from Dixon's garden party was that I nearly retched on his shoes when I realized it wasn't him I'd accosted at Milbank's. I was going to take the secret to my grave that I'd been so foolhardy, but it seemed my Merlin had plans of his own and came looking for me."

"Ah." It was Drake's turn to indulge in pleasant memories. "The arboretum."

"The arboretum," she echoed. "And then you gave me your card and— Well, you know the rest, Drake."

He stood and came over to take her hands into his. "My God, that was the most terrifying story I've ever heard."

"It was not!" she protested, struggling not to laugh at the wry look in his eyes.

"Of course it was. I almost wore a pirate costume that night."

Merriam rolled her eyes. "You are a villain, you realize this, yes?"

"Oh, yes"—he pulled her against him—"and clearly in need of constant supervision, my familiar." His lips just grazed hers, a teasing, tormenting, ghostlike kiss. "I'm a wretched man with nothing to recommend me. Come back to me."

"You're not." Her eyelashes fluttered as she struggled not to lose control, her fingers itching to touch him. Instead she pushed away, gaining her freedom at his gentle release. "But I . . . No matter what has happened, I'm not sure I have the strength to be your mistress again. It isn't about courage so much as . . . I don't think I have the character for it, Drake." Her eyes filled with tears. "I'm dying without you, but . . . I think I'm too practical to live in a constant state of scandal."

With one hand, he reached up to wipe tears from her cheek. "Merriam—"

"Please forgive me, Drake." She began to step away, but he caught her arm and held her there.

"Do you have the character to be my wife?"

The universe stuttered to a halt, and Merriam was sure her heart had stopped. "W-what?"

"It probably takes more courage to be my duchess than to be my mistress, but if anyone has the moral courage and ability to tie me in delicious knots without even trying, I would say that it was you." He knelt before her, her hands held in his like a bird he was unwilling to free but was equally determined not to hurt. "Marry me."

"Oh." She was speechless.

"Shall I interpret that sound as a yes, or must I begin a full campaign that will undoubtedly continue to ruin your reputation as a practical, beautiful, scandal-free widow?"

"You wouldn't . . ." Merriam smiled, imagining all the wonderful ways that Drake would seek to court her.

"As you wish. I believe I'll begin with a long bubble

bath—isn't there a fountain just outside in Bellingham Square?"

"Oh, no you don't! I should marry you just to see that you behave, Drake Sotherton!" She started laughing and pulled him to his feet, and then she was in his arms. The room spun as he whirled her about in celebration.

"Yes, Merriam, say yes!"

"Yes, yes, oh . . . yes!"

Epilogue

"What are you doing?"

"I'm leaving flowers." Merriam stood to step back from the fresh-picked arrangement of wildflowers she had dropped against the grass in front of the gravestone. "I felt that I should. I owe her . . . a debt."

"A debt?" Drake eyed her with wary tenderness. He'd buried Lily here almost nine years ago in his family's plots on their ancient country estate. On their walk he'd not intended to stop, but Merriam's eyes were keen and the beautiful stone chapel and markers had drawn her off the path. "I'm not sure I understand."

"Lily . . ." Merriam blushed at the awkward conveyance of her feelings. "I want her to be at peace. I feel like I've stolen the happiness that was her due."

He smiled and stepped closer, drawing his beautiful

new duchess up against his side. "You didn't steal anything, Merriam. If anyone is indebted, it would have to be me. What a villain I became, and for all the wrong reasons . . ."

She elbowed him in the ribs with a sideways look. "Sotherton, there are no right reasons to be a villain. You do vex a person, you realize."

"Yet you still love me." His look was pure innocence, and Merriam felt the familiar pull of languid heat through her veins.

"You are incorrigible, Your Grace."

"I fail to see how this is a terrible thing, my familiar." He smiled down at her, ending the mock battle. "A better behaved man would never have dared to trust again, or looked for happiness where he least deserved it, and of course"——he bent down, his mouth hovering over hers——"he would never do this in public."

"Drake!" Merriam whispered in a panic, stealing one guilty glance at the white marble gravestone next to them, as if expecting Lily to be looking on in horror. "We mustn't!"

He pulled her closer, a wicked gleam in his eyes that warmed her to her toes. "How else are we to maintain our scandalous reputation?"

"We have— Th-there is a new scandal?"

"Haven't you heard?" He put a finger under her chin to tilt her head back, lowering his voice to a seductive growl. "The Duke of Sussex is madly in love with his wife and can hardly keep his hands to himself. Unheard of . . . and most improper."

"Oh." Her color changed as a mischievous light answered his. "I'd heard he married his mistress . . . a most wanton creature, wild for him morning and night."

He kissed her in a commanding claim that melted her bones and made her arch against him. They both lost track of their surroundings, the world disappearing until nothing could distract them from each other.

"Oh, my." He framed her face with his hands. "You see? Scandal is inevitable."

"Yes, my love." She sighed happily. "I suppose so."

Acknowledgments

I want to thank everyone at Romantic Times Bookreviews for their phenomenal support and introduction to the wild world of romance, and especially to Kathryn Faulk, Lady of Barrow, Carol Stacy, Tara Gelsomino and Kathe Robin. It was through the pages of the magazine that I met my great friend and arch-nemesis, Cindy Cruciger, who has provided endless inspiration, goaded me into triple-dog-dares, and credited me with more weird craziness than anyone on the planet. I can't imagine my days without her warped stories to make me laugh even when I want to cry.

I have to thank Robin Schone, who proved that brilliance and kindness can come in the same package and who made me feel brave as a writer (just when Cindy was poking me in the ribs and making chicken noises). I'm in awe of her, and for her encouragement and support, I'll never be able to say enough.

To my agent, Meredith Bernstein, a very special thanks for believing in me and opening that door. You made it look so easy! And to my phenomenal editor, Maggie Crawford, go the greatest thanks of all. Thank you for your talented guidance and gentle advice. When people describe their dreams coming true, I just smile and remember the first time we talked on the phone. And it's only gotten better . . .

And finally, I want to thank Geoff, for being my very own romantic hero and making all things possible again.

Watch for Renee Bernard's
next stunningly passionate historical romance

Madame's Deception

**featuring Jocelyn Tolliver, Madame DeBourcier,
and Alex Randall, Lord Colwick**